Dexter Gordon

A MUSICAL BIOGRAPHY

Dexter Gordon

A MUSICAL BIOGRAPHY

Stan Britt

DA CAPO PRESS

Library of Congress Cataloging in Publication Data

Britt, Stan.
  Dexter Gordon.

  (A Da Capo paperback)
  Original British ed. has title: Long tall Dexter.
  Discography: p.
  1. Gordon, Dexter, 1923–   . 2. Saxophonists – United States – Biography. I.
Title.
ML419.G665B7   1989   788.7′092 [B]   89-11843
ISBN 0-306-80361-5

This Da Capo Press paperback edition of *Dexter Gordon* is an
unabridged republication of the edition published in London in 1989
under the title *Long Tall Dexter*. It is reprinted by arrangement with
Quartet Books.

Published by Da Capo Press, Inc.
A Member of the Perseus Books Group
Visit us on the World Wide Web at www.dacapopress.com

Manufactured in the United States of America
10 9 8 7 6 5

'Dexter? This is one of the few giants left'

Milt Jackson

Contents

Overture: Dexterity

The fair-haired drummer bends quickly to make a slight adjustment to the wing-nut holding his hi-hat cymbal. Simultaneously, his left foot pumps downwards on the pedal attachment. The rapid-fire triple rhythm betrays a slight nervousness. Satisfied with the final soundcheck for this part of his kit, he relaxes, retrieves a half-burned Disque Bleu from the edge of the cowbell, and inhales deeply. The serious-faced pianist trails a long index finger of his right hand from one end of the keyboard to the other, making gentle, if unrelated chordal patterns with the other hand. He glances sideways to the slim, tall bass player, permits himself a smile and relays a short message. The boyish features smile a return message. A pause. Then, he hums a unison figure to a restrained, yet perfectly articulated, bebop line lasting no more than eight bars. The pianist's friendly black features crease to a wide grin: 'Ye-e-e-a-ah, Niels!' The response, delivered at something approaching a loud whisper, breaks the tension. All three musicians relax visibly as they enjoy the pleasure of a private joke, one which doesn't quite communicate to the crowd which has been gathering, slowly but in increasing numbers, for the past thirty minutes and more . . .

The punters who wait expectantly this evening at the Montmartre Jazzhus are no different from those who've packed its four walls three nights so far this week. They're basically a warm and friendly audience, readily appreciative of the various sounds which can be heard at Copenhagen's jazz emporium. And even though the present (second) version of the Montmartre has been open for business for less than five years, it has seen and heard some of the greatest names in jazz, both from the

United States as well as from the length and breadth of Europe.

The audience is just beginning to show signs of restlessness. There is an expectant buzz from all areas of the semi-darkened club. As usual, the crowd comprises a goodly percentage of students – teenagers and those in their twenties – mostly from the local art college. There's a fair sprinkling too of older men and women, some in small parties, occasionally seated or standing alone.

As ever, a string of non-performing local jazz musicians has gathered for what they know is almost certain to be a Very Special Occasion. Most are lounging inelegantly near to or against the bar. They're acting cool, like jazz musicians do . . . but they're not here just to demolish a few drinks, take in a little of the music, then leave. They might well consume considerably more than a cognac or beer or two, but they'll stay for the opening set – maybe the second. And they'll dig the music, *and* the efforts of the star performer of the evening and his superbly integrated rhythm trio.

It is no coincidence either that among their number the knowledgeable Danish jazz fan can pick out a half-dozen or so local tenor saxophonists, who perhaps will be recalling the imposing list of visiting tenormen who have played the Montmartre thus far, either as officially booked players or temporary visitors, sitting in at the invitation of the resident guest performer. That impressive list would include such gifted players as Ben Webster, Stan Getz, Booker Ervin, Don Byas, Coleman Hawkins, Johnny Griffin, Archie Shepp and Paul Gonsalves. And, of course, the man they've come to see that very evening, someone who has long since become a kind of local hero, and who is now apparently a permanent resident in Denmark. Something of a true Living Legend, a giant (in more ways than one) of his chosen instrument. An important link in the noble chain of great tenor saxists, started by Coleman Hawkins. A charismatic personality, whose very appearance generates the kind of electric atmosphere few others could command. Indeed, as now, that electricity is present at all times even before he's made his customary attention-grabbing entrance. Something with which the Montmartre aficionados were familiar, but something which never failed to happen . . .

The general restrained hubbub partially dissolves as the club's PA crackles briefly, then a friendly voice breaks through: 'And now, ladies and gentlemen . . . the Montmartre Jazzhus is proud to present – once again – one of the great tenor players in jazz history . . . and a resident of Denmark . . . the one and only DEX-TER GORDON . . .!' Well before the house lights – other than those which continue to criss-cross the bandstand – have dimmed, the response to the introduction is instant and vociferous. A genuinely spontaneous reaction, even though but a handful of those grouped near to the dressing-room entrance have actually caught more than a glimpse of the evening's star attraction. For the few patrons present who have never seen him at close quarters at the club – or any other venue – before now, there are a few gasps – easily audible – of genuine astonishment.

Which is in no way an overreaction on their part. Even more so for those who were catching their first sight of the giant who ambles, loose-legged, towards the stand. A towering figure of a man, stretching all the way up to six feet five inches, and seemingly destined to come into sharp contact with the Montmartre's now invisible ceiling at every step.

Dexter Keith Gordon makes an exaggerated – half-spoken, half-waved – greeting to the three waiting musicians. Turning full-circle, he acknowledges the ever-increasing volume of rapturous applause with something approaching a half-bow and a smile that is as broad as it is warm. In his right hand he carries a Selmer saxophone, which looks like a miniaturized version of the real thing. Gordon's long, arching trunk is lean and muscular, with little or no superfluous flesh anywhere, rather akin to the classic outline of the American-style footballer. An impressive physique indeed for a man who six months previously has celebrated his forty-sixth birthday . . . and for someone who has been comprehensively involved in practically every aspect of the jazz life, from age fifteen.

If the first time visitors to a Dexter Gordon gig have evidenced a profound surprise merely at his onstage appearance, they are soon to be positively stunned into shocked silence at what is to happen next: first, a hoarsely whispered instruction to the piano player, both hands raised, almost touching, an inch above the middle keys. More like a distant rumbling of an impending thunderstorm, still far off, or a sound that seems to have emanated from some deep well. Followed, after a pause lasting no more than four seconds, by a sudden rhythmic snap of thumb and forefinger, dictating an unmistakable tempo guideline. A neat, eight-bar introduction from the pianist, with bass and drums lending close support. From the opening keyboard phrase, Dexter Gordon steps closer to the microphone to commence what will be his first solo of the evening. One which will range over no fewer than seventeen expressive choruses. The mouthpiece is clenched, vicelike, as the big man straightens to more or less his full height. The expanding chest muscles indicate a mighty intake of air into the lungs . . .

The sound which issues from the bell of the saxophone is, by any standards, exceptionally large. It appears to fill the four corners of the Montmartre. Not even long-time habitués can recall a saxophone sound more overpoweringly huge than this. Hawkins . . . Byas . . . Ervin . . . Webster . . . these tenorists have big-toned reputations, but Gordon's . . . Leonard Feather has probably best summarized Dexter Gordon's playing, in relation to his first period of ascendancy: 'Perhaps more than any of the others [tenormen of the 1940s] he transferred the characteristics of bop to the tenor.' That, too, is manifestly obvious during this opening Montmartre offering, a solo which seems to grow progressively more exciting with each succeeding chorus. The drive is unremitting. The man's harmonic skill is impressive; he negotiates the changes effortlessly. The emotional power is almost unbearable. The ideas flow unceasingly, from one chorus to the next.

From time to time, and at exactly the right juncture, a succession of craftily inserted interpolations, from a variety of sometimes unlikely sources, add touches of humour . . . without ever interrupting the flow of the improvisations. These include undisguised references to such as 'Alice Blue Gown', 'And the Angels Sing', the 'Habanera' from *Carmen*, and 'Anything You Can Do (I Can Do Better)'.

The entire length and breadth of the instrument's range is utilized, including some high-register screaming that Adolphe Sax never dreamed of, contrasted with a few startling honks tossed in with almost disdainful casualness – and false-fingered well below the 'official' bottom range – which rebound off the mike like the sound of elephants round the waterhole. The solo is, if nothing else, a hair-raising lesson in dynamics. As he builds to the last of several climaxes, Gordon's left leg – slightly inverted – trembles, as if its nerve centre has lost control. Just when it seems there will be no end, it is over . . . the final portion comprising a marvellously executed surge into the upper register once again.

Just a split-second of unnerving response, then the by now capacity crowd of 150 spellbound observers are given a much-needed release from the tension they have suffered gladly during the kind of individual performance they are scarcely likely to forget. The applause is memorable in its density, even by the Montmartre's past standards of generous response. The beating of nearly 150 pairs of hands is punctuated by sporadic shouts and screams and nervous, high-pitched, tuneless whistles.

The tall figure beams, wipes his sweat-soaked forehead with a large white handkerchief, mouths a silent 'thank you', grins a joyful grin. Then, the saxophone – gleaming like its owner's face in the main spotlight – is pushed gently outwards, in front of the huge frame. For several seconds it is held in space, horizontally. It is Dexter Gordon's highly personal salutation to the audience, from his beloved Selmer and himself . . .

Finally, the clapping and yelling subside. Gordon blinks, smiles again and steps forward to the microphone. Another swab of the wet brow. Then, in a voice as deep as the Grand Canyon, he reiterates his grateful thanks, both for their warm response and their presence at the Montmartre Jazzhus this very evening. The little speech is delivered with warmth and in measured tones, as if to make sure everyone will understand his message. There is a strategic pause. Then, one by one, he introduces the members of his quartet, encouraging applause as he relays their names and birthplaces: '. . . on drums, from this fair city of Copenhagen . . . Al-ex Ri-el . . .!'; '. . . on the double bass, that extraordinary young man from Osted – also Denmark . . . Niels- . . . Hen-ning . . . Øo-o-rsted Pedersen . . .!'; '. . . and, at present a resident of Copenhagen . . . via New York City . . . and an old buddy of mine of the past . . . on pi-an-no . . . Mr Ken-n-y Drew . . .!'

The large face becomes slightly more serious for a moment.

'And now, ladies and gentlemen . . . we'd like to kinda slow down the pace and play you a lovely old standard ballad, from . . . way back.' Another pause. And then something of a delightful surprise – especially for those who have not witnessed this unusual contribution to a typical Dexter Gordon in-person performance – as, once again, he steps forward to the mike. With Drew and his companions poised for their sensitive introduction, that impossibly deep-down voice identifies both the title of the ballad – and speaks the opening stanzas of its refrain.

Another up-tempo swinger – but closer to fast-medium than fast. More humorous asides spill from the first two choruses following an almost summary despatch of the fine Jule Styne melody – one which Gordon had been using at fairly regular intervals after he'd first recorded it in 1961. Always played at or around that same tempo. This is another solid solo statement. The high quality of soloing is diminished not at all by the fleet fingers of the young Danish bassist, whose outstanding all-round performances are already making him something of a legend . . . and not only in European jazz circles. His fellow countryman, Alex Riel, is learning fast, as his ensemble drumming and his own rapid-fire contribution indicate. Learning fast in the company of the gifted, demanding Americans with whom he has been working, with increasing regularity, during the past two years or so. Especially someone like Dexter Gordon . . .

Next up, a classic pop ballad. Another Jule Styne standard, Sinatra-associated. During his introduction to 'Guess I'll Hang My Tears out to Dry', Gordon mixes in a smattering of Danish; it sounds quite authentic, hardly the expected American-

Danish. Another side of Dexter. A tender-tough ballad performance, in the classic tenorist's tradition. Something very personal. The big man with the big sound. Muted, deliberately, here, but with the unashamed 'cry' one hopes the best, the most moving, jazz can impart. With Dexter Gordon revealing much of himself, his emotions, his fears, his sadnesses ... but imparted with dignity and infinite good taste.

The repertoire for the rest of the evening is archetypal Gordon-at-Montmartre fare. An Afro-Cubanized 'I'll Remember April', with more massive sound and robust swinging. A personalized approach to Luiz Bonfa's sensitive 'Manha de Carnaval'. Plus bebop classics such as 'A Night in Tunisia' and 'Scrapple from the Apple', and Gordon original pieces like 'Cheese Cake' (with an awesome coda that seems endless) and 'Soy Califa'.

The intensely rapt attention and respect shown during his solos is complemented at the conclusion of each with the kind of rapturous applause some might be forgiven for believing must be associated more with the hysterical response of pop fans to their idols. After the final encore, the ovation is even more unstinting.

A deep resonant 'Thank you ... ladies and gentle-men!' The friendly voice rumbles through the amplification. Once again, the Selmer is proffered in salutation.

A group of teenage girls laugh and smile, almost adoringly.

A conspiratorial wink. A gently guffawing laugh. Then, an ambled turn to the right. A half-wave. A half-stoop to negotiate a threatening overhead beam. Finally, a dozen relaxed strides to the dressing-room.

Long Tall Dexter has been reaffirming his pre-eminence once again ...

Obviously, all of the afore-written is fictitious. But even fiction can be based on absolute truth – however fanciful, or even far-fetched either might seem. In fact, it is based on the author's personal memories: of having been present at literally dozens of club or concert or outdoor-festival appearances by someone who, without a shadow of doubt, can be called a Living Legend of Jazz. And it doesn't matter that the majority of my personal memories of hearing Dexter Gordon in live performance are centred on, not the Montmartre Jazzhus, Copenhagen, but Ronnie Scott's, London.

It was in 1977 – the year he was, once again, firmly ensconced in the land of his birth, after many years of living and working in Europe – that I first got to meet Dexter properly. That first time, too, I conducted my first interview with him. It wasn't a very long chat, but it was revealing. The huge figure that ambled casually into a room thoughtfully provided by a member of the promotion staff at CBS Records, in Soho Square, proved to be a warm, friendly individual, whose natural humour never disguised the obvious intelligence of the man. As an interviewee, he exhibited all these facets – and a few more. These included an at first slightly disconcerting manner of taking his time to think about a question and then proceeding to answer it – lucidly and interestingly – in his own time, at his own tempo. Very similar, in fact, to his marvellously laid-back approach to playing what is often called 'boss tenor'.

The basic reason for Gordon's appearance in London in 1977 was to allow him to undertake a two-week engagement at the Scott club (a mere stone's throw from where our first meeting took place). It was indeed rather extraordinary to be reminded that this was the first time British jazz fans had heard him locally since 1962, the year of his unforgettable first-ever appearances here for a month at the club.

Dexter returned to the Ronnie Scott Club as leader of his own fine quartet the following February. Then, and on subsequent return trips to London – annually, for the next few years – it was readily apparent that his much-publicized elevation to a kind of jazz superstardom in the States was much appreciated by its recipient. Obviously, he was benefiting, both financially and personally, from all the mass attention he was receiving (albeit long, long overdue).

Our third get-together, in 1980, was just as enjoyable for me as any of the others, before and since. But it assumed proportions of genuine importance (and if I may say so, a sense of personal fulfilment, with an aura of real, all-pervading excitement). For I had been commissioned, less than six months before we met in his hotel room, to write a full-length musical biography on Dexter. When I passed on the news, he seemed pleased, and said he would be happy to answer some more questions about his now lengthy, and certainly colourful, life in the jazz world. (Already, I had acquired sufficient material from our previous conversations to form a solid basis for a comprehensive survey of Gordonia.)

Unfortunately, before that same year was out, the book found itself in limbo. The small publishing house which had commissioned the work went out of business (like so many of its contemporaries at the end of the 1970s and the beginning of the 1980s). It resurfaced less than a year later. I withdrew my incomplete manuscript from its file on the shelf, and started where I'd left off. Alas, the same thing happened again, less than a year later . . . with the book still far from completed. Back on the shelf went the manuscript. It was to remain there, unfinished, and I was certain, unlikely to be published for years . . .

Unfortunately, my gloomy forecast proved only too true. That is, until Chris Parker, Quartet Books' Jazz Editor, rang me at home, one morning towards the end of 1986. He'd heard about my unfinished musical biography, and he wanted to publish it with Quartet.

So, now – for the third time of trying – *Long Tall Dexter* has become reality! I can scarcely believe it. I am most beholden to Chris Parker for giving me the chance of completing a project which was always close to my heart. Throughout a longer-than-anticipated period of revision, etc, he has been infinitely patient, wholly supportive and, when necessary, marvellously sympathetic to the eminently valid reasons for the unavoidable stop-and-start 'technique' needed to finish the work . . . at last. While thanking Chris, I must not in any way omit ample credit to the man who started all this in the first place. Sadly, I lost contact completely, several years ago, with Phil Edwards (one of the two partners in the long-since-defunct Davison Publishing/Millington Books). In all probability, the final appearance of *Long Tall Dexter* (albeit ten years after he officially sanctioned its premature birth) might not have occurred without Phil's perception, encouragement and indeed his gallant effort to salvage the project after its initial demise.

Readers will find an impressive list at the foot of this introductory chapter of the many who have helped me, right from the outset and indeed during the actual putting together of the final manuscript. The first list comprises jazz musicians – with a perhaps not unexpected bias to those who play, or have played, the tenor saxophone, but also including several players who have worked with Dexter Gordon, in a variety of settings, through most of his years as a professional (and in some cases, even before that).

The second list is no less important, and the various persons involved know just how much their individual contributions, however seemingly small, have been in helping me to try to do justice to a major jazz figure, who in more recent times has even been rubbing shoulders with some of the screen's major contemporary personalities.

However more involved he becomes with films, for those who have known and respected the name of Dexter Gordon for any length of time prior to the production and release of *'Round Midnight*, its very utterance creates an instant image of a charismatic man who, in getting on for half a century, has remained one of the great individualists of the tenor saxophone. For me, Dexter Gordon has provided some of the most exciting moments in a not inconsiderable period spent listening to jazz, in the one setting above all others where its uniqueness as a vital musical art form of the present century is best appreciated: in live performance. Many of his recordings I have cherished for years, and will remain, I know, among those to which I will return at regular intervals in the future – in no matter what configuration they might become available – as much as any of my other great jazz heroes of the past and present. Other Gordonites will know exactly what I mean . . .

On an even more personal note, I still retain the many memories of meeting and talking with Dex, on several occasions in the past. My thanks to him for both his time and patience, in answering what might have seemed to him an endless list of questions. His answers were never less than interesting, and in their own way help immensely in documenting the history of the music we both love passionately during his many years of total commitment to and unswerving involvement with jazz. (All the numerous quotations reprinted throughout this book, by Dexter and so many others, emanate from interviews arranged with the author. Any remaining personal remarks are credited to the appropriate sources.)

It's something of a cliché, I know. But *Long Tall Dexter* has been, for all its fragmented history, a real labour of love.

Stan Britt
London, 1988

Pepper Adams	Red Holloway
Art Blakey	Freddie Hubbard
George Cables	Helen Humes
Red Callender	Milt Jackson
Arnett Cobb	Illinois Jacquet
Al Cohn	Stafford James
George Coleman	Pete King
Junior Cook	Yusef Lateef
Nathan Davis	Howard McGhee
Kenny Drew	Jackie McLean
Allen Eager	James Moody
Billy Eckstine	Dick Morrissey
Art Farmer	N.-H. Ørsted Pedersen
Frank Foster	Cecil Payne
Benny Golson	Art Pepper
Al Grey	Rufus Reid
Johnny Griffin	Sonny Rollins
Chico Hamilton	Ronnie Scott
Jimmy Heath	Tony Scott
Joe Henderson	Bud Shank
Billy Higgins	Zoot Sims

Bill Skeat
Sonny Stitt
Buddy Tate
Barbara Thompson
Stan Tracey

Cedar Walton
Don Weller
Bobby Wellins
Spike Wells
Trummy Young

Roy Carr (*NME*)
Gabrielle Clawson
Michael Cuscuna
Fred Dellar
Mike Hennessey (*Billboard*)
Chris Howes
Dave Kay (Kay Jazz
Productions)
Alan Luff
Brian O'Connor

Maurice Rolfe (*Jazzlink*)
Ali Shadwick/Jo Grant (EMI
Records)
Peter Vacher (*Jazz Express*)
Joop Visser (Charly Records)
Tony Williams (Spotlite
Records)
Nils Winther (SteepleChase
Records)

My grateful thanks to Don Tarrant for his splendid Dexter Gordon Discography. This is an absolutely essential adjunct to the book.

And, of course, most warm thanks to Sonny Rollins – himself one of the absolute giants of the tenor sax – for his typically warm tribute, included on the jacket.

1

Long Tall Dexter from LA

Dexter Keith Gordon was born in the city of Los Angeles, California, on 27 February 1923, the only son of Dr Frank Alexander Gordon and Mrs Gwendolyn Gordon.

Dexter's father was born in Fargo, North Dakota. He was to become one of the precious few blacks not only to graduate with distinction from medical school, but to go on to run his own successful practice on the West Coast. Gwendolyn Gordon, a native of Detroit, Michigan, was the daughter of parents who had settled in Canada. Her father's forebears were French; he rode the Canadian prairies as a full-time cowboy.

The Gordons' son grew to his adult height of six feet five well before he'd officially reached manhood. An intelligent boy, academically bright, Dexter always treated his parents with much respect, especially his father, for whom he had real and meaningful love and admiration, despite the fact that Dr Gordon was to die, prematurely and suddenly, and at a tragically early age in his son's development.

From as early as he can recall, Dexter Keith got to know about music, particularly jazz music. For Dr Gordon had become a great jazz fan, from his time at medical school, when he'd also played a little self-taught clarinet. Jazz records spun regularly in the Gordon home; then, of course, at the frantic speed of seventy-eight revolutions per minute. And when Frank Gordon observed that his son was responding – eagerly and spontaneously – to practically anything he was played, on the record player or from the radio, he was quick actively to encourage that interest.

Young Dexter also had extra incentive to develop his musical precocity. For one thing, his father numbered among his patients such jazz luminaries as Duke Ellington, Lionel Hampton and Marshall Royal. If Dexter didn't get the chance to meet them when they came to Dr Gordon's surgery, he was often taken backstage at local theatres when the top visiting bands played Los Angeles, as they did at regular intervals. Singers, too: as a shy boy, he was once introduced to the great Ethel Waters, in her dressing-room, after a concert. Actually seeing and hearing the great jazz bands of the thirties – Ellington, Lunceford, Basie, Calloway, Kirk – was the ultimate thrill for a wide-eyed, open-mouthed fast-growing boy. Just occasionally, too, there was the rare treat of meeting one of these super-heroes at home, following their acceptance of an invitation to dine with the doctor and his wife. It was all part of what Gordon, Jr, was later to call his 'cultural upbringing'.

Then, again, he would save his pocket money to buy jazz discs of his own, starting with the acquisition of a stack of used 78s rescued from possible extinction from the garage of a jukebox dealer.

Ultimately, though, the single most significant event in Dexter's rapidly developing involvement with music came when his father bought him a clarinet, with the proviso that he must take lessons, not only in learning to play the instrument, but also to study harmony and theory. So, at seven, Dexter studied clarinet and music, his father paying for the lessons.

The youngster's clarinet tutor was a New Orleans-born clarinettist, John Sturdevant, who favoured the classic Creole approach, and whose favourite soloists were Barney Bigard, Albert Nicholas and Buster Bailey. Gordon himself soon learned to appreciate the playing of these, and others, including Benny Goodman. At the same time, he continued his jazz studies by listening to more recordings, including those by Roy Eldridge (an all-time favourite performer), Benny Carter, Pete Brown and, significantly, the leading tenor saxophonists of the day: Coleman Hawkins, Chu Berry, Dick Wilson, Herschel Evans and Lester Young. There was something about the whole sound and concept of the saxophone in general and the tenor member of the family in particular which began to exert a fascination for him.

The switch from clarinet to sax soon became an inevitability. But before he obtained an alto, which got him into his school band, disaster struck the Gordon family. Suddenly, without any warning, his father collapsed and died of a heart attack. For Dexter, at twelve, it was a cataclysmic event. His father's shock passing, just when his only son was most in need of his father's love, encouragement and intensely practical approach to life, was to haunt him for many years. Indeed, he has said on more than one occasion that he never has truly recovered from that terrible personal tragedy, and there have been many times when he has wished his father were still alive.

The first saxophone he possessed – a Conn alto – he remembers as being a sound instrument.

> I think I used a hard reed, with a rubber mouthpiece . . . I tried a metal mouthpiece on alto, but it didn't project. Don't forget, at that time I'm only fifteen years old. The only one I've heard on alto who played a metal mouthpiece was Benny Carter, and he does it OK. But all the other alto players choose rubber. Of course, on tenor, it's another story . . .

His membership of the sax section of the school's dance band was not, however, the first time he played in grade school. Previously, he had made a most unusual debut, with a local kids' jug band. The instrumentation included washtub, pie pans (surrogate cymbals), kazoo, a snare drum . . . and the obligatory jug. The jug band played at amateur shows in Gordon's neighbourhood. Even before leaving school he had started making live appearances at what he has called 'sailor joints . . . for a dollar and a half a night and the kitty'.

As a saxophone convert, Dexter had already changed tutors. Lloyd Reese, a multi-instrumentalist who had played with several name bands, was also a highly respected teacher. Reese was playing lead trumpet for the Les Hite Orchestra during the period he spent teaching Gordon. His effect on the fledgling saxophonist was, as Dexter has recalled, positive and extremely rewarding.

Dexter's improvement continued with further studies at Jefferson High School. Jefferson High rated the study of music high on its curriculum. It is not at all surprising, perhaps, that, Gordon apart, several other young aspiring musicians at the school – contemporaries – went on to become celebrated as jazz players. These included drummers Chico Hamilton and Bill Douglass; trumpeters Ernie Royal, Lammar Wright, Jr; and altoist/vocalist Vi Redd. (One other Jefferson High pupil was Jackie Kelso. A brilliant altoist/clarinettist, and a gifted writer, Kelso's reluctance to leave the confines of LA robbed the jazz world at large of a superb talent – as any of his ex-schoolmates, Dexter included, will readily testify.) Certainly, the city and its neighbouring districts were blessed with burgeoning talent of extraordinary potential at this time. For, apart from the Jefferson High School prodigies, several students of another Los Angeles high school (Jordan) would in later years achieve varying degrees of fame. They included bassist Charles Mingus (who hadn't developed in any way as a composer at this stage), multi-reedsman Buddy Collette and trombonist Britt Woodman (and brothers).

Dexter Gordon's teacher at Jefferson High was Sam Brown, known more affectionately by his students as Count. Brown was responsible for the school's three orchestras – a marching band, an ensemble which featured light classics and a swing-type band – its repertoire included Goodman and Basie stock arrangements – the outfit which included Dexter Gordon and his jazz-conscious buddies. Before he left school, he was also to perform in a band comprising students from both Jefferson and Jordan high schools.

And leaving school was fast becoming almost a foregone conclusion for Gordon, because he knew exactly where his future lay, the only direction he wished to take. Already, he'd begun to gain access to some of the late-night clubs in downtown LA, only because he looked older than his slender years, his huge frame doing nothing to diminish this impression. These visits were all unofficial, of course, as by law he was under age. And the more he managed to observe, at close quarters, of the star performers who worked Los Angeles – at after-hours jams as well as official gigs – the more sure he was that one day he, too, would be trying to earn a living doing the same.

While still trying to make his mind up about splitting from Jefferson High – and offering a satisfactory explanation to his mother, who had just bought him his first tenor sax – he accepted an invitation to join the Harlem Collegians.

Long Tall Dexter, the tall, handsome, friendly young man from LA – who looked remarkably like Joe Louis, the reigning world heavyweight champ – was about to take the first step on the way to a lifetime in music.

2

The Real *West Coast Jazz . . .?*

For anyone interested in jazz's evolution and development during the past thirty-odd years, the term West Coast Jazz means, almost inevitably, one thing: a brand of light, airy, often delightful, sometimes downright anaemic, occasionally pretentious jazz music which originated from a fair-sized collection of musicians – mostly white – who either resided in California at the time, or who chose to put down roots in the sometimes sunnier climes of the second largest US state, during the early 1950s. The prospects, professionally, for the more well-read jazz musician, who decided to become an adoptive Californian – clement weather and glorious local scenery apart – were not inconsiderable. For one thing, there were ample opportunities for those with a proven ability to sight-read a variety of scores – classical, pop, even, occasionally, jazz – to earn impressive sums of money in the capacious area of film-soundtrack music. Recording studios too were plentiful, in and around Los Angeles and Hollywood. Playing jazz for a living – full-time, anyway – might well have to take second, or even third place in the lives of those musicians who would take the decision to make California their homes during this period. Even so, chances to play jazz, in live performance as well as on record, were there – although nowhere near so prolific as in, for example, New York City or Chicago.

Among the vanguard of West Coast jazz musicians of the 1950s, it is curious that few of the notables actually originated from California itself. For example, saxophonists Bob Cooper (Pittsburgh, Pa), Clifford Everett 'Bud' Shank, Jr (Jersey City, NJ), Bob Gordon (St Louis, Mo) and Gerry Mulligan (New York) were all strictly 'foreigners' to the western state. So too were other bastions of the new-wave Californian jazz movement, such as drummer/writer Shelly Manne (NYC), trumpeter/composer Milton 'Shorty' Rogers (Great Barrington, Mass), trombonist Frank Rosolino (Detroit, Mich), and saxophonist/clarinettist/composer Jimmy Giuffre (Dallas, Texas).

Much of the jazz exodus to the West Coast came about when a succession of big bands led by Stan Kenton and Woody Herman ended their respective lives by disbanding there. The early arrivals thus included Shank (ex-Kenton), Cooper (ex-Kenton, Jerry Gray), both in 1951; and Rogers (Herman, Kenton) and Manne (Herman, Kenton), both in 1952. Bassist/pianist Keith 'Red' Mitchell completed a European tour with Red Norvo (another adoptive Californian) in 1954 to take over the bass spot from Carson Smith in the prestigious, innovative pianoless quartet put together by Mulligan (who had left the Elliot Lawrence Orchestra to live and work in California two years before). Rosolino left Kenton after approximately three years as a principal soloist. Gordon, who was to die tragically in a motor accident in 1955, never really lived long enough to become an established Californian; he was touring continuously at the start of the fifties with the big bands of Alvino Rey (1948–51), Billy May (1952), Horace Heidt (1952–3), George Redman (1954), and Pete Rugolo (whose San Diego gig Gordon was driving to when he met his untimely death).

The groups put together by Mulligan, Manne and Rogers notwithstanding, the focal point of much of the 'new' 1950s West Coast jazz scene was Howard Rumsey's Lighthouse All Stars, a constantly changing band of erstwhile touring musicians fronted by a California-born bassist who had been a member of the first ever Stan Kenton Orchestra, remaining as a pivot of Kenton rhythm sections from 1941–2. After freelancing extensively throughout California, with outfits fronted by such as Charlie Barnet and Barney Bigard, Rumsey established a regular spot as leader of the house band at the Lighthouse jazz club, at Hermosa Beach, California, in 1949. The arrival of Rogers, Manne, Shank *et al*, coincided with the advent of Howard Rumsey's Lighthouse All Stars, an outfit which worked at the club until 1971, and which was recorded comprehensively during its lifetime.

The West Coast Jazz movement of the fifties did produce some fine music – but there was also a plethora of diluted jazz. Flutes, oboes, English horns – even occasionally harps and bassoons – became very much part of the Californian jazz scene. So too did an over-concentration of written scores and compositions.

It is significant that where the West Coast expatriates did produce some healthy-sounding music, this invariably occurred when they were supported by other musicians, who were either born in the region or who had lived in the state for some time. It is significant too that most of these were black. Included among this happy breed were pianists Hampton Hawes, Carl Perkins, Dolo Coker and Russ Freeman; reedmen Sonny Criss, Teddy Edwards, Harold Land and Buddy Collette; drummers Forrest 'Chico' Hamilton, Frank Butler and Chuck Thompson; trumpeters Chet Baker, Carmell Jones and Gerald Wilson (the latter to become much better known as big-band leader and composer); guitarist Barney Kessel; and bassists George 'Red' Callender (also an excellent tuba player) and Curtis Counce.

Widespread attention became focused upon the activities of these players – as well as other arrivals and/or welcome visitors, such as vibist Terry Gibbs, pianist Claude Williamson, trumpeter-brothers Pete and Conte Candoli, saxists Joe Maini, Bill Perkins and Richie Kamuca, drummer Stan Levey, and Red Mitchell. But for the established Californian fan, the early-1950s invasion did not mean that, at long last, jazz was being brought coastwards for the first time. The true jazz buffs of Los Angeles, for instance, were amply aware that a thoroughly stimulating jazz scene had for years been in operation *before* 1950.

The pre-1950s West Coast scene, as evidence unearthed in more recent times shows with much conviction, was indeed a fascinating, rewarding and yet shamefully neglected part of American jazz history. Mostly involving black musicians who had been born in and around Los Angeles, as well as those who were to become later residents, a whole portion of jazz of the

1940s remains clouded in what amounts almost to secrecy. This is partly due to poor documentation, but is also attributable to the ignorance of those who might have helped spread the word at the time so much superb jazz music was being made. Records that have been issued for the first time have appeared at infrequent intervals during the past ten to fifteen years; some others, recorded for then obscure labels, long since lost in the mists of California, have been rediscovered and reissued. Together, these help provide much valid evidence that while New York and Chicago were undoubtedly the focal points of jazz activity during the decade, much superior music was also being produced on the coast . . . even though some California residents too seemed unaware of its whereabouts.

Apart from a network of local radio stations which helped spread the local jazz news, as well as the records made locally which did manage to proliferate at least within the state, very little documentation, or even ground-level information seemed to be available to punters at that time.

During the early 1940s, the first real jazz event came with the rejuvenation of trombonist Kid Ory – already something of a jazz veteran – first through regular exposure via the popular Orson Welles radio show, in 1944. Later that same year, another local event took place that was to have far-reaching consequences inside a couple of years. A young film producer and avid jazz fan named Norman Granz decided to promote a live jazz concert at the Philharmonic Auditorium, Los Angeles. The date was 2 July. Among the featured artists were pianist Nat Cole, tenorists Illinois Jacquet and Jack McVea, and a young trombone player then with the Benny Carter Orchestra, J.J. Johnson.

But there were other, more regular, jazz events in Los Angeles that concerned mostly local musicians. It was in this latter environment that a youthful Dexter Gordon learned so much about jazz playing – and in the most practical and decisive way. Patricia Willard, a well-informed American writer, has produced what is probably the most comprehensive survey of the Los Angeles jazz scene during the mid-1940s, with her notes for a two-LP collection of recorded music, either originating from, or more currently released by, Savoy Records. Titled *Black California*, the set contains material recorded on the coast by such as Slim Gaillard, Sonny Criss, Harold Land, Wardell Gray, Roy Porter, the Farmer twins – Art and Addison – a youthful Eric Dolphy, plus the results of a 1950 date featuring singer Helen Humes, with Dexter Gordon, no less, playing fine blues tenor.

Patricia Willard, in her liner notes, has traced the kind of outlets at which jazz could be heard, either in more convention-al club times, or at after-hours sessions with only the participating musicians – and selected friends – present. These were sessions which could, and did, last through the night, finishing between 7.30 and 8.30 a.m. The focal point of club activity was Central Avenue. The most popular clubs to be found in the Central Avenue locale included the Club Alabam (on the east side of the avenue), the Down Beat (at the junction of Central and 41st Street), Lovejoy's (sometimes known as Papa Lovejoy's, and sited on the avenue itself), Jack's Basket, the Elk's Club, Backstage & Brothers, the Hi-de-Ho, the Swing Club, the Brown Bomber (named after Joe Louis, the most respected of all the US heavyweight boxing champions), the Club Finale, the Black Flamingo and the 331 Club.

The 331, on Eighth Street, was the joint which showcased the piano artistry of Nat King Cole in the days before he became one of the most respected pop singers in the world. Later, he was to graduate to his own King Cole Room, at El Trocadero on Sunset Strip. Cole, whose keyboard work – itself influenced by Earl Hines and Teddy Wilson – had enabled him to be ranked within the upper echelon of top jazz pianists of the era, was generally acknowledged as the leader of the pack as far as after-hours jamming in LA was concerned.

Drummer Chico Hamilton was part of that mid-1940s Californian jazz scene. Before that, he'd played with a local school jazz band which had an interesting line-up: Buddy Collette (the eldest of the group), on saxophones and clarinet; Dexter Gordon, tenor sax; Gerry Wiggins, piano; Charles Mingus, bass; Hamilton, drums. After finishing school, Hamilton became an eager participant in much of the late-night jamming, involving the younger as well as the established musicians.

The jazz scene in California, man, was fantastic . . . and as far back as I can remember. There was only one type of music, you know, and that was music to swing by. *That* form of music. There were good orchestras around, always. And the calibre of musicians in LA was always excellent. They were very learned. Everyone read music. They *had* to read, because the arrangers out there – Phil Moore, and people like that – everybody arranged . . . the whole world was cognizant of orchestras and orchestrations, because that was mostly what they had in the forties. Because there was no such thing as small groups and things like that.

The small-group scene evolved, remembers Hamilton, when the smaller clubs appeared and became popular.

Joints like Lovejoy's, Jack's Basket; places like that. Where Ben, Illinois would mix with Dexter and myself . . . this was about '39–'40. Dexter and myself, we were playing, first, when we were about thirteen to fourteen years old! Dexter confirmed recently [in 1980] that he and I were the only two guys to get an 'A' in English in the whole of our class at high school. Dex and I grew up together – we've known each other since, I guess, we were about twelve. We were all in a band led by Al Adams. He was a bass player. Wasn't very good, but he was the oldest guy in the band, so we made him the leader. That band consisted of Buddy Collette, Ernie Royal, Dexter, Jackie Kelso [an altoist], and myself. Oh yes, and a guy who's now deceased – James Nelson, we called Hawk – also on tenor. Charles [Mingus] used to come by and play . . . We were in high school [then]. Our band, man, was so heavy that when Basie and Jimmie Lunceford and those bands would come to town, they'd come over to our *rehearsals*! They flipped over us. We were kids. But remember, they weren't really *that* much older than us . . .

At this time, the all-star youth band rehearsed constantly. Its repertoire consisted mostly of the Basie/Lunceford-type charts that were popular at the time, using stock arrangements.

Chico Hamilton remembers Dexter Gordon's early work, in and around Los Angeles, as an aspiring tenor saxophonist:

> Like Pres? Yeah, but who wasn't, man? We all idolized Pres. And I [also] idolized Jo Jones. In California, it was mandatory in the educational system that music be compulsory. You had to take some form of music at school . . . either music appreciation or an instrument or something. It was very hip at that time. I guess that's why all of us [jazzmen] got into music.

Hamilton recalls too that the young enthusiasts got to hear about major jazz events through a series of jazz-conscious radio disc jockey-enthusiasts.

Patricia Willard has noted that the important radio stations in California for the jazz-minded, together with the respective presenters, included KWKW (Bill Sampson, whose regular jazz programme eventually was beamed direct from Jack's Basket); KALI (Roy Loggins and his 'Blowin' with Roy' presentation); KOWL (Joe Adams – the station's 'Mayor of Melody'); KFWB (Sunday nights with Dave Dexter, soon to become a successful record producer/executive with the fledgling Capitol Records company, and a noted jazz scribe); KLA (Al Jarvis, whose varied programme included some jazz); KFVD (Jack the Bellboy, succeeded later by Hank the Night Watchman); and KFWB (respected local jazz concert promoter Gene Norman's two-hour jazz programme). The last-named was to receive some kind of jazz immortality, like Norman Granz, for his highly respected jazz concerts at venues such as the Civic Auditorium, Pasadena, and the Shrine Auditorium, LA. (Dexter Gordon was just one of an impressive number of star instrumentalists who appeared at Norman-sponsored Just Jazz concert presentations.)

Chico Hamilton was an avid listener to the radio stations which beamed so much great jazz music over the airwaves.

When an orchestra or a band would come to the West Coast, it was an *event*! You heard about it on the radio. They used to let us out of school to go see these bands perform. We used to go and meet them at the railway station. Because when a band got to California, that was it – you couldn't go any further! Literally. So I was always cognizant of jazz music. But you didn't think in terms of 'jazz'. It was *music* – it was the only kind of music you knew . . .

Altoist Art Pepper was destined to become one of the greatest saxophone players on the West Coast. Born in Gardena, California, a predominantly black area, Pepper was two and a half years younger than Gordon. Yet, despite their slight age difference and their ethnic dissimilarity, they hung out together as teenagers – and, not surprisingly, got the chance to play in each other's company. In those days of youthful innocence, Pepper didn't experience any kind of racialism.

When I got off the street-car into the black neighbourhood people would be walking down the street. And they'd say: 'Hey, man, saxophone?' I'd say: 'Yeah.' And they'd say: 'Sure like to hear you blow, man. Come on down to the club.' People I'd never met. I'd be alone – yet I was never robbed. Nobody called me 'White motherfucker', and all that. They'd just say: 'Come on, get that horn out and blow.' First time I met Dex? It was before I went into the Club Alabam. I think I met him on the street, in some club. I thought he was marvellous. I loved the way he played – he played like Pres. Only it was a little bigger, the sound. Whereas Zoot, then, sounded exactly like Pres.

Pepper's next musical association with Gordon came about when he accepted an offer to join a small combo led by Lee Young, drummer-brother of the legendary Lester. Pianist Gerry Wiggins and bassists Mingus or Joe Mondragon also worked with Lee Young's band when Pepper was a member. Already, the youthful giant was beginning to make a definite impact as a tenorman who was obviously going places. Pepper recalls from this period that there were other, non-musical reasons for remembering their friendship.

> What happened next was Dexter and I became very close. Unfortunately, we both liked having a good time. He started using sulphate, which is like an upper . . . it makes you feel like there's electricity running through your body . . . you couldn't even think of going to sleep. It made you play fast. He was like an influence on me. And Lee Young was very down on drugs, or too much alcohol. He liked me. He just felt like I was a kid – which I was. Dexter and me, we just had a ball. And Lee Young saw this. He talked to me a coupla times. And finally he said: 'Art, whatever you're doing, it's really not good for you. It's gonna spoil your life. You're gonna spoil your career and everything. You might die from too much of something.' He said: 'Dexter's a bad influence.' I said: 'No, no, no!'

When Dexter Gordon returned to the West Coast in 1946, he was already something of a local hero with the jazz fans, especially those who had heard him solo with the big bands of Armstrong and Eckstine, most notably his 'Blowin' the Blues Away' duet with Gene Ammons, as a member of the legendary Eckstine Orchestra. By which time, the electrifying message of bebop had well and truly invaded all areas of jazz in California in general and Los Angeles in particular.

Bebop began to make a significant impact on the West Coast in 1945, which more or less coincided with the arrival of the Coleman Hawkins Sextet, present for a three-month season at Billy Berg's Club, Hollywood. Hawkins, the accepted Father of the Jazz Tenor Saxophone, had become intrigued with the new sounds that were being heard nightly on 52nd Street, in New York City – a location in which Hawkins's name had become something of a legend. Hawkins brought with him to the coast a mostly 'mainstream'-based sextet. Youngest member of the sextet was Howard McGhee, an often brilliant soloist, whose trumpet had been heard with the bands of Georgie Auld, Count Basie and Charlie Barnet. Oscar Pettiford, three and a half years

younger than McGhee, had co-led (with Dizzy Gillespie) the
first real bebop combo to work 52nd Street. He shared with
McGhee and, to a lesser extent, Hawkins, a profound interest
in and involvement with bop. Sir Charles Thompson, the
Hawkins band's piano player, although basically a middle-
period performer, had recorded and worked with Charlie
Parker – and Dexter Gordon – in New York, in September
1945. Pettiford left Hawkins towards the end of the Berg's
engagement, working first on the coast with the remarkable
Boyd Raeburn Orchestra then, in November of the same year,
joining Duke Ellington. His all-round brilliance enabled him to
become, together with the already deceased Jimmy Blanton, the
most gifted of all bass players to work with Ellington.

McGhee left Hawkins after the Hollywood engagement, then
put together his own band, from the pool of local musicians, as
well as participating in numerous jam-session promotions,
during which time he became something of a catalyst at
after-hours blowing sessions. Originally a mid-period trumpet
player, with experience in the orchestras of Lionel Hampton,
Andy Kirk and the other previously-mentioned big bands, he
had been deeply influenced by Dizzy Gillespie. His playing,
during this time, found him successfully making the transition
from swing to bop. During his stay on the coast – McGhee left,
finally, to make a Stateside tour for Norman Granz's Jazz at the
Philharmonic troupe in 1947 – his became a distinctive and
respected solo voice on trumpet. It was McGhee's sheer
professionalism that was to salvage something from the
infamous, somewhat horrifying 'Lover Man' record date, for
Ross Russell's local Dial label, in 1946.

But it was Parker's first visit to Los Angeles which had really
ignited the local bebop scene. Together with Dizzy Gillespie,
Milt Jackson, Al Haig, Ray Brown and Stan Levey, Parker
arrived in the City of the Angels from the Big Apple during the
second week of December 1945. The sextet had been booked to
play Billy Berg's. Parker's personal problems meant, in the
event, that not only did he relinquish the leadership of the band
to Gillespie before the season ended, but he would also
undertake that terrifying Dial date – made under Howard

McGhee's name – which would produce jagged, tortured, incomplete playing by the altoist that mirrored only too well his already shattered mental state. Even so, for those present at the opening of the Berg's season, Parker's playing electrified everyone, including the local musicians who helped pack the club – even though, ultimately, the non-musician jazz locals didn't respond over-warmly to Bird and his colleagues.

On his arrival in Los Angeles, Howard McGhee had soon linked up with some of the best local jazzmen, including altoist Sonny Criss, pianist Hampton Hawes, drummer Roy Porter and tenorist Teddy Edwards (the last-named having arrived himself in LA recently after playing alto with the Ernie Fields combo).

One other musician with whom McGhee became acquainted – socially as well as musically – was tenorist Wardell Gray. Gray, born in Oklahoma City, had established an enviable reputation with several bands, including that of Earl Hines, before deciding to settle in California in 1945. Still to become a familiar name among jazz soloists, he was, at all times, very much a musician's musician. His style – always individual – developed into an almost perfect synthesis of Lester Young and Charlie Parker.

Dexter Gordon met Wardell Gray first when the former was touring with Hampton. They struck up an instant friendship and a mutual admiration society.

> We met in Detroit. He was gigging there. With Howard McGhee, Lucky Thompson, Tommy Flanagan . . . all those people. They too were all kids. We became friends. And next time I saw him he was playing with Earl Hines. At a place called El Gratto, in Chicago. And the girl he married was in the chorus line at the club.

When Gordon decided to leave the whirlwind atmosphere of 52nd Street and New York for the first time, he turned, not surprisingly, to the state of his birth, where he and Gray were able to cement their friendship at greater length. Musically too they were, from their first association, very compatible. No surprise here, again, as Gordon's initial Young influence had been suffused with the message of Parker and bebop. Both, of course, were already supreme individualists: Gray, with his lighter, more serpentine phrasing, Gordon with his huge sound, hard tone and more rugged way of phrasing rhythmically. Playing together, they made for intriguing contrast – yet their overall messages, and the way in which they delivered them, were not so far apart.

The marvellous empathy between the pair is simply displayed during their friendly battle on a two-sided recording of a number appropriately titled 'The Chase', wherein both engaged in a series of genuinely exciting chase choruses, reducing gradually from thirty-two bars apiece to sixteen bars, then eight, finally four. Such 'duels' between the two tenors were to become a regular occurrence in concert and club performances for several years.

'The Chase' was recorded for Dial with a fine local rhythm section in support – pianist Jimmy Bunn (who had performed at the Parker/'Lover Man' date), bassist Red Callender and drummer Chuck Thompson (later to become an integral member of the fine 1950s Hampton Hawes Trio). In allowing Gray and Gordon the luxury of a six-and-a-half-minute recording of the number, producer Ross Russell's idea was to present a studio re-creation of some of the heat and excitement generated by the two tenors, who had established 'The Chase' in nightly performances at the Bird in the Basket club – to almost riotous acclaim. According to Russell, 'The Chase' became Dial's biggest-selling disc – even Parker's recordings for the label were less successful.

Russell was to bring Gordon back into the studio again the same year – in December – for another 'Chase'-type tenor battle. This time, however, Gordon's friendly opponent was Teddy Edwards, already well established as one of California's top men on his horn. Re-creating the marvellously spontaneous quality of the Gordon–Gray duel – with a view, presumably, to achieve at least its musical and artistic equal – was, of course, asking much from both Gordon and Edwards. 'The Duel', with the two protagonists accompanied this time by another fine rhythm section – Jimmy Rowles, piano; Roy Porter, drums; and Callender again on bass – produced much fine music during two takes – the longer of which was issued under the alternative title of 'Horning in'. But rewarding as the results were, the session did not quite match up to the overall excellence of its predecessor.

Dexter Gordon has fond memories of working with Gray. He and the slim, quiet-spoken Middle-westerner first got together, he recalls, after Gordon had left the Eckstine band and started working on 52nd Street.

Then, I came back to LA in '47. And the jam-session thing was going on very heavily at that time, at several different clubs. At all the sessions, they would hire a rhythm section, along with, say, a couple of horns. But there would always be about ten horns up on the stand. Various tenors, altos, trumpets and an occasional trombone. But it seemed that in the wee small hours of the morning – always – there would be only Wardell and myself. It became a kind of traditional thing. Spontaneous? Yeah! Nothing was really worked out. It was a natural thing. We were coming out of the same bags – Lester and Bird . . . Bird was never really a mystery to me because he was coming out of Lester. And others, too. When he evolved, he came out of Lester – that line. It was just a natural-evolution-type thing. Plus his *own* thing, of course. But it was the same lineage. That's where I was. That's where Wardell was . . .

Although the reception to his and Gray's nightly involvement with 'The Chase' was never less than enthusiastic, did it surprise him that the recording of the number did so well?

I guess so. 'Cos I never made any money . . . same old story! We used to work around LA. It wasn't that regular a thing . . . there wasn't anyone who had that kind of foresight to put all these things together – properly, that is. All these things occurred happenstance-wise. Which is why I think there is something so special about my present manager, Maxine Gregg – she has that foresight and understanding to do something for you correctly; putting it all together. The direction is settled upon. Of course, there have been agents – like Joe Glaser and Monte Kay and Billy Shaw – who know how to handle things. But, usually, these things go straight through booking agents. They book you OK, but that's about the extent of it. I guess it would have happened with someone like Louis [Armstrong], somebody of that calibre. He had Joe Glaser, and therefore there was some kind of directional thing. But basically, agents will say we'll get a week for you here . . . and that's about it. The only one I can remember really doing anything was Monte Kay, with the MJQ. He did fantastically well for them for twenty-one years or so. But he was the only one in all those years. Until right now, that is, and Maxine and me . . .

Even though neither Gordon nor Gray made a financial score with their otherwise successful recording of 'The Chase' – or indeed through the medium of live performance on the concert stage or at the Bird in the Basket – the sheer enjoyment and fulfilment it gave the big man does not fade from his keen memory. And even though his friend and erstwhile partner in those titanic tenor battles has been dead now for over a quarter of a century, his feelings towards the other man, both as a friend and as a musician, remain deeply warm. In the latter capacity, Gordon summarizes thus:

Wardell? He was a *beautiful* player. Very musical. I learned a lot from him. Yes, of course, his death was something of a tragedy. It was from an OD – overdose of heroin. It happened when he was in Las Vegas, appearing at Joe Louis's Club – the first black hotel/club in Vegas. After rehearsal, he'd gone back to the hotel, and he and Teddy Hale, the dancer, got high. Teddy told me he then went to his room to get clean, to get ready. He came back to fetch Wardell, to go to the gig, and he found Wardell was out, cold. Hanging over the bed, you know. He and a friend tried to revive him . . . there was somebody else about – maybe his connection, I don't know. They got scared. Panicked. Took him out of the hotel . . . making it appear he was drunk – you know, one on each side of him. And they put him into a car, drove out to the desert and dumped him. In the process – because he was deadweight or something – they cracked his neck. There was no mystery, really. Teddy's not that big, although I don't know who the other guy was. But it was just through deadweight . . .

Gray, as Gordon rightly says, was indeed a 'beautiful player'. He was also one of the most consistent of performers on his instrument, turning in one superb solo after another, whatever the context, wherever the venue. During his residence on the coast, Gray was also one of the most popular players, taking part in a regular succession of studio recording dates and live performances, many of the latter having been captured for posterity on record. Although the bulk of the recordings that find Gordon and Gray working in close proximity readily demonstrate a marked individuality – as well as a difference in approach – there was one occasion at least when the former did exhibit definite traces of Gray's style.

In a particularly perceptive analysis of Dexter Gordon, written in 1961, British jazz writer Michael James noted that Gordon's playing on a recording date for the Swing Time label (which took place in Hollywood, in June 1952) incorporated certain devices essential to his buddy's own style.

. . . The figure with which Gordon follows his quotation from 'I Hear Music' at the start of his solo in 'The Rubaiyat' was also one of Gray's favourite phrases. This is not the only occasion on which Gordon borrows from his partner's vocabulary, but there is no doubt that he plays very well. His strident tone and incisive swing make an intriguing contrast with the smoother texture of Gray's solos, as they do elsewhere on the record . . .

Probably the last occasion that Gray and Gordon appeared together – in concert, in tandem – took place at the Pasadena Civic Auditorium, in February of 1952. Accompanied by pianist Bobby Tucker (at that time celebrating nearly four years as singer Billy Eckstine's personal accompanist), Don Bagley (then bassist with the Kenton Orchestra) and Chico Hamilton (soon to become the first drummer with the Mulligan Quartet), the two tenors were part of the last 'official' Gene Norman Just Jazz concert presentation. Not surprisingly, but Gordon and Gray chose to reprise 'The Chase'. Fortunately, too, Norman had decided to record both this and 'The Steeplechase', a Parker blues line which had been based on Gray's own 'Easy Swing' (which the composer had recorded two years before Parker's Savoy version of 'Steeplechase'). At three seconds over eleven minutes, this is very much of an extended version of 'The Chase'. Both musicians are not far from the top of their game, obviously relishing the opportunity to flex their musical muscles, and stimulated by the sympathetic support of a solid accompanying group, together with the spontaneous response of an audience, obviously hip to the excitement engendered by the pair. The result is chorus after chorus of truly fine jazz from both men, with Gray probably taking the honours. For 'The Steeplechase', the principals are joined by the trumpet of Conte Candoli (perhaps best remembered for his wide big-band experience), for nearly fourteen minutes' work-out. The presence of the tenor 'twins' inspires Candoli to produce one of his finest recorded solos. For the remainder of the date, Candoli is absent; unusually, perhaps, Les Thompson (a little-known, if competent accordionist) is added. The sound of Thompson's instrument doesn't exactly enhance the proceedings. And although there are more fine sounds from both Gray and Gordon – especially during a fast 'Take the "A" Train', and a consummately swinging 'Robbins' Nest' – nothing else improves upon either 'The Chase' or 'Steeplechase'.

Among other distinguished jazz musicians who remember Dexter Gordon fondly from his West Coast days of the 1940s and early 1950s are tenorists Zoot Sims and Buddy Tate, drummer Billy Higgins and trombonist Al Grey.

Higgins, later to become not only a frequent associate at recording sessions of the 1960s and thereafter, but also one of Gordon's top three all-time drummers, recalls hearing that huge saxophone sound at a very tender age.

Central Avenue used to be the focal point of LA. Because whenever any of the cats came through there – Bird, Miles ... others – that's where they would play: in the Central Avenue clubs. There was a lotta good music at that time. Teddy Edwards was another of the locals. He was one of the first guys who took me out and taught me a lot, too. When I first started playing with Teddy, I must have been about eighteen years old ... I knew Dex since when I was a little kid. We were all born around the same neighbourhood. Near Central Avenue, and near 42nd Street. Dexter's folks lived around the same part. I first met Dexter outside my house. He was going with my sister. I was a little bitty guy. I looked up one day and there was this huge cat. I must have been about five or six years old. That's when I met him. Oh yeah – he was *the* guy around there, musically ... he'd been playing with Louis Armstrong and Hampton and all. He was a local hero.

John Haley 'Zoot' Sims was born at Inglewood, in those days a country district of California, not too far from Dexter Gordon's birthplace. He was another aspiring musician who started gigging locally during his early teens – and yet another Californian who has vivid memories of the Central Avenue jazz scene. Seemingly, there were few problems even for a fifteen-year-old to gain access to the clubs.

That never bothered me! I mean, they never bothered me in the club. I guess I knew one guy or something ... they knew me, and I could sit in. I remember the Swing Club – that's where I met Jimmie Rowles. I was about fifteen. The all-night sessions came later. But then I started going to Central

Avenue. I used to get out of Honey Murphy's about six in the morning. I remember Dexter being around, then. Buddy Collette . . . Wardell Gray, too – actually, he was a little more advanced than I was. Yes, and I played with Mingus out there, and Chico Hamilton. I used to hang out with Herbie Steward a lot. I met him also at one of those sessions . . .

As far as he can recall, Sims first met Dexter Gordon at the Swing Club. As a fellow Lester Young follower, Sims naturally was able to relate easily and avidly to the playing of the tall, black tenorman. Even at an early stage in the latter's development, was he fairly certain that Gordon possessed the kind of ability that would make a lasting impact on the jazz-saxophone world – and, moreover, become one of that genre's most celebrated exponents? 'I never thought of it in those terms, that he'd go somewhere. I just went around with my ears wide open. I *knew* that he was good. Maybe, even at that time, I thought he *was* somewhere! But he's *always* been a good player. And, naturally, he was right up my alley . . .'

One other celebrated jazz soloist, a man over two years younger than Gordon, is Al Grey. A veteran of many big-band associations, including considerable years' playing with leaders such as Count Basie (the band with which he has gained most international popularity), Dizzy Gillespie, Lionel Hampton and Jimmie Lunceford, Grey had first met and heard Gordon play in and around Los Angeles when he (Grey) was visiting with one of his name-band jobs. 'At that time, he didn't actually have that much of a name. But I knew that he had arrived when he played with the Billy Eckstine Band, with Gene Ammons and the others. I just *knew* that he was a tremendous talent . . .' At that time Grey was working with the Benny Carter Orchestra, which also included Miles Davis in its ranks at that time. The Carter band was gainfully employed for some time on the West Coast.

Charlie Parker was working in LA at that time at a hotel where they'd go to work at one o'clock in the morning. In those days, there used to be sessions every night, because the musicians used to be going out jamming every night. Used to blow with Bird at that time at one of the clubs – used to be scared to death. They had the Casablanca, where they had the Three Blazers – Oscar Moore and his brothers. We'd go to the Elk's Club, though we'd go to Ivie Anderson's Chicken Shack first. We'd see Art Tatum, who'd come on late at night . . . and they'd have Erroll Garner . . . they'd have all these sessions every night. Teddy Edwards . . . Bumps Myers . . . masses of people, every night. Because sessions would go on until daybreak. It was allowed then. But when the musicians' union came along, they didn't allow any more jamming and everything. That also created less great musicians, because they didn't have the opportunity to do their experimental work – to experiment is *another* thing, you see . . .

And Dexter Gordon was a vital component of the nightly 'experimental work'. Grey remembers:

Like I say, he was there, on the scene, every night. Just blowing. No job – he'd just be out for jamming, you know. At least I had a job . . . you see, I was with Benny – Dexter, too, but for only a little while. We'd get off at twelve o'clock, and we'd be zooming downtown, which was on the east side, all up and down Central Avenue. Lucky Thompson was blowing, too; he had a band that was a kinda jazz workshop: Buddy Collette, Charlie Mingus, Oscar Bradley, Jr . . . Britt Woodman, Lee Young. And they used to have jam sessions out at Billy Berg's, in Hollywood. Dex would come out and play on Sundays. Because we could play on a radio show, we could pick up that little extra money right there on the scene. You had to make it early, because all the cats would be there. But you'd be *paid* for that. In the meantime, there was no recording, so this is why you hear some things today perhaps [only] on V-disc records . . .

During those sessions – impromptu or otherwise – Al Grey got to blow with Gordon on numerous occasions. And the trombonist remembers him as being an inveterate jammer.

Grey, too, was impressed by what he heard of the young Californian. The reasons were, perhaps, obvious:

> His *sound*, of course, plus the fact that he was running his chord changes different than the others. I suppose he had more knowledge of the chords. That was the whole thing about Wardell, he had complete knowledge of his instrument and he was running them all kinds of ways himself. But Dex had that big sound going for him as well.

George Holmes 'Buddy' Tate was already an established and much-respected tenorman when he first heard Dexter Gordon. A mainstay of many territorial big hands of the Midwest, Tate's reputation had been cemented by a ten-year tenure with the Count Basie Orchestra. Tate had joined Basie, in 1939, as a replacement for Herschel Evans, who had died prematurely. Tate and Gordon first met when the former made his first-ever trip to California with Basie.

> He was a young, strong, healthy 'little' kid . . . now, I'm six-two, and still I had to look up to Dexter! I looked like a little boy next to Dexter. Jo Jones, incidentally, named him King Joe – after Joe Louis, who was the world heavyweight champion, then. Jo said: 'This man's a prize-fighter, man, he's gonna be a protegé of Joe's.' We became friends because he was hanging out with us on the Basie band. I didn't hear him play, then. When I first heard him, was about 1941. Lionel Hampton had organized his [first] big band and he [Dexter] was with this band. He and Illinois were the featured tenor players. We liked him very, very much – and so did Pres.

Of Gordon's abilities in 1941, Tate is absolutely certain:

> He swung, and he always had a good sound. And he had some nice ideas. He made them and you could follow him – you knew what he was doing. He's *always* been a good player. He's played good all through the years. After leaving

Hamp's band, he did a lot of beautiful things. Like he and Wardell Gray – 'The Chase'; then, with Gene Ammons. They actually started the two-tenor thing. I'm very pleased to see his success now. Because he's always been playing good. It's not just that he got better and then got the break. I'm so happy to see him finally acknowledged . . .

Trumpeter/flugelhornist Art Farmer is another graduate of Jefferson High, although Dexter had long since been and gone. Farmer and his twin brother Addison had been born in Council Bluffs, Iowa, in 1928, but moved to Los Angeles seventeen years later. After serving his apprenticeship in various local big bands (including that of Benny Carter), Art Farmer became a much-in-demand soloist at the end of the forties and beginning of the fifties (just prior to touring for a couple of years with Lionel Hampton). During his pre-Hampton period on the coast, Farmer accepted a job as a member of a Dexter Gordon-led sextet, during one of the latter's return trips to California. Other members included Hampton Hawes, drummer Chuck Thompson, plus two musicians who never made significant reputations: trumpeter Kenny Bright and bassist Clarence Jones. The sextet played only a few dates together, mostly dances at ballrooms.

I thought he was a great player. Because that was, without doubt, a person of *that* stature, and you don't even judge them at that time. You figure, well, whatever he's doing it must be great. You're not even critical. The great big sound . . . the swing . . . the ideas that are so clear – there was never like he was fumbling or just playing a bunch of notes. He's always playing phrases. He's making a statement all the time. He always amazed me that he was able to play chorus after chorus. And each chorus would find him coming up with something new. It wouldn't be a matter of repetition. And it was an outgoing thing; it was very attractive to the people. He was able to communicate so well with the audience, with the listener . . .

Sonny Stitt, a one-time section mate of Dexter's in the Billy Eckstine Orchestra, was one of the first saxophonists to gain a reputation of some distinction in the jazz revolution of the forties. Equally adept on both alto and tenor saxophones (for a time, at the end of the decade, he also played baritone with great fluency), Stitt's twin influences throughout his career remained, i· equal proportions, Lester Young (tenor) and Charlie Parker (alto). Stitt's admiration for Dexter Gordon dates from the very first time he heard the Californian play.

> I rode thirty-five miles on my bicycle, from my home to Flint, Michigan, to hear Dexter, with Hampton. The only drag was, he was going home. But he was good, what he had to play. Later on, of course, I really heard him when I joined Billy Eckstine, in '45. Boy! He was out front of that band, shouting like a trumpet man. He was doing it right, then! And Dexter used to really show off on 'Airmail Special'.

Bassist/tuba player George 'Red' Callender has been a resident Californian since 1936, when he was twenty. A vastly experienced musician who has worked with many of the greatest jazzmen (Parker, Armstrong, Tatum, Young, Garner, Hampton, *et al*), Callender first met Dexter Gordon in 1939. Dexter was still attending Jefferson High. Already, though, he was hanging out and jamming in the Central Avenue after-hours joints, in the kind of jam sessions where Callender's rock-solid bass playing was an always welcome and wholly dependable part of proceedings.

Callender and Gordon became friends.

> Dex was always quite a ..acter. Soon, unfortunately, he had got into some drug trouble. But he was always a big, strong young guy. Still, today, I love him. Always did. Always the same guy, to me. He is a really dear person. You judge how people relate to you. He's a beautiful guy. Warm. But, then, that has always been the way with him.

A twenty-one-year-old saxophonist from Dayton, Ohio, who

had moved to California after university, in 1947, was destined to become one of the protagonists of the West Coast Jazz movement of the fifties, after he'd gained experience with the big bands of Charlie Barnet and Stan Kenton. Bud Shank, a raw, completely unknown player when he too took his alto sax into the jam-session arena of Central Avenue in 1947 (prior to joining Barnet later the same year), first heard Gordon at several of the after-hours haunts.

> Naturally, I loved what he was doing. I was a Lester Young disciple – and fan. And Dexter was right out of that mould. So, naturally, I was intrigued by him. Yes, he was a star already, and I was a young punk white kid. So, there was a lot of looking up to do . . . literally, of course, as he's so tall! There were a lot of top guys working around town, but the two big heroes were Dexter and Wardell. I might have jammed with him once or twice, but I don't think so. I wasn't in his league, so I don't think I would have been permitted to play with him. Of course, I saw him when guys like Mulligan, Shorty, Shelly and myself were popular in the fifties. But not too often. Sadly, he was off the scene for a long time. And the scene couldn't be quite the same without him . . .

3

Po'k Chops with Hamp/All Love with Louis

Dexter Gordon's ever-increasing musical activities, in and around Central Avenue, continued to bring his burgeoning talents to the attention of numerous visiting jazz musicians, especially those who were, almost obligatorily, drawn to the nightly jam-session scene in that area. They were impressed not only by his Pres-ian tenor-playing, with its already big sound, but also by the teenager's onstage charisma.

For Dexter himself, the completion of academic studies could hardly come soon enough. There was never any doubt, by the time he'd reached seventeen, that he would become a full-time musician – and, of course, a *jazz* musician. Exactly how that career would shape up, both inside and outside Los Angeles, had not been mapped out in his mind. But that was the *only* direction he could think of . . . nothing else mattered.

One telephone call was sufficient in deciding when, and in which direction, Dexter Gordon's career-proper in music would take a definite step forward. The all-important caller identified himself at once as Marshall Royal, one of Dr Gordon's musician/patients, and a respected clarinettist/saxophonist of some experience. At first, the younger man assumed it was one of his mates, engaging in a smart joke. He was assured that the call was for real. Indeed, said Royal, he was ringing with the serious intent of asking young Dexter if he'd be interested in taking the second-tenor position in a new big band Lionel Hampton – with Royal's comprehensive assistance – was assembling, in LA.

Not unnaturally, perhaps, Gordon's immediate reaction was one of stunned silence. Royal probably sensed the youngster's shock. 'Hamp knows of your playing,' he assured Dexter, 'and he's impressed. Otherwise, I mightn't be ringing you . . .' As an afterthought, Royal tagged on the news that a couple of Dex's jazz-mad friends would also be working with Hamp – drummer Lee Young, and Marshall's trumpet-playing younger brother, Ernie Royal. Finally, Marshall Royal invited Dexter to bring his horn to Hampton's house the same evening.

This time, there was no hesitation. Horn in hand, Gordon presented himself at Hampton's, around six o'clock, as Marshall Royal had suggested. Royal himself was there. So, too, were pianist Sir Charles Thompson, guitarist Irving Ashby, Lee Young and, of course, Hampton. The latter was friendliness itself, welcomed Dexter into a front room, then invited him to join those present in a little impromptu jamming. Hampton seemed pleased, smiled one of his wide smiles and asked the youngster: 'Well, would you like to come into the band?' Dexter's reply – an emphatic '*yeeah!*' – came automatically, almost before Hampton had finished his question.

Hampton told him to settle things at home, pack his gear, and be prepared to hit the road, with the rest of the guys, aboard what turned out to be a none too comfortable – and definitely second-hand – band bus. Dexter assured his new boss that the situation, home-wise, was cool. That he'd be at the point of departure on time.

Then, he returned home. He told his mother he was about to leave, that he was about to embark on a long tour with the new Lionel Hampton band. She asked him, a little worried, about his schooling. He said he'd probably return to school at a later date. But Mrs Gordon didn't press him to stay, or try to make him wait for a year or so before trying his luck as a full-time professional musician. She knew that any such entreaty would be useless. Her son was absolutely certain he was going.

By 1940, Lionel Hampton had become internationally recognized as one of jazz's premier soloists, and indeed the one musician above all others who elevated the vibraphone from being simply a novelty member of the percussion department to a status equal to that of the more conventional jazz instruments like trumpet, trombone, piano and clarinet.

Hampton was born in Louisville, Kentucky, in 1909. Originally, he rose to some prominence at the very end of the twenties, principally as a powerful, hard-driving drummer, with the Les Hite Orchestra. A recording session in 1930, with Louis Armstrong fronting the Hite outfit, proved to be of signal importance for Hampton, for it was the first occasion which found him doubling on vibes – albeit in this context his use of the instrument found him playing a purely accompanying role.

Hampton spent four years with Hite, with occasional appearances as a member of Nat Shilkret's Studio Orchestra. He also took time off from playing full-time to study music more formally, at the University of Southern California. A reunion with Armstrong came in 1936, with Hampton appearing as a masked drummer in the film *Pennies from Heaven*. During the same year he put together his own big band, resident for a while at Hollywood's Paradise Cafe.

But the most important happening in his career thus far came when Lionel Hampton became a vital, full-time member of the Benny Goodman Quartet. Later, he would further enhance a constantly growing reputation by performing with other Goodman units, including a short period as drummer with the big band, following Gene Krupa's much-publicized departure. Outside of his freewheeling contributions to Goodman-led outfits, from 1936 until his own exit, finally, in July 1939, Hampton's most important contributions to jazz of the thirties relate to a unique series of recording dates he was to undertake, as leader, at the bidding of the RCA Victor company. Between 1937 and 1941, he fronted a succession of pick-up studio bands, comprising an impressive cross-section of top soloists and rhythm-section players of the period. Ranging in size from five to nine – occasionally ten – pieces, these truly all-star recording ensembles were borrowed, perhaps inevitably, from the leading big bands – Ellington, Calloway, Basie, Hines and, not at all surprisingly, Goodman. The overall standard of music emanating from these legendary sessions – resulting in almost 100 individual performances in all, including several alternative takes deemed worthy of issue – is astonishingly high.

Certainly, as a major soloist in his own right, Hampton proved at all times to be an inspiring colleague to have in your corner, whether the situation involved live performance, or within the confines of a recording or TV or radio studio. In fact, in the succeeding years he has continued to make a comfortable living out of being the catalyst supreme, something which has continued well into the late eighties. As a bandleader, Hampton has continued to demonstrate a passionate conviction that personal deeds are more effective than mere verbal instructions, in persuading his sidemen to follow Duke Ellington's basic tenet: It Don't Mean a Thing if It ain't Got that Swing.

Although he has stoked the fires of innumerable small combos through the years, Hampton's undimmable catalytic powers have never been surpassed within the genre of big-band jazz. The resultant electric atmosphere and built-in excitement of the occasion have sometimes caused near-riot scenes among audiences wherever a typical wild-and-woolly Hampton orchestra has appeared, most especially, perhaps, within the context of an outdoor jazz festival.

Right from the beginning of his first significant venture into big-band leadership, in 1940, Hampton's policy of basic communication has tended to be delivered in a style that has often horrified, even offended, the most purist element of jazz appreciation. The brash, often torrid, presentation by Hampton & Co in live performance has been much vilified by those whose views on the subject tend obviously towards a more sedate approach to jazz playing. The purists have sometimes gone one step further, in tending to be generally dismissive of much of the music produced by Hampton bands, as much as anything because it is more than marginally related to basic rhythm and blues. Which, happily, is at least partially correct. Hampton-led bands have concentrated on an extrovert mode of delivery, achieved through the dynamic combination of a powerfully swinging rhythm section (with the drummer – and sometimes even two drummers – laying down an unrelenting, near-sledgehammer, beat), allied to a roaring, take-no-prisoners saxophone section, topped by a team of leather-lunged trumpet players screaming collectively through a succession of triumphant finales. Many music historians have rightly credited the various Lionel Hampton big bands of the forties, and thereafter, with being of seminal influence on the rock 'n' roll revolution that turned pop music inside-out during the first half of the 1950s. Certainly, Hampton's method of presentation in live performance must have had some direct bearing on the onstage extroversion of many rock performers and bands, in much the same way as other important solo influences like T-Bone Walker, Wynonie Harris (who also vocalized with Hampton for a while) and Big Jay McNeely. Unashamed exhibitionistic, delightfully outrageous, performer–audience communication at the most basic level . . .

Hampton's own brand of showmanship was the focal point. Always a physical performer on any of his chosen instruments, he has long since established an additional non-musical reputation – whether one is for or against him – with regard to his apparently inexhaustible in-concert activities, activities which have included periodic demonstrations of simple athleticism, concerned principally with leaping sweatily on and off one or more of his own large individual drums, as part of a triumphant, if rather over-dramatic, conclusion to a typically rip-roaring big-band performance. Of course, such physically excessive capers have gradually been phased out with the arrival of middle age, as well as several periods of serious ill-health, during the present decade and even further in the past. So too with Hampton's long-established routine of encouraging his tenor-sax soloists physically to gyrate, out in front of the band, while delivering the kind of appositely blistering solos scarcely to the liking of many of those who prefer their jazz less bombastic and ferocious. The same can be said of the frenetic outpourings of a succession of powerhouse trumpet players who spent regular periods blowing in the altissimo region.

And it was Lionel Hampton who probably first instigated the regular practice of ending a live session by leading his men offstage – mostly in single- or double-file – while still blowing fiercely. Sometimes the route took the musicians in and around various sections of the audience.

Whatever final and overall assessment is accorded the various Lionel Hampton orchestras, there is little doubt that their ranks have been populated by a more or less continuous stream of superior talent. Many, like Dexter Gordon, were young, raw and inexperienced when they joined Hampton, and were usually much the better for their incumbency. Many significant post-World War II jazz personalities worked for Hampton in their formative years. Included among an impressive list of alumni, who were Hampton sidemen *after* Gordon's own departure (in 1943), are the following – just a handful of top players to have honed their individual talents as employees of the indefatigable native of Louisville, Kentucky: Earl Bostic, Clifford Brown, Alan Dawson, Johnny Griffin, Quincy Jones, Charles Mingus, Wes Montgomery, Fats Navarro and Joe Wilder.

When Dexter Gordon joined Hampton's first post-Goodman orchestra, as second tenor saxophonist, he soon found he was in hot company. For one thing, at seventeen he was the kid in the band. The only other members who were close in age were principal tenor soloist Illinois Jacquet (four months younger), trumpeter Ernie Royal (brother of reedman Marshall, Dexter's former high-school buddy, and almost two years his senior) and guitarist Irving Ashby (almost three years older). He and Royal, naturally, stayed close, and Gordon's own acute sense of humour soon homed in on the quick wit and flexible attitude of the slim, dapper Joe Newman.

Most of Gordon's colleagues found him an amiable, friendly and courteous individual, albeit with his own brand of zany humour and basically laid-back attitude to life in general: an oversized, real-life definition of the classic jazz preoccupation with acting cool. Already, too, he often evidenced a natural acting ability, in the way he conducted himself in the company of fellow jazzmen; and a tendency towards poor timekeeping – later something of a classic Gordon trait – was not uncommon.

Joe Newman remembers this latter failing. As he related to jazz author Ira Gitler, with regard to an appearance by the Hampton band at the Paradise Theatre, Detroit:

Dexter was always coming late. He'd come in at the last minute, and we were playing this tune he was supposed to play on. There was no Dexter, and just as it got to his solo, he walked out of the wings with his horn, man, like Pres, man, blowing away, man, and broke it up. Because that was a hell of a thing for those people. They didn't expect it, and we fell out, too. And Hamp was – normally he would have been angry – but he couldn't be angry because it broke it up.

The two tenormen in the band provided an extraordinary contrast, whether seated or standing side by side. Illinois Jacquet, short and in those days fairly slim, measured around a foot shorter in height, but what he lacked in stature, Jacquet made up for in his ability to blow with unbridled passion and considerable force. He possessed a powerful sound and had a rare ability to rouse an audience to near-hysteria, something he was to capitalize on, with the Jazz at the Philharmonic concert troupe as well as his own various bands, after leaving Hampton. He remains the archetypal Hampton tenor player; and, of course, he was the yardstick against which practically all his numerous successors were judged in the years following Jacquet's departure from the Hampton aggregation.

For both Jacquet and Hampton, that early-1940s association was mutually productive. Indeed, it was Jacquet who helped put the band on the map because of his personal contribution to its first recording of 'Flying Home', a Hampton original the composer had first worked as a member of the Benny Goodman Quartet. Jacquet's 'Flying Home' solo – one he was to repeat, night after night, at each and every Hampton appearance, with inevitable results – stands as a classic example of big-band solo work, building, logically and skilfully, to a truly climactic end. Although there was precious little difference in their ages, Jacquet had the kind of on-the-road working experience Gordon lacked. Indeed, he had spent much of the late 1930s touring, as a precocious teenager – and playing mostly alto – touring the Midwest with 'territory' bands, like those of Milt Larkins and Floyd Ray. In fact, Jacquet had arrived in California in 1940 with the Ray band, and had decided to hang out for a while in Los Angeles, especially attracted by the nightly facilities for jamming in and around Central Avenue. Jacquet remembers Dexter Gordon's first appearance as a newly-signed Hampton employee. He was immediately impressed by the local boy as a person.

> When we got to the bus depot, there's Dexter Gordon sitting in the bus. Ten feet tall. Cramped all up . . . at that time he looked like Joe Louis – they used to call him Joe Louis. Wasn't drinking too much at that time. Nothing much. For a big guy, he was so *kind*. So big and warm. I didn't know how anybody could be that big and yet be so humble. We became very close . . . I mean *close*, man . . . They sat him right side of me. And we took a liking to each other . . . we were hanging out together in the hanging-out places. Marshall Royal sat the other side of him. So, he was sitting, like, between two universities, really. So he had to learn . . .

And as far as Illinois Jacquet was concerned, Dexter had lots to learn in terms of playing the saxophone.

> Frankly, he couldn't play at all. Dex told me he'd studied under Lloyd Reese and, OK, he knew about his [chord] progressions pretty good. But he hadn't had the exposure like me. So, he wasn't quite ready . . . I'm telling you, every time he'd go to do something, I'd say: 'Hey, man, you played the bridge before you got there!' He couldn't get it together. And his feet would be all out of time. His co-ordination was bad. You could tell he needed help. And by him being such a beautiful person, man, I helped him. This is my friend. To ourselves, he was Pres and I was Herschel.

Jacquet and his fellow tenorman talked for hours about how the latter might improve his playing. Gordon proved to be a good listener – and a quick learner. Suddenly, Jacquet saw the difference.

> One day, he walked out to the microphone – and I knew he

had it. He was on his way. He was beating his feet in time. He was holding his horn right. He was beginning to get it together. He was a little awkward at first, but then he started getting it all together. Man, he was *determined . . .!*

Dexter himself was immensely grateful for the advice he was given by the more experienced players. As a fellow tenorist, Jacquet helped him in many ways. And there is little doubt that Gordon's ability to project an above-average sound on his horn owes a great deal to sitting next to and observing just how the man from Broussard, La, was capable of a really large sound, and one that was at all times distinctively Jacquet.

However quickly he continued to improve, it was only rarely that Gordon was given the chance to show his paces in a solo capacity – certainly, in direct proportion to Jacquet's own handsome allocation of solos. In fact, one of the few opportunities which came his way was a two-tenor showcase for them both. Unfortunately, Hampton never did get around to recording 'Po'k Chops', the Jacquet–Gordon feature. Apart from anything else, a most helpful recording contract with Decca Records did not allow the full band into the studios until December 1941 – a full year since it first took to the road – and 'Po'k Chops' was not on the menu that Christmas Eve. And just to make absolutely sure that Dexter Gordon would not make his solo debut on record with Hampton, the president of the American Federation of Musicians called a strike of his members the following July, which kept them out of all recording studios until November 1944. By which time Dexter had long since relinquished his second-tenor position with Hampton.*

Certainly, it would be instructive to be able to refer to one version at least of the 'Po'k Chops' duel, but up to now not even an aircheck of the number has been discovered.

Disappointed as he was, as the months went by, that more solo opportunities failed to come his way, Gordon contented himself with the realization that his all-round improvement,

*In fact, Dexter played on only the single Decca session of 24/12/41.

though at times slower than he might have wished, was actually happening. It was due, he knew, to the band's increasing schedule of appearances, including the sometimes routine commitment of more than one show per night. His reading, too, was sharper.

One other important contributory reason for Gordon's all-round improvement was working alongside Marshall Royal. Not only was he a consummately gifted saxist/clarinettist, but Royal led the section in flawless style – something, of course, he was to repeat for many years with the Count Basie Orchestra of the 1950s–60s. Gordon responded willingly to the older man's expert advice.

> Marshall was the straw boss, as well as the section leader. Taught me *everything*. Before, I didn't know anything. I was just a kid. He gave me tips on the lot. Tone. Tuning up. Intonation. Breathing. Phrasing. When to use vibrato. *How* to use vibrato. Pianissimo, forte ... the whole scope. *Everything*.

Of inestimable importance, too, was the invaluable advice imparted by Jacquet and Royal – especially the former – in respect of the vital component part of the tenor saxophone: the mouthpiece, something which obviously hadn't meant too much to Gordon before joining Hampton. Having the wrong mouthpiece, he was to discover, was a major factor in helping to retard his progress in attempting to project, and was preventing him from acquiring the kind of powerful sound he was hearing, but unable to reproduce, the kind of ample sound he admired in masters of the tenor such as Hawkins, Byas, Webster ... and, more recently, Jacquet himself.

With the Harlem Collegians, Gordon had used a Conn alto ('a good instrument'), with which he'd tried both rubber and metal mouthpieces. With the latter, the fifteen-year-old Dexter Gordon experienced little but frustration. Seeking advice from his section mate proved to be the turning point. After listening to his colleague's problems, Jacquet suggested, as an experiment, that they swap mouthpieces.

They were both [Otto] Links. Illinois, he loved my mouthpiece – it was smaller than his. He had a medium . . . I think
he had a Coleman Hawkins Special, like a No. 6 or
something like that . . . mine was smaller – maybe a four. I
didn't know at the time but this horn I had was a very
Mickey Mouse-type; a Modern tenor.

That it was hardly an instrument with which a young,
aspiring player could hope to develop a sound and style of his
own was demonstrated during this period when one of Dexter's
own heroes asked to use it . . . and found it palpably lacking.

Once, we were working in Chicago – at the Grand Terrace –
and Ben Webster came in, with Georgie Auld . . . they sat in
with the band. I think Georgie played Jacquet's horn and Ben
played my horn. Afterwards, he just said: 'Man, what's this
little boy's horn?' He couldn't get a sound out of it. I knew,
then, that it wasn't just me – I was in need of an *instrument*.

It was not too much later that the Modern was summarily
despatched, in favour of a brand-new Conn tenor saxophone,
something which set back its new owner what must have
seemed a daunting sum of somewhere between $300–$400.
The former Jacquet mouthpiece proved an equally worthwhile
acquisition, even though it was to be replaced by another, years
later. However, the mouthpiece Gordon passed on to Jacquet
remains in constant use with the latter, over forty-five years
later.

As the band's principal soloist – the leader, of course, apart –
Jacquet's personal reputation continued to grow. His always
extrovert playing was becoming even more outrageous and
uninhibited, especially with an increasing use of upper-register
harmonics. Still, by the autumn of 1942, Jacquet took his leave
of absence from the Hampton outfit, to recharge his batteries,
away from the non-stop touring and one-night stands. After
which, he spent time with two other major jazz orchestras,
those of Cab Calloway and Count Basie. (The latter composed
a feature item for Jacquet during his tenure with the Basie band:

'The King'.) In between these commitments, Jacquet's extremist approach gained him all-time immortality (or notoriety, depending on your personal point of view) as the torrid centre-point of the earliest Jazz at the Philharmonic concerts, in 1944.

Naturally, Lionel Hampton was not at all pleased when Jacquet informed him of his intention of leaving. Jacquet himself had been reluctant to leave. Hampton had treated him fairly, and the almost-two-year stay had made the tenorman a star in his own right. Jacquet, not anxious to offend, added that he had a worthy, ready-made replacement, his former colleague in the Milt Larkin band, four years his senior, and the kind of hard-blowing, big-sound tenor saxist Hampton preferred. And, like Hampton's personal favourite on the same horn, he was a native of Texas – and thus one of the noble tradition of so-called Texas Tenors.

Arnett Cleophus Cobb was to prove a more than able replacement. Joining the band in November 1942, Cobb – an immensely likable individual who in later years was to suffer much from ill-health, and later still be permanently semi-disabled, following a serious automobile accident – remained a Hampton sideman until early 1947. During Cobb's tenure with Hampton, his became as famous an individual sound as Jacquet's, as exemplified in particular by his blistering showcase performances such as 'Air Mail Special', the eponymous 'Cobb's Idea', and a reborn 'Flying Home'.

As an even more experienced player than Jacquet, Cobb automatically took over the premier tenor seat. Dexter Gordon's status thus remained practically as before; even though, as he continued to grow in confidence and proficiency, his solo allocation increased, albeit fractionally. Like his predecessor, Cobb took an instant liking to his new acquaintance – personally as well as professionally – and tended to cast an avuncular eye in Dexter's direction. It soon became obvious to Cobb that, even though he still had much to learn, this friendly and fun-loving young man had certain positive ideas of how he wished to express himself on his horn; even though it was even more apparent that his whole approach and concept was based on one of the two most influential – and significant – tenorists in jazz at that time.

When I joined the band, Pres was obviously his idol, 'cos he tried to play like him. Of course, he plays different now, though off that style. Actually, I think he was more important to me then – loved his playing. What really impressed me about Dexter – as young as he was – he'd be so relaxed and cool. Didn't get excited over anything. That really stuck in my mind. Live, Dexter just played a few things [alone]. Yeah, we had some tenor battles, Dexter and I but, solo-wise, Hamp went for the Texas tenors, on account of Herschel.

Even though he still had little to do in a solo capacity, Dexter Gordon's personal charisma gradually asserted itself, most obviously when he rose to take a solo. Ex-Juilliard student Tony Scott, an arch-enthusiast and at that time a promising young clarinettist, has vivid recall of one incident which gave ample demonstration of just how that charisma could affect an audience. It happened one evening at the Savoy Ballroom.

All of a sudden the break came. This guy – Dexter Gordon, of course – a giant even from the seat up – he started to rise as he played the break . . . and the break was Lester Young's break from 'Miss Thing' . . . oo-be-oo-bee-doo-bee, ba-ba-bee, boo-ba-bee-doo, ba-woo-wah! And he kept rising . . . and rising. And you know, he's about seven feet tall . . . he kept going up as he was playing this break. And the people *screamed*. I was standing there, in this all-black audience – it's Harlem, you know – and he kept going up and up . . . it was like if *I* started going up – and I'm over six feet and I kept going up till, finally, I stood on a chair, and still kept going up . . . And the people are watching as, first, he's bent over . . . coming up slow . . . *bee*-doo-be-*bee* . . .! And the people screamed . . . it was very impressive.

Early in 1943, Dexter Gordon decided he needed a break

from the more or less non-stop touring with Hampton. He gave his notice to the leader – who seemed not at all pleased to be losing his services – and Dexter returned to Los Angeles, feeling life, on the whole, had been good to him during the past two and a half years. Of course, he had learned to make continuous adjustments to combat the rigours of being on the road for such a length of time. He still remembers, to this day, that very first time the Hampton crew left LA, crammed in a ramshackle vehicle which barely passed muster as a band bus. First date: Fort Worth, Texas. The start of gruelling schedule, taking young Dexter many hundreds of miles away from his home town. An initial trip by Hampton's brand-new band which, because of the inadequacies of the transport provided, was almost curtailed by the time it reached El Paso.

By which time the Californian temperature had assumed more wintry proportions, and heating was not one of the precious few facilities to be found inside the band bus. The newly-assembled ensemble rebelled. They would go no further, they informed a harassed and unhappy band manager, unless the present mode of transport was changed . . . immediately. The band manager realized there was no alternative. A distinctly superior bus was purchased in El Paso. The aggregation arrived – safely and decidedly warmer – on Boxing Day.

Despite any shortcomings or personal deprivations, Dexter was thrilled to be touring as a member of what might well become, at some time in the future, a celebrated addition to the already overcrowded big-band field, even though he was painfully aware of his own deficiencies. ('Every day, at the beginning, I expected Hamp to give me my return ticket.') His anxieties had been helped not at all by the fact that, outside of that front-room audition, there had not been time for him to rehearse – once – with the full band. But thanks to the help and patience shown by the others, he painstakingly began to shape up in all the requirements needed to become at least a functional big-band sideman.

Outside of the obvious desire to make a comprehensive all-round improvement in his playing and reading, Gordon was looking forward, with no little anticipation, to visiting as many new places as possible – places, like New York, which for years he'd only dreamed of. New York topped his own fantasy charts since he was a not-so-little kid. The Big Apple – for Dexter, this was *the* City of Jazz . . . And New York City was part of the Hampton band's first itinerary.

Although the band's stay in New York was tantalizingly brief, the place was all that Dexter's fertile imagination had hoped for. He knew, even before the band bus pulled out of the city, he'd be returning again. And again after that. New York gave a warm welcome to the Lionel Hampton Orchestra. The reviews were uniformly good. Including that of *Metronome* magazine's enthusiastic young critic George Simon, who gave Hampton's second tenorist what was most certainly his first-ever namecheck in a major jazz publication: brief, to the point and kind: 'Young Dexter, a handsome six foot four [*sic*] eighteen-year-old, comes across with some fine melodic ideas as well as a mighty pretty tone.'

Simon's comments referred to the Hampton band's appearance at the Savoy Ballroom, the same venue, of course, at which Tony Scott had witnessed the spontaneous audience reaction to Dexter's presence as well as his playing.

Although New York was a personal thrill for the Los Angeles teenager, he admits that the most successful portion of that memorable first cross-country tour concerned the band's season at the Grand Terrace, in Chicago. Originally, it had been booked to play a two-week season, but so great was the reaction that the management kept extending the stay. Eventually, the band stayed a full six months, during which time its nightly commitments included, apart from its own sets, supplying accompaniment for the Grand Terrace's resident dancers, vocalists and sundry other acts.

Nevertheless, for Dexter and most of his colleagues, the visit to New York topped everything. For the band's youngest member, there was an extra-special reason why his first experience in that particular city proved so utterly memorable. That reason came when the Hampton band played opposite that fronted by pianist/singer Jay McShann. Like Hampton's, the McShann band was in the process of making its New York debut. Both outfits played opposite each other at the Savoy Ballroom. Gordon liked the McShann band, especially its relaxed swing and natural affinity for blues (Midwestern variety). Most of all, though, he was impressed by the solo work of a slim, sometimes intense alto saxophonist named Charlie Parker.

Although Parker was, quite obviously, a natural – and indeed superior – blues player, Gordon was also fascinated by Parker's overall concept. True, his playing evidenced a deep appreciation of Lester Young – something which the twenty-year-old from Kansas City confirmed, during their first conversation, backstage at the Savoy – but Parker had his own way of improvising, the like of which Gordon had not heard before this time. (Gordon had heard Parker previously – on record, with the McShann band – but by the time of their first meeting, it was easy to hear that his phrasing had become more adventurous; that his playing – rhythmically, melodically, harmonically – had many more individual qualities.)

As impressed as Dexter was with Parker's effortless, declamatory playing, it did not need any extended hanging out by the pair for the younger man to discover that, off the stand, his newest musical hero had an apparently insatiable interest in social high flying. When their paths crossed, on subsequent occasions, Gordon was to understand, even more emphatically, just how much Parker's lust for life, so to speak, continued on an upward spiral.

Going back to Los Angeles – something he'd looked forward to for months – was tinged with the knowledge that he would be unable to spend many hours with his father, relating all, or most, of the numerous highlights and events of the Hampton episode. Dr Gordon, he knew, would have been so proud that his son had embarked on a full-time professional career, had benefited by his lengthy spell with a band like Hamp's, and that he had learned so much more than the little he knew before leaving home. Dexter, who retains a deep and lasting affection for both his parents, never has forgotten his father's love, and the care with which he'd tried to ensure his son's obvious interest in becoming a full-time pro should be preceded by as thorough a knowledge in music as possible. Time heals, but it would take years for Gordon, Jr's tremendous sense of loss at his father's passing to recede . . . although never completely. Now, on his return home, his thoughts would be concentrated on his mother. And he was determined to find a way of spending as much time in her company as possible, although, as events were soon to prove, for much of the next two or three years he would be resident in Los Angeles for only brief periods, when future itineraries decreed he make temporary returns to his birthplace. For phase two of a burgeoning career was about to unfold.

When remembering the impact of that debut tour with Lionel Hampton, at all times during the following years, Dexter Gordon never has failed to voice his warmest respect for the way the bandleader looked after his youngest sideman – indeed, all the members of his orchestra. 'Hamp's a beautiful man. Treated me great. I couldn't have asked for anything more. And, of course, that first band of Hamp's was really something. Very, very special. A mixture of older, experienced players and talented young ones.'

It was indeed something of an extra incentive for any youngster in a comparable position to have been afforded the pleasure and inspiration of a benevolent leader. And it can be said that as far as Dexter Gordon is concerned he was fortunate in the extreme to find that his next major employer – another of jazz's top solo performers – adopted a similarly kind and encouraging attitude on his behalf. Louis Daniel Armstrong had long since been recognized as the most significant soloist in the admittedly still youthful history of jazz, a trumpet player of ineluctable power and majesty, a singer of immense warmth and real style, and an all-round catalytic figurehead whose surpassing brilliance alone would have ensured that jazz be categorized as an art form of the twentieth century. Armstrong's innovative trumpet work in the 1920s – with mentor King Oliver's Creole Jazzband, and even more devastatingly through a remarkable series of recordings with his own Hot

Five and Hot Seven studio combos – had helped brush aside practically any barriers which might have confronted the more forward-looking jazz musicians of earlier days. By 1944, however, Armstrong had become all too comfortably ensconced as the virtuoso soloist (which he was anyway), permanently in the spotlight, and backdropped by a succession of big bands which, at most times, provided the great man with little or no real inspiration. Armstrong's singing, too, had become almost as important as his still electrifying trumpet playing. And his personal exuberance and sometimes overtly amiable character had also ensured him of a fairly comfortable, if somewhat irregular, involvement with movieland.

Despite the dissatisfaction voiced by many of his army of admirers – critics, fans and even some fellow jazz musicians, who invariably idolized him for his natural superlative talent – at what seemed to most to be the continued wasted opportunities to present Armstrong's genius in a more appropriate setting, the former New Orleans waif seemed happy and content with the big-band set-up. Certainly, his financial status, for the future as well as the present, seemed secure. And in all media – concerts, records, radio, films – his reputation continued to expand. In fact, it might be said that even as long ago as the early 1940s, Louis Armstrong's reputation extended impressively outside a strictly jazz-only following, something he shared with the widely popular big-band leaders of the so-called Swing Era.

Of course, with the United States finally entering World War II, Armstrong's own outfit, like every one of his contemporaries', had been raided by Uncle Sam. By 1944, its line-up changed frequently; not that personnel changes seem to have bothered the playing of its leader at all. Whatever the inadequacies – and there were shortcomings, ensemble-wise, in terms of arrangements which never seemed more than average-to-good, performed by a band which didn't always appear to be particularly well-drilled – Armstrong remained definitively the superlative individualist. And the sheer thrill for a promising, twenty-year-old musician like Dexter Gordon to be asked to share the same stage as such an undisputed living legend virtually removed any possible artistic disappointments or frustrations.

Not that Dexter had been completely idle or inactive since leaving Hampton. During much of 1943 he had worked with the small bands of drummers Lee Young and Jesse Price in Los Angeles. He also grabbed the opportunity of working with one of the seminal figures of big-band jazz. Fletcher Henderson arrived in LA with the nucleus of a big band which he completed by adding a handful of local players. Gordon shared tenor-sax solo duties with Woodrow Key, one of those who had arrived in California with Henderson. Approximately one week after the line-up had been finalized, the new Fletcher Henderson Orchestra opened for a season at Joe Morris's Plantation Club, in late April of 1944. Although his association with Henderson was to last only a month or two, Gordon reckons it was an experience that represented another stepping stone along the route to becoming a fully-fledged professional. Playing Henderson's music nightly – including many of the charts which had helped make Benny Goodman the King of Swing during the previous decade – helped sharpen his technique as well as improve his reading. As he was to explain later to British writer Les Tomkins:

> ... it was true what they said about Fletcher writing in all those sharp keys; but it wasn't a catastrophe – he wrote it in such a way that it felt good. You weren't even aware of it. Not everything was like that, because in his arrangements there were modulations. In the blowing choruses, of course, you weren't playing in B-natural – something a little more reasonable. It was a very good experience.

Not surprisingly, Dexter filled in time between his gigs with Young and Price and Henderson with regular after-hours blowing along Central Avenue, including several enjoyable sessions with Nat Cole at the 331 Club, and Charles Mingus and Gerry Wiggins at the Ritz.

It was partly due to Cole's help that during this period Dexter Gordon was able to make the first recordings under his own name. In fact, the late-'43 session was only the second occasion he had worked inside a recording studio; and, of course, it was the very first time he had been heard as a soloist in this context. The entire four-number date appeared, finally, thirty-odd years later. These performances are important insofar as they remain, outside of a solitary Hampton airshot item from 1941, the only examples of his playing, in solo, prior to 1944. For the occasion, Dexter fronted a five-piece which also included trumpeter Harry Edison, Cole, Johnny Miller (bassist with the King Cole Trio) and a still unidentified drummer. Apart from sparkling piano from Cole, it is the playing of the leader which registers strongest throughout. That he is profoundly influenced by Lester Young is indisputable; but even a poor recorded sound fails to hide the fact that, even at this stage in his development, Gordon projects an ample sound with real conviction. A splendid opportunity, then, to document his musical progress at this time. But it was to be almost two years before he would be asked to take another pick-up band into the studios.

It was during the short period he played with Kansas City-born Jesse Price that Dexter received an invitation to become a member of Louis Armstrong's band, at one of those busy after-hours joints, and from the mouth of the great man himself.

I didn't know he was there until after one set he came up to the stand and said: 'Hey, son, I like that tone you got.' All I could say was: 'Thank you, Mr Armstrong.' Then, he asked me, personally, to join his band. The next night, Teddy McRae – who was at that time his musical director as well as tenor saxophonist – asked me, officially . . . they were in California to do a couple of films. Then, they were going on the road, up the coast, up into Canada, and back down through the States. The band was fully booked for the next six or seven months. So I said, OK . . . I really wanted to dig Pops, because, of course, I'd heard him on records, et cetera. But before this, I'd never gotten the opportunity to be around him, or to work with him. So, this was it, right?

For Gordon, that golden opportunity proved to be even more advantageous than he might have hoped. Naturally, he most certainly had first-hand experience of observing Armstrong's extraordinary instrumental-vocal art in nightly concert performance, including the numerous broadcasts by the band. In addition, Gordon had a first-time taste of the world of movies. In respect of the latter, he appeared, together with Armstrong-fronted big bands in brief sequences in *Atlantic City* (1944) and *Pillow to Post* (1945). Although Dexter is seen on-screen in the former – with Armstrong performing 'Ain't Misbehavin'' – the actual music for the soundtrack is supplied by Louis and a collection of studio musicians. There is a club sequence during the Ida Lupino-starring *Pillow to Post* featuring the Louis Armstrong Orchestra, including his young tenorist.*

Financially, Gordon remembers, he had no complaints. And although solo opportunities for Armstrong sidemen generally were even more restricted than with Hampton, Dexter found himself allowed probably more solos than anyone outside the leader himself. Ironically, though, during the six months spent with Armstrong, only three titles were commercially recorded by the band, for Decca. Of which one ('Groovin'') has a tenor-saxophone solo . . . by Teddy McRae.

Still, Gordon remained happy and contented. The honour of appearing with a jazz giant like Louis Armstrong was one thing; but for Dexter there were additional pleasures. For one, Armstrong took a personal, avuncular interest in his new saxophone player, both musically and personally.

The actual music that the Louis Armstrong Orchestra performed wasn't exactly inspiring. And the band itself didn't over-impress Dexter. 'A mediocre band. They were just playing Luis Russell arrangements from the thirties. Plus "Ain't Misbehavin'", some new pops of the day; things like that. So nothing was happening. For me, it wasn't anything special. All those big bands he had seemed to be almost like that.'

*David Meeker's *Jazz in the Movies* (Talisman Books, 1981) contains a still from the picture, principally of Armstrong, but which also shows, unmistakably, the young, handsome Dexter Gordon, with sleeked-back hair and white jacket.

At least, though, there was the chance to demonstrate, in solo, his ever-improving Young-influenced tenor sound at fairly regular intervals. Very few of the radio transcriptions of the Armstrong band of 1944 that have appeared in subsequent years have an over-abundance of Dexter Gordon at this stage in his career, solo-wise. But those which have been transferred to disc do lend credence to the comments of those who heard him at this time, and who remember he was improving in most areas of saxophone technique – and already he was developing a comprehensive sound.

Apart from Armstrong and the two tenor players, the rest of the band of 1944 comprised young players who were largely unknown. A handful, like altoist John Brown (later with Dizzy Gillespie's big band), trumpeter Andrew 'Fats' Ford (a future Ellingtonian), and trombonist Taswell Baird (destined to become a colleague of Gordon's in a new and exciting big band, later the same year), attained reasonable reputations after leaving Armstrong. Vocalist Velma Middleton was to remain in Armstrong's employ, on and off, for the next seventeen years. (She died in Sierra Leone, in 1961, while touring with the All Stars.)

Finally, Gordon decided, again, he wanted a change of musical scenery, so it was back to LA, for more jamming and a little local work, along Central Avenue. Not for the last time was he to return in this way to his birthplace, preparatory to undertaking some fresh venture, or perhaps to recuperate from some kind of stress or strain.

He had time to pause and reflect on the past six months: a little frustrating, maybe, in terms of dated charts and stock arrangements to play, but in a general sense, something he would remember with lasting affection and no little pride. 'Working with Louis? Oh, great. *Love, love, love* . . . that was what it was all about. All love. He was just beautiful – always beautiful. It was just a gas being with him. He let me play all the time. He really dug me.'

It was not too long after returning to LA that Dexter Gordon received a call from Billy Eckstine. A slim, handsome native of Pittsburgh, nine years Dexter's senior, and a fine vocal stylist in his own right, Eckstine had left the Earl Hines Orchestra in 1943 after spending almost five years carving out an enviable reputation.

Although never really a jazz singer *per se*, Eckstine's always musical approach – not to mention a distinctive vibrato – had earned him an ever-increasing following, especially among fellow blacks. With Hines, Eckstine had racked up a small handful of record hits – 'Jelly Jelly', 'Stormy Monday Blues' and 'You Don't Know what Love is' – which augured well for his future as a solo artist. When Frank Sinatra left the Tommy Dorsey organization in 1942, he created a precedent whose significance not only meant a long-term dominance by solo vocalists but also signalled the decline and, ultimately, the demise of the big-band bonanza, the latter already being gradually decimated by the increasing involvement of the United States in the widespread World War II commitments. Sinatra . . . Haymes . . . Bob Eberle . . . Peggy Lee . . . Ella . . . Jo Stafford . . . Pearl Bailey . . . these, and many others, were gradually leaving the confines of big-band work, both in the jazz and dance-band fields. Eckstine's departure from Hines took an intriguingly different tack. For Billy Eckstine took the decision to front his own orchestra, the commercial aspects of which, admittedly, were to become centred on his own vocals.

When Eckstine called, his band had been working for only a couple of months. Nevertheless, various personnel changes had taken place already, and the new singer/bandleader urgently required the services of a solid replacement for Eli 'Lucky' Thompson, another promising tenor saxist. Thompson, sixteen months younger than Dexter, had just accepted a tempting offer to replace Lester Young, making his final departure as a full-time member of the Count Basie Orchestra. Eckstine didn't have to engage in any full-length explanation about his band. The news of its inception, and the early gigs, had been proliferating rapidly among the jazz community, nationwide – particularly among the young lions like Dexter Gordon.

When Eckstine asked him, well, will you take Lucky's place? there was not a second's hesitation.

'Where do you want me to meet you, B?'

4

Blowin' the Blues Away with Jug and B

Billy Eckstine's career as a nightclub singer began in Buffalo, following his graduation from Howard University, Washington, DC. Less than two years later, he was working, as a singer and emcee, in Detroit; after this he spent a two-year period playing various clubs in Chicago, which is where his burgeoning vocal talent was spotted by the ever-alert Budd Johnson, who offered a strong recommendation to his boss, Earl Hines. Hines badly needed a class vocalist, and agreed with Johnson's enthusiastic report.

After a short audition, the former William Clarence Eckstein was taken on the Hines payroll. Between 1939 and 1943, the Hines–Eckstine association proved to be a mutually productive one, the singer proving a visual as well as vocal attraction. Although he could handle a rhythm number without any problems, Eckstine never could be truly classifiable as a jazz singer, in the strictest definition of that often controversial piece of terminology. Primarily, he has remained through the years a superior singer of ballads.

During his Hines tenure, Eckstine proved not only the ideal out-front performer-cum-verbal-linkman, but an arch-enthusiast for the music produced by the Hines band in general and its soloists in particular. His warm and friendly disposition enabled him to mix freely with jazz musicians of many schools and different ages – both inside as well as outside the band. During his last year with Hines, he also took up playing trumpet, helped no little by colleague Dizzy Gillespie (who joined early in 1943); eventually, Hines utilized his singer's services as a sometime extra member of the trumpet section.

In addition, Eckstine, together with Budd Johnson, proved to be something of a talent-spotter, bringing new talent within the ranks, including Gillespie, altoist Charlie Parker (who played tenor), and a teenaged singer, Sarah Vaughan. Eckstine heard the shy, eighteen-year-old Vaughan at the Apollo Theatre, where she won an amateur talent contest. His sharp ear recognized, at once, the makings of a remarkable singer. As well as helping Eckstine with vocal duties, Sarah Vaughan's basic musical upbringing enabled her to act as second pianist with the Earl Hines Orchestra.

Gillespie's presence turned out to be significant in relation to Eckstine's own big-band plans. And in addition to both Vaughan and Gillespie, several other members of the 1943 Hines ensemble were to form the nucleus of the band Eckstine assembled the following year: trumpeters Gail Brockman, Maurice 'Shorty' McConnell, Little Benny Harris; trombonist/ arranger/composer Jerry Valentine; drummer Rossiere 'Shadow' Wilson; and tenorists Tommy Crump and the ubiquitous Budd Johnson. Unfortunately, both Wilson and Crump were drafted before the new band had played its first gig, and Wardell Gray, a promising tenorist who had joined Earl Hines in 1943, couldn't persuade the by now hard-pressed pianist/ leader likewise to take his place with the proposed new outfit.

Billy Eckstine left Hines, finally, in September 1943. His own big band would not be operational until early in the New Year, before which time he was to operate as a solo performer – playing occasional trumpet to augment his singing – at the Yacht Club, on 52nd Street, early in 1944 – billed, to Billy's embarrassment as 'X-Stine'. Billy Shaw, of the William Morris Agency, who had taken over as his manager, promised him a tour with the George Hudson band out of St Louis, following the closure of the Yacht Club. Eckstine had other ideas. He returned to Chicago, collected the Hines sidemen whose services he needed – including Parker, who was back on his premier instrument and wailing with the Carroll Dickerson Orchestra – and returned, with his ex-Hines colleagues, to New York.

Eckstine had already acquired his two most important associates for the new adventure. Johnson, although operating in a part-time capacity – he had firm commitments, not only to Hines but other big bands of the period – would contribute to the writing, appear in the sax section whenever possible, and would continue to act as a talent-spotter and all-round enthusiast. Gillespie had agreed to become the Eckstine band's musical director and principal arranger, as well as one of its most important soloists.

Thanks to Shaw's hard talking, a one-off record deal was completed with the independent DeLuxe Records label – with the proviso that the emphasis would be firmly placed on Eckstine's singing. Billed as 'Billy Eckstine, vocal, accompanied by the DeLuxe All-Stars', the embryo Eckstine big band contained only six musicians who were to become full-time members of the 'official' aggregation: Gillespie, McConnell, (trombonist) Howard Scott, Johnson, (guitarist) Connie Wainwright and, of course, the leader. Shadow Wilson and Tommy Crump made token appearances before their draftboard appearances; other notable studio participants included Wardell Gray, pianist Clyde Hart, trumpeter Freddie Webster and bassist Oscar Pettiford (in town with the Charlie Barnet Orchestra). And Charlie Parker? His reputation for unreliability precluded his appearance at the 13 April DeLuxe session. When Eckstine's studio band was cutting three titles, Parker was working with the Noble Sissle Orchestra . . . back in Chicago.

By the time the Eckstine band proper had left for a southern tour, in June, the first line-up was complete: Gillespie, Brockman, Hazel and Bernard 'Buddy' Anderson (ex-Jay McShann), trumpets; Valentine, Scott, Arnett Sparrow, Rudy Morrison, trombones; Parker, Robert 'Junior' Williams (another former colleague of Parker's, with McShann), altos; Lucky Thompson, Gene Ammons (ex-King Kolax, and son of boogie-woogie virtuoso Albert Ammons), tenors; Leo Parker, baritone; John Malachi, piano; Wainwright, guitar; Tommy Potter, bass; Art Blakey, drums. Vocals were handled by Eckstine and his former Hines associate, Sarah Vaughan. Of the newcomers, Leo Parker – no relation to Charlie – had joined as an altoist; Eckstine purchased the larger horn for him, and his namesake taught him how to play an instrument he'd never used before this time. Malachi, who was to prove useful also as an arranger/composer, had been a member of Gillespie's Yacht Club combo.

The DeLuxe All-Stars discs were released prior to the tour, to generally favourable response from the jukebox community – based totally on Eckstine's continued popularity as a singer. As a result, DeLuxe had signed the band to a one-year contract.

Repertoire-wise, the Eckstine orchestra's book was practically non-existent. But such was the goodwill its appearance had engendered, that before it departed for that first ground-breaking tour, both Count Basie and Boyd Raeburn had donated charts and sent warmest best wishes. Even though the potential popularity of the band depended primarily on its two vocalists, it would take an extraordinary amout of luck – plus a much-increased book – for commercial success to come its way. For the Billy Eckstine Band was a brand-new outfit in rather more than the obvious interpretation of that description.

It was to be, in fact, the very first large-size ensemble to purvey the sounds of bebop, nationwide . . . and to an audience scarcely ready for both the new music or the explosive manner in which this once-in-a-lifetime orchestra would deliver the goods. Of that pioneering first trip, former *Down Beat* columnist George Hoefer was to recall, twenty-one years later:

> When Eckstine's enthusiastic modernists first hit the road, they had but two jazz arrangements of their own, plus some ballad backgrounds devised by Valentine for the vocalist/leader. The jazz arrangements were old scores, Gillespie's 'A Night in Tunisia' (originally written for the Hines band) and Valentine's 'Second Balcony Jump' (another Hines special).

But whatever the outcome of the tour – or indeed whatever was in store in its lifespan *after* that tour – Eckstine knew from the beginning he had the kind of sidemen who were utterly dedicated to the kind of music they would be performing, other than the more desultory ballads and pop features which in comparison must have seemed like music from another planet.

And such was the fierce cameraderie, the unswerving commitment to the overall task ahead, that anything the band might
well be called upon to play – good, bad or indifferent – would
be performed with the kind of personal commitment that is in
itself an absolute rarity. Many might say that Billy Eckstine was
extremely fortunate in acquiring the kind of sidemen he did,
especially with regard to the war-affected general shortage of
musicians at the time – the kind of sidemen, too, who projected
the music they believed in with an almost demoniacal passion.
In retrospect, the leader doesn't agree. 'Lucky? Not really . . . it
wasn't a case of being extremely lucky at all. You must bear in
mind that in America at that time this style of music was being
played by certain people, and that certain little cliques of people
were all buddies. We all hung out together.' For Eckstine,
leadership of and involvement with that proto-bebop big band
will remain, for as long as he lives, his most cherished single
memory, his personal *ne plus ultra* achievement.

> I can say it now, without any fear of braggadocio accusations
> . . . but it was *the best band*. There's never been a band that
> had its moments like that band! I don't care what band you
> name – and anybody who was ever in that band will tell you
> that. There was never excitement created like that band
> created. You see, it was so *happy*. It was a case of a bunch of
> guys who got together, strictly because this was what we *all*
> wanted to do. And they found an outlet where they could
> play the kinda music they dug. The fact that it wasn't
> commercial was where market-values angles came in. I
> couldn't give a damn whether it was commercial or not.

For the leader the sometimes precarious venture contained
'very many happy moments'.

> One in particular was a little-publicized event . . . we played
> the Brooklyn Armoury once, in a Battle of Jazz with Jimmie
> Lunceford's band. Now, again, it's long since over, and I can
> say, now, that there was no comparison. It was like night and
> day. That band was asked to really play . . . a battle between

the old and the new. And let me tell you, it was a night to remember! You never heard a sound like that in *any* big unit.

Art Blakey joined the Eckstine band when it arrived for its first gigs in St Louis. Blakey, who previously had been fronting a band in Boston, became Shadow Wilson's permanent replacement. Together with Ammons and Valentine, he was to remain with Eckstine up to and including the day the final bars were played out. His was an absolutely vital role, for Blakey's fiery, explosive drumming helped comprehensively in stoking the fires of an already raging inferno. His personal contributions to the artistic success of the Eckstine orchestra proved to be of inestimable importance.

Blakey, a no-nonsense talker at any time during an illustrious career in jazz which now spans over half a century, waxes enthusiastic about the band's short lifetime and his personal involvement, but that enthusiasm is tempered with, at most times, a thinly disguised bitterness at its eventual demise. For the latter, Blakey lays the blame squarely on the doorsteps of the companies for which the band recorded which, he says, were ill-equipped really to get behind it as they ought to have, and were really only interested in Billy Eckstine's career as a singer – and in a strictly solo capacity.

They didn't have that much foresight. They wouldn't have been that stupid if they'd been good businessmen. Every time I saw 'em [the bosses of the record companies], I'd say: 'Look, here, man, we've got Sarah Vaughan ... Charlie Parker sitting there; there's John Jackson ... for a while, too, we had Lady Day as vocalist; she sang lots of times with us ... But they goofed – they didn't *know*. Ahead of its time? No, it wasn't that. It was the business end of it. The record industry hadn't grown up – they'd just gotten stereotyped. It's like anything: when the winds of change blow, people grow afraid of it. They feel threatened ... But you know I can appreciate Billy Eckstine for what he *tried* to do. And Charlie Parker. For those are the two guys who put that band together. At that time Dizzy and Bird, they were the musical directors of the band, they really got the men together. And Billy would go along with anything. He just loves musicians. His attitude was, look here, these are all my buddies, they're going out on tour with me . . . Billy was the one who kept that band together.

Blakey, like Eckstine, still reckons the band compared favourably with any other comparable unit. The ultra-enthusiasm of the new and younger breed of jazz musicians who were beginning to appear with increased frequency in most parts of the US during the mid-1940s meant that there never was a shortage of instrumentalists in any department. Blakey remembers that sometimes the sax section would comprise five players, at others it would increase to seven; similarly, the trumpets might vary in size and strength, from one month to the next – he recalls at one time at least a nine-strong trumpet section. And there was no opting out of rehearsals by anyone in the band. In fact, it was commonplace for the members to rehearse most of the day – then play long hours in the evening and nighttime. 'All that . . . but, ultimately, we never really got anywhere, just didn't make it. And that was heartbreaking. So, Billy just broke it up and went out on his own. I stayed with the band until the last because I hated to see it go. Yeah, I loved that band so much.'

Dexter Gordon remained with the band for only eighteen months of its total existence. By the time he took his place among the reeds – altoists John Jackson and Bill Frazier, fellow-tenorist Ammons and baritonist Leo Parker – there had been significant personnel changes. Apart from Thompson's departure, trumpeters Bernard Anderson and Miles Davis (Juilliard-bound) had both come and gone. So, too, had Charlie Parker and fellow-saxist Robert 'Junior' Williams. Parker, in fact, had left in somewhat typically dramatic fashion. At the Club Plantation, in St Louis, he had caused a rumpus by drinking water out of glasses placed on dinner tables, ritualisti-cally breaking each glass on the floor. As a result, and to no one's surprise, the band's potentially important engagement was cancelled by an incensed management. Nevertheless,

Gordon was more than happy to be a part of this constantly stimulating organization. He was especially glad to join what he considered to be the band's strongest individual section. His succinct explanation of the basic difference between working with the big bands of Armstrong and Eckstine? 'You grew up overnight with Billy. It was night and day, you know.'

Dexter's inception was to be important in at least one other significant way, for with Eckstine he was to make his first important solo statement – one which would impress most of the critics, and thus bring him to the attention of a wider audience. Even so, it was one which he had to share with Gene Ammons. The two-tenor feature on Eckstine's recording of 'Blowin' the Blues Away' remains one of the first – and certainly one of the finest – of such duets (or duels, or even 'battles', as some prefer to call them). Eckstine's forgettable lyric is delivered in a friendly manner (even if its blues content is only slight); his contribution ends with the singer exhorting: 'Blow, Mr Ammons, blow, Mr Dexter too!' In response, both tenorists play a series of chase choruses, in a friendly but combative style, obviously stimulating each other to greater heights of musical excitement. For Dexter, it was a logical development from the 'Po'k Chops' feature-duet with Jacquet, and he enjoyed the even more regular chance to engage in friendly battle with Ammons – 'Blowin' the Blues Away' proved to be a most popular item of the Eckstine orchestra's growing book.

Gordon was especially happy to be a member of what he considers one of the all-time greatest saxophone sections in jazz big-band history. During the shortish period when ex-Tiny Bradshaw altoist Sonny Stitt worked with Eckstine, part of that fiercely blowing section – Stitt, Jackson, Gordon and Leo Parker – was known as the Unholy Four. That unusual title was bestowed due to the ultra-zestful quartet's extrovert offstage behaviour, which sometimes caused even the generally easy-going B to become exasperated.

For Dexter Gordon, just being part of such an exciting outfit as the Billy Eckstine Orchestra was sufficient to confirm that this – and nothing else – would be his present and immediate future. Although, already, he was thinking in terms of performing as part of the front line of a much smaller jazz combo – maybe his own group? – the involvement with Eckstine was all he could have hoped for. The challenge and inspiration that came from working with such an exhilarating ensemble was indeed everything an aspiring young musician could wish for. And the kind of off-stand lifestyle that accompanied such artistic attainment – particularly during this period in history – made life seem idyllic in the extreme. 'People say Hamp's band was wild-and-woolly . . . not that it wasn't, but it was a more conservative kind of wild-and-woolly. With B, *everything* was going on. In every way, *this* was your final schooling, man.'

As one gig followed another, as Gordon remembers, the band's all-round improvement rate was little short of astonishing. The individual sections worked hard to effect the kind of togetherness of other bands, like Lunceford and Goodman. The soloists became just that little more adventurous and inspired. The rhythm section, lifted at every turn by Blakey's herculean efforts, was the band's engine-room, working at full capacity at all times. As a soloist, Gordon was growing in confidence, projecting with more authority, showing a definite improvement in terms of improvising, as well as with regard to tonal production. Dexter's large sound still evidenced his early appreciation of Hawkins, Webster and Byas – not forgetting the later influence of Illinois Jacquet, with Hampton, but there was no doubt whatsoever that Lester Young provided the fundamental source of inspiration. The definitive Dexter Gordon sound was still just around the corner. With Eckstine, he tended to sound rather like Young with a meatier sound, as indeed did his tenor-playing companion Ammons.

It was during the Eckstine period that his fellow-musicians really began to take a keen interest in Gordon's playing. The younger saxophonists, some not even as old as he, became aware of his abilities at this time, mostly because of the Gordon–Ammons duet on 'Blowin' the Blues Away'.

Johnny Griffin was studying clarinet at Du Sable High

School, in his native Chicago, when he first heard the records. His interest in the exciting saxophone playing was twofold. For Griffin had known Gene Ammons at Du Sable, even though Ammons was three years his senior. It was hearing Ammons and Gordon doing battle on 'Blowin' the Blues Away' that was further to inspire Griffin, then sixteen, in becoming a professional saxist. Indeed, the following year, Griffin was himself to join the Lionel Hampton Orchestra.

> Dexter and Gene – they were both idols of mine at school. Saw them both with Billy's band. What did I think of Dexter, then? Well, he was so *exciting*. First of all, I heard that record – 'Blowin' the Blues Away'. Ow, man! I'd spend my money in the school's store to play it, at lunchtime, which was the only opportunity I had at that time. That record, and 'Solo Flight' – Charlie Christian with Benny Goodman . . . boy, those two records did it for me. Then, of course, I saw Dex with Billy . . . *that* was something else!

What excited as well as intrigued schoolboy Griffin about Dexter Gordon's playing was a combination of the way he phrased, his humour, and that already ample sound.

> I think it was the humour that influenced me more than anything else. And, of course, that amazing sound. Important for me, too, 'cos *I* had to do those tenor-saxophone battles with Arnett Cobb – with Hamp – and Arnett had a *huge* sound. It took me three or four months to get myself together. But, like Dex, I always wanted to have a big sound. I wanted to be heard. And, remember, in those days, in some places we played, there'd be no microphones . . .

Chico Hamilton noted his school buddy's musical growth when the Eckstine band arrived one weekend in California, for concert and radio appearances.

> Yes, he'd taken a giant step forward. He'd visited New York and virtually become a New Yorker. I was more or less still

on the West Coast – I didn't go to New York until after I came out of the service. Had Dexter improved some? Oh, yeah! And he'd become hip and cool, too.

Billy Eckstine lost four-fifths of his saxophone section – the aforementioned Unholy Four – almost at one and the same time. The lure of the New York jazz scene in general and 52nd Street in particular had proved too much. Sonny Stitt would soon become a member of Dizzy Gillespie's combo; Leo Parker, whose highly individual baritone playing – an almost unlikely combination of basic rhythm and blues and bebop at its most declamatory – was to become familiar on the New York jazz scene, working with all the leading boppers at some time or another; John Jackson, a much-talented performer, who could play with equal facility as lead altoist and jazz soloist, never did attain the heights and, following an accident in which he was badly burned, quietly disappeared from the musical scene.

For Dexter, of course, much was to happen in the years ahead. But for the immediate future, the New York scene – socially as well as musically – would become the focal point of his activities . . . even though there were to be periods during the latter half of the 1940s when, for one reason or another, he would return home to Los Angeles.

5

On the Street where You Bop (with Bird, Miles, Bud, et al)

By the time Dexter Gordon dropped off in New York in 1945 for his first substantial involvement with that city's pulsating jazz scene, Charlie Parker had become the focal point of interest among the community of younger musicians (and he was making a deep impression too on such well-established figures as Coleman Hawkins, Don Byas, Budd Johnson, Buddy Tate and Ben Webster).

More than anywhere else in the States at this stage, the term bebop (alternatively known as rebop or, more succinctly still, just bop) was becoming an everyday piece of terminology among the forward-looking jazz cognoscenti of New York. In addition, it was later to inspire an emerging breed of hipsters, whose influences outside of Parker, Gillespie and the other 'modern' jazz musicians, included the writings and utterances of Jack Kerouac, and his followers, like Allan Ginsberg and Neal Cassady. Bebop, though, was the subject of intense derogation by the die-hard traditionalists, who were to become intensely involved in a predominantly New Orleans-styled revival, which included the resuscitation of such pioneer figures as Bunk Johnson (who'd been revitalized, in part at least, by the acquisition of a pair of false teeth), George Lewis, Kid Ory and other less celebrated figures of jazz's earlier days.

Bop's incubation had taken place in various places, most notably in the Earl Hines Orchestra (1942–4) and, of course, the innovative Eckstine big band. Off the commercial stand, much experimentation, exchanging of ideas and the initial development of bop generally could be observed in after-hours blowing sessions, at two New York clubs – Minton's Playhouse (on West 118th Street) and Monroe's Uptown House (133rd Street and Seventh Avenue) – which have long since been recognized, historically and geographically, as important locations for the music's embryonic period.

Dexter Gordon's first exposure to bebop in its undeveloped (yet assuredly developing) form had come through that first encounter with Charlie Parker, when bop's principal genius was working with the Jay McShann band (first, on one or more of McShann's Decca recordings, then in live performance at the Savoy Ballroom). Parker's whole approach was new to the then Hampton sideman – although, as Gordon has always emphasized, he had all the accepted requirements of a gifted saxophonist whose playing never lost its Kansas City blues heritage. What made the still inexperienced youngster extra-curious was the Midwesterner's forward-looking harmonic and rhythmic approach. And Parker's overall concept excited him.

The Parker influence was to grow during the next two years, accelerating swiftly when Gordon joined Eckstine's sax section (even though Parker, an Eckstine sideman himself for a brief period, had left bebop's big-band cradle just a few weeks before).

Gordon had first jammed at Minton's Playhouse shortly before he was due to leave Hampton. He'd made a beeline to the club after work one night, hoping that Parker would show. He didn't. Consolation was forthcoming, however, as a slightly nervous young West Coaster was pushed onstage, with his horn, and he discovered that among the friendly combatants were Ben Webster and his first major hero, Lester Young. Despite the big names, he managed to hold his own. Moreover, Dexter learned, at first hand, what the term 'sitting in' really meant ('at that time, all the musicians when they played were sitting down . . .')

Gordon loved the atmosphere to be found at Minton's counterpart, Monroe's Uptown House. When he first visited the latter, he was merely an observer – albeit a very interested one. It never opened until well after 1 a.m., so if a working musician, having just finished for the night, wanted to go somewhere simply to relax and drink and talk – and to dig some fine music – Monroe's was ideal. And even as a spectator, Gordon discovered, as relaxed and unforced as these after-hours sessions might appear, the participants were accomplished players.

Oh yeah. All the cats who went there had to know their horns. I didn't go there *that* often, but I remember seeing Bird ... Charlie Christian. That kind of musician. They had a regular band. Had two trumpets – or two cornets, I don't remember which. There was George Treadwell, and a guy named Little Vic [Coulsen], who was a favourite of Miles's. Miles learned a lot from him. Played very beautifully. Like Miles does, that lyrical kinda style ... The music was always at a certain level of quality.

Gordon didn't get a real opportunity to talk music with Charlie Parker at great length when first they met at the Savoy, or when he heard him next (playing tenor with Earl Hines) – or even in 1945, when Dexter got a call from Bird to work as a regular member of an all-star Parker-led sextet. But talking came second to Dexter, after listening to the coruscating outpourings from Parker's alto.

Just to hear him play was such an education and a thrill ... In McShann's band, he was still developing. You could hear it ... it was fresh and new. But it hadn't reached the maturity and the stage of development that it had three years later. By 1945? [*Silence: stares ahead, mouth wide open in disbelief*] And that's the way it was ... *every night*! Unbelievable. If you listened to him on the McShann things, his tone was very nice but it was weak and light. By this (later) time, I had gotten *my* sound fully developed. But Bird had gone even farther. He always used a rubber mouthpiece, but a very stiff reed. Once, I tried to blow his horn. Didn't get nothing out of it. Could have been that very high reed he used – a No. 4 or a No. 5 – which he could control. Could play from top to bottom, with no strain. He had very powerful jaws which he clamped on to the mouthpiece. Incredible ...

Although Gordon missed Parker at his Minton's induction, he managed to blow informally with his new idol on numerous occasions later on in this more free and easy situation. Just as exciting, though, was that wonderful two-month gig with Parker's sextet, at another Clark Monroe-run club, the Spotlite, situated on 52nd Street; in company with, Parker apart, pianist Bud Powell, drummers Stan Levey or Max Roach, Miles Davis and bassist Curley Russell. Sir Charles Thompson sometimes deputized for Powell. For some numbers during most sets, a special guest would add his unique talents to the Parker combo, legendary jazz dancer, Baby Lawrence.

> He wasn't on the stand all the time. But when he came out to dance he was just part of the band. He was playing fours and eights. He'd come out and play the melody for two or three choruses. Somebody would play and then he'd start doing some eights. We didn't have any special music for him, it was just whatever we were playing that was right for him, he just joined in.

Working with Bird at the Spotlite remains 'totally memorable' for Gordon – and for the other sidemen. Not only were he, Davis and Levey in awe of the music pouring nightly from Parker's horn – and not forgetting Powell's electrifying keyboard excursions – but they had to keep constantly alert. Gordon agrees it was comparable to undertaking a crash-course in pure bebop, delivered in absolutely definitive fashion, as well as an unofficial graduation in the art of jazz performance for the sidemen.

> Crash-course? Oh, yeah! Because I never knew *what* he was gonna call. Nobody else did, either! It was the time when he started playing all these sophisticated standards – show tunes and stuff. Things like 'All the Things You are', 'I didn't Know what Time It was' . . . these were the new tunes at this time. And every night he'd just call these tunes . . . Next day, I'd find out what I could from the piano player – George Wallington worked with us occasionally, too. And the next

day I'd try to piece [it] together, and be ready. Out of the blue, Bird would call something and you'd think: 'What the fuck is *that*?' Sometimes Miles just stood there, open-mouthed. We all did.

As smitten as he was with Parker's playing alone, Dexter Gordon was in seventh heaven at this time because of the Spotlite's location, the immortal 52nd Street, the most famous jazz block of all time – even more famous than Bourbon Street, New Orleans, or Central Avenue, Los Angeles – tucked in between Fifth and Sixth Avenues. Sometimes known as Swing Street (or Swing Alley). A veritable market place of jazz and show-business talent whose lifespan covered the years 1934 to 1950. At the peak of its extraordinary existence (during the first half of the 1940s), any unsuspecting visitor would pass clubs with names like the Three Deuces, the Famous Door, Jimmy Ryan's, the Onyx, Kelly's Stable – and the Spotlite – and without paying too close attention to all the advertising banners casually encounter door-to-door references to such as Billy Holiday, Art Tatum, Charlie Parker, Erroll Garner, Dizzy Gillespie, Coleman Hawkins, John Kirby (and Sextet), Max Kaminsky, Maxine Sullivan, Oran 'Hot Lips' Page, Stuff Smith, Slim Gaillard, Don Byas, and many more.

When Dexter first hit the Street, it was to be another crash-course in music appreciation. He totally shares the author's pipe-dream, to be time-warped back to 52nd Street in the forties.

Apart from all the guys like Hawk, Dizzy, Bird, Tatum and such, they had so many singers. Billie, of course, but others, like Thelma Carpenter, Billy Daniels. And Pearl Bailey, Maxine Sullivan, Lee Wiley. Every night was a *thrill*! I'd just go in and out of all them clubs . . . sometimes when I stop and think about all those things, those times, it all seems like a movie. 'Did that really happen?' All the activity and enthusiasm . . . Of course, there was a lot happening in Los Angeles and Chicago. But in New York – specifically on 52nd Street – it was right there. It was just door-to-door. *Unbelievable!*

Dexter Gordon's first illuminating (and extensive) New York experiences lasted until the middle of 1946. His playing had reached a peak during this period, and both as a tenor saxophonist and as a personality in his own right he had succeeded in making his presence felt, in no uncertain way. From a personal standpoint, he rarely failed to attract attention. His giant frame helped, of course, but so did some of his delightfully eccentric behaviour, on and off the stand. Like the incident as reported by Ira Gitler, in his *Jazz Masters of the Forties*, when Dexter, after a successful meeting with his connection, played a solo for his heroin supplier – on request – while standing on the corner of 111th Street and Fifth Avenue. Or another occasion, inside a club, when a drunk stumbled up to the stand where Gordon was playing a ballad and dropped a handful of coins into the bell of the saxophone. Without pausing for a second, he opened one eye, clocked the event, closed his eye and completed his solo. After which, he tipped up the bell, pocketed the money and ambled to the bar nearby and ordered himself a drink . . .

From a more practical point of view, Gordon's impressive progress during this important 1945–6 period was documented for future reference by a series of recordings he made in New York. Between September 1945 and January 1946, he was to make a series of uniformly superb records under his own name for the Savoy label – two separate sessions, the second of which found him in particularly triumphant mood, stimulated no doubt by the presence of Max Roach and some magnificent piano playing from Bud Powell. In addition, he was present at a Benny Carter big-band date, for DeLuxe, and had what was an obviously uplifting experience of recording – for the first and only occasion – with Charlie Parker. This was as a member of a pick-up group, fronted by Sir Charles Thompson, whose individual jazz pedigrees ranged from a New Orleans-born guitarist (Danny Barker) who had worked with Cab Calloway and other big bands; Buck Clayton (ex-Basie trumpet star, currently on leave from the army); a swing-period rhythm section (with Thompson flirting with bop); and Parker and Gordon.

But Gordon's comprehensive involvement with the frantic New York scene of the mid-forties was to end in the summer of 1946. For one thing, he w   .   ' to spend some time with his mother, and old friends in   .. And he needed a temporary respite at least from the personal extravagances he had encouraged. First, though, there were two welcome months in Honolulu, after accepting a job with the R&B-based Cee Pee Johnson band. Then, back to California, to recuperate as well as to forge the partnership with Wardell Gray. And more journeys up and down Central Avenue.

Time, too, to reflect on the host of memories of the past year or so. So many magic moments to recall with pleasure. Perhaps none more exhilarating than the time spent in the company of a genius named Charlie Parker. Over thirty years after that unforgettable experience, Dexter Gordon was to offer his own summation of Bird and his profound contributions to jazz: '*Music!* All music. The fluidity and the freedom of expression, musically and emotionally, are still unbelievable. So, what's new?'

6

Detour Ahead: The Lean Years

The fifties should have been the decade for bebop's premier tenor saxist to capitalize on his arrival, acceptance, continuing development and the achievements of the previous four or five years.

Unfortunately, the natural progress of a career which still more or less fell into the 'immensely promising' category was to become severely retarded, due to Dexter Gordon's personal problem, a problem whose acceleration was already beginning to disrupt both his personal and professional life. The major problem was not fully to resolve itself for many years to come, but in the fifties it all but destroyed, if not the extraordinarily resilient man himself, then his hard-earned reputation as a gifted musician, someone whose talents could be appreciated by fellow-performers within the jazz world, almost irrespective of style or era. He was regarded as a soloist of real significance and individualism, who impressed both a majority of critics and a growing body of fans (especially those with a predilection for the exciting developments which had been, in many important ways, continuing to refresh and reinvigorate jazz's evolution). Slow though the integration process was, bebop was gradually becoming a part (and a fundamentally important part) of jazz history. Many of those, including certain noted jazz critics, who had previously denigrated bop and had pilloried its practitioners, had either accomplished a sometimes humiliating *volte-face* and were now among its cheerleaders, or were prepared to concede, albeit grudgingly, that the music had some real validity.

For all those who had never really bothered to listen closely to the playing of bebop's leading practitioners, content merely to be utterly dismissive and contemptuous, some now paid keener attention to the work of Parker, Monk, Gillespie, Navarro, Powell, Roach, Gordon and others. And for anyone prepared to make a genuine effort, it was becoming increasingly apparent that, far from being removed from any previous approaches to the art of jazz playing, even the often frenetic aspects of bop could not disguise the fact that the work of the forties revolutionaries had basic roots. Parker's Kansas City blues heritage remained with him to the end of his tragically short life. Monk's apparently other-worldly, idiosyncratic piano playing, as forward-looking as it was in bebop's embryonic years, stretched back in time and stylistic derivation to the Harlem/stride era of James P. Johnson, Fats Waller and their contemporaries. Gillespie's innovatory trumpet never has lost contact with the greatness of his personal idols of his own formative years. Powell, the most gifted of all the pianists of his era, and yet another supreme individualist, never cut himself off from his lineage, which continued to evidence certain elements of such outstanding keyboard practitioners as Tatum (predominantly), Cole and, most understandably, Monk. The same kind of influences can be found, with minimal effort, for Navarro and Roach, as well as for the majority of those who constituted the first wave of bebop. The same scenario can be enacted with those who followed the early crusaders. In the decades that have followed, similar comparisons can be found, although matters tend to become complicated from around the 1960s and thereafter, with the developments of what some might call extreme elements of the music, the kind which, for reasons of convenience, incomprehension or sometimes utter disdain, is generally allocated the description of avant-garde; probably the most unsatisfactory piece of terminology to be inflicted thus far on jazz music and its unsuspecting performers and followers. But that highly complex subject – something which might never be resolved to the complete satisfaction of even a sizeable majority – is, of course, outside the scope of this musical biography.

In retrospect, it seems beyond conjecture that, like that of his close buddy and fellow tenorman Wardell Gray, Dexter

Gordon's playing has never lost contact with the basic jazz roots in general and the stylistic contributions of the great figures of the pre-bop eras. Naturally, certain harmonic elements derived from Parker's comprehensive influence had become an integral part of his musical make-up since the mid-forties, but although Dexter had been developing his own voice since his big-band days, his admiration for the playing of Hawkins, Wilson, Byas and, most importantly, Young remained. Indeed, Young cast the longest shadow.

Unfortunately, Dexter was able to consolidate his substantial progress only during the first couple of years in the fifties. Thereafter, his was to become something of a half-forgotten name among jazz personalities of the decade. Jazz was changing, yet again, and the emergence of the basically white West Coast Jazz movement tended to push hard-hitting performers like Gordon into undeserved second place – indeed for some of his contemporaries, their fate was near-oblivion. But the prime cause of Gordon's long spells of fifties inactivity lay with his addiction to heroin. Not that he was alone. Bebop's guiding light, Charlie Parker, was to die prematurely, aged thirty-four, in 1955. A predictable happening, to state the obvious, considering his unbelievable appetites, for drugs, booze, sex and eating. The other significant bebop casualties of the fifties were: Navarro (who passed in 1950); Serge Chaloff (probably bop's premier baritone saxophonist, 1957); altoist Ernie Henry (also 1957); and Wardell Gray (just two and a half months after Bird).

Gray's sudden death hit Gordon hard, even though he was sufficiently preoccupied at the time with his own drug difficulties.

However, the start of the decade found the pair locking horns for numerous live appearances in California, at various, if irregular, times. In 1950, for instance, their reunion on the coast was documented through two numbers recorded at the Hula Hula Club, on Sunset Boulevard in Los Angeles, in August. Trumpeter Clark Terry (a colleague of Gray's in the octet Count Basie was leading at that time) was present; so too were a couple of Californian stalwarts, altoist Sonny Criss and pianist Jimmy Bunn. Singer Damita Jo sat in for one number only. Gray was leader for the session. Gordon's expansive tenor sound makes its presence felt on what is an organized jam on Denzil Best's 'Move' which, at ten minutes' duration, gives everyone – including an in-form Gray – ample chance to relax and give of their best. Damita Jo's solitary outing – a dynamically performed, if regrettably off-mike, 'I Can't Give You Anything but Love' – is much shorter, and only Criss gets a chance to solo. Dexter's tenor is heard, like Terry and Gray, in sympathetic obbligato.

Another – better-known – vocalist gave Gordon an opportunity to record, three months later, also in LA. This was for Discovery, one of the numerous small independent labels which came into existence between the mid-forties and the mid-fifties. The lifespan of these labels was invariably brief. Helen Humes had come to prominence, as Billie Holiday's replacement, with the Basie band, singing mostly ballads. She worked regularly with Basie between 1938 and 1941. Following a big hit with her definitive recording of 'E-Baba-Le-Ba' (with Bill Doggett's combo, in 1945), Humes's work concentrated in the main on an infectious rhythm-and-blues direction. She first recorded for Discovery in May of 1950, with an eleven-piece band fronted by Marshall Royal; then, in August, backed by Roy Milton's Band, reprising her hit number in electrifying style, in front of an obviously stimulated audience at the Shrine Auditorium, in Los Angeles, the city which had become her home after leaving Basie. The billing for her third (and final) Discovery session, which took place three months later within the same studio as the first, was credited to 'Dexter Gordon's Orchestra'.

Much excellent, blues-based music emanated from that date, with Dexter proving himself to be a superb blues tenorist, supplying apposite obbligatos to Humes's suitably expressive vocals on four mastered titles, including 'Helen's Advice' and 'Airplane Blues'.

During what proved to be her last London appearance, at the Ronnie Scott Club at the end of 1980, Helen Humes remembered the occasion with obvious delight and spoke with genuine affection of Dexter Gordon and his contributions to the date.

She recalled too how much she had enjoyed his company – on a personal as well as musical level – at previous in-person dates they had shared in clubs along Central Avenue. 'Guess I first heard him around '44. I felt he was one of the greatest out there, even then. Had such a big, beautiful tone. He used to play such *pretty* things, you know? But all the boys used to play such pretty changes, then.'

The sporadic recording dates included further reunions with both Humes and Gray. These were live affairs, emanating from the previously noted concert recording (for Decca) at Pasadena in 1952, with Dexter returning to the stage, following the two-tenor portion of the programme, to offer substantial support to the singer on four recorded titles. An unusual session, in an otherwise unknown small band accompanying noted R&B performer Lowell Fulson, took place around June 1952 (from which only one number is known to have been issued). And then there was nothing else until the autumn of 1955, apart from a final studio get-together with Gray (also in June), after which this fruitful partnership was not to be renewed.

Towards the end of 1952, Gordon was busted for possession of heroin and commenced a two-year incarceration at the minimum-security prison in Chino, California. It was shortly after finishing his sentence that Wardell Gray was found dead.

Naturally, it wasn't that easy to pick up the threads of a career after being off the scene completely for so long, but at least Gordon did manage to find the occasional gig. And, perhaps even more astonishingly, he was given two opportunities to record – within a period of less than a fortnight – for a youthful jazz label called Bethlehem. First, he was given leadership status, performing in front of the splendid rhythm section of Kenny Drew, piano; Leroy Vinnegar, bass and Lawrence Marable, drums. Nine days later, he was back inside Bethlehem's Los Angeles studios, this time as part of a fine-sounding group of West Coasters, including Frank Rosolino, trombone; Conte Candoli, trumpet; and an old 52nd Street associate, drummer Stan Levey, whose opportunity it was to act as session leader. Amazingly, the tenorist is in consistently visceral and inventive form throughout both recordings.

Two years away from regular jazz work is scarcely adequate preparation for even a temporary 'comeback' as a recording artist, the personal suffering of prison – physical, mental, spiritual – aside.

For Dexter Gordon, imprisonment had to be faced in as positive a way as possible. His personal lifelong philosophy has been to make the best out of unfortunate situations. One quintessential attribute has been his unflagging, highly developed sense of humour. However disastrous – and painful – a particular problem might have been, he never fails to find something irresistibly funny in relation to at least one element of the actual circumstances. Of his involvement with narcotics, and the resultant price he paid for it, Gordon merely tells it like it was: 'It was all mechanically inspired. It was just a thing that I got caught up in, as many cats did. And I went through these periods, y'know . . . It wasn't all that bad [in prison], I had fun, too.'

Where others with a similar problem might have given in to complete despair, Dexter says that never at any time did he feel that he wasn't going to make it.

> But finding the where and the how was another thing. Some of the guys – after their first 'accident' – they stop and never do any more; other guys take a little longer. It took me several years to finally accomplish this. As a matter of fact, I probably owe my life to the fact that I had a few enforced 'vacations', in order to build my body back and to lead a fairly normal type of life – meaning, you know, uninvolved. With regular hours, regular meals. So, each time this would happen, my body would rebuild. Because there were a lotta guys, like Bird, they never had any 'vacations'. Their thing was continuing, twenty-four hours. Day in, day out. For years. With no break. It's no fun being incarcerated, and all that. But it's not *all* negative. You have plenty of time to think and to read . . . study and utilize the time. Et cetera . . .

In a revealing moment in 1966, Dexter Gordon told Mike

Hennessey (the *Melody Maker*'s Paris jazz correspondent at that time) about the ceaseless battle it was to keep straight – or at least to resist the ever-present temptation further to line the pockets of the pushers.

It got to the stage where I told myself it just couldn't go on. I was spending up to 200 dollars a day on smack, my kids were getting their father's addiction flung in their faces. So I fought it and went clean. But I was getting phonecalls every day from pushers, and they were approaching me in the street. 'Aw, come on, Dexter, let's swing . . .' I had to tell them over and over again that I was determined to kick it.

The Hennessey feature – still one of the most constructive and sympathetic articles on the subject of hard drugs and a distinguished jazz musician, composed by one of the most respected writers on the subject – concluded when Gordon was asked whether he really did want to kick the habit. The answer was as straightforward and honest as one would expect from him: 'Of course I want to beat it. I'm a perpetual optimist and I feel I can. I hope I can. But I just don't know whether I'll be able to. I've just got to try to kill the habit before it kills me.'

Of course, 1966 was a long way ahead of the fifties – and jail. Still, Dexter's eternal optimism was something which would prove of inestimable help in getting him through each night and day. There was another, perhaps more fundamental, reason for his believing that life – even inside Chino – wasn't as awful as it might otherwise have been: 'I was playing all the time. Because they always let me have my horn with me.'

Not only was that luxury available, but Gordon's playing was further kept to a reasonable standard by the fact that he was given permission to get together with other inmates who could also play an instrument. As he related some years ago (the brief comment followed by one of his huge, bellowing outbursts of laughter): 'In fact, some of the best bands I played with were in the jug!'

A rather unusual event occurred towards the end of his first incarceration, something which, although it remained a comparatively insignificant, unimportant happening for years, was to assume some significance, intriguingly, some thirty years later. Dexter participated in a movie, about prison life inside Chino. Entitled *Unchained*, and based on Kenyon Scudder's *Prisoners are People*, it starred him both as a musician and as an actor. Regrettably, Dexter's musical contributions were not heard on the final soundtrack; another tenorist overdubbed his solo work ...

Even though parole, in 1955, was a relief, work outside didn't come too often. Miraculously, there were opportunities to record – three in all, during the last quarter of the year: two sessions for Bethlehem (September) and one for Dootsie Williams's Dootone label (November). Naturally, though, there was always the terrible inner struggle to avoid temptation. And the pushers, hip to his release even before he was free, were as vigilant as ever. The inevitable happened: rearrest, conviction, and back, once more inside; off the scene.

Still, Gordon could not complain. As before, his request for retention of his beloved tenor sax was granted. So too were the opportunities to put together informal 'jug' bands, which provided welcome entertainment for those inmates who were interested, as well as a sense of personal fulfilment for the musicians involved.

When Gordon once more tasted freedom, there was no automatic way to recapturing his place among the upper echelon of top jazz soloists. Sadly but inevitably, his had become something of a forgotten name. During the previous decade – he was paroled in 1960 – jazz had experienced further fundamental changes – and there were more significant developments just around the corner.

Out of sight, out of mind is a phrase that might have been invented as part of the jazz language, and being 'off the scene' can have more connotations than the (obvious) one. Jazz polls might not seem to some the ultimate in identifying the musicians who really deserve to be voted in top spot for a given year – or even a totally accurate assessment of the popularity of one particular jazz musician over another. Dexter Gordon's name hadn't figured too frequently in the leading US jazz polls in some years – and this despite the fact that there are those loyalists who continue to cast votes for their favourite player, irrespective of whether he (or she) has been performing on a regular basis in the previous year.

Certainly, both the *Down Beat* polls for 1959 carried no listing of Gordon. Coleman Hawkins, not surprisingly, topped the Jazz Critics' Poll, followed by Stan Getz, Sonny Rollins, Ben Webster, Zoot Sims and John Coltrane. In the companion Readers' Poll, Getz racked up his eighth consecutive victory, easily ahead of both Rollins and Coltrane, with Hawkins, Sims, Benny Golson, Bill Perkins, Webster, Al Cohn and Paul Gonsalves even farther back in the list of final qualifiers. Getz's long reign, however, was about to end . . . in the following Readers' Poll, anyway. For in terms of major influence on the tenor saxophone during the second half of the 1950s, Rollins and Coltrane, in that order, were the major names. And it was to be the last-named who would be *the* dominant figure on tenor (and indeed soprano), right up to his premature death in 1967; Coltrane's innovations and resultant influence were to remain widely felt right up until the end of the eighties.

Ironically for the neglected Gordon, it was his own influential sound that would be apparent in some elements of the playing of both Rollins and Coltrane. It was most apparent with Coltrane during his 'modal' improvisations, and discernible more easily during the ballad playing of both, and in the tonal similarities of each player. The Gordon influence on Rollins is less obvious, being confined mostly to the latter's impressively large sound and to his dry – often sardonic – wit, and his frequent and humorous use of phrases interpolated from other sources.

Although there seemed little on the 1960 horizon, two events occurred which definitely helped to alleviate the depressing prospects. The great alto saxist Cannonball Adderley, appointed by Orrin Keepnews as A&R chief of Jazzland, subsidiary label to the famous Riverside Records company, got to hear of Dexter's release. He contacted Gordon and there was immediate agreement that Adderley should produce an album date, on 13 October, in Los Angeles. Gordon would be given the role of leader and personal choice of sidemen. The LP, titled by Adderley, was suitably optimistic: *The Resurgence of Dexter Gordon*.

An even bigger break that year came about when Dexter was leading a band at the Zebra Lounge, in Los Angeles. One evening, he was approached by playwright Carl Thaler, who asked him to read for his play *The Dying of the Light*, which was to have a musical background. But nothing happened.

Later though, it was as a result of Thaler's personal recommendation that Gordon was asked to lead a jazz quartet, solo, compose music for and act in a Los Angeles production of *The Connection*. Written by Jack Gelber, *The Connection* had opened in New York, at the Living Theatre, in July 1959. Gelber's story concerns a group of junkies who are waiting for their dealer to arrive with a fresh supply of heroin. As an afterthought, Gelber decided to incorporate music, to be performed onstage by four of the protagonists. Not only did they perform that function, but they were also given lines to speak. Freddie Redd played piano and composed the music, and altoist Jackie McLean not only blew superbly but also proved himself a fine, natural actor.

The play was not at all well received by some of the critics who attended its opening, but a second wave of critics disagreed and treated it with more sympathy and understanding. In 1961, a critically acclaimed film adaptation of *The Connection* was produced – featuring the identical Freddie Redd Quartet – thus bringing its powerful message to an international audience.

The New York stage production was still running when Dexter Gordon accepted the principal role in what was to be known as *The Hollywood Connection*. For his three musical associates, he selected pianist Charles 'Dolo' Coker, bassist George Morrow, and drummer Lawrence Marable. The Los Angeles production received mostly favourable reviews (surprisingly, its only out and out condemnation came from John Tynan, *Down Beat*'s West Coast Editor). Dexter himself was singled out for individual praise from several critical sources, notably for his ad-lib contributions to the dialogue.

Compositionally, Dexter retains a personal pride in the music he wrote for *The Hollywood Connection*, especially 'Ernie's Tune', a delightfully melodic ballad, with a tender, yearning quality all its own. (It is rather surprising that a suitable lyric hasn't been written. Even with a title-change, 'Ernie's Tune' might still become a standard-type song to which the more sensitive, intelligent vocalists would wish to return.) And as for Dexter Gordon, Thespian, he is pleased at any time to recall how well his contributions were received – both by the general audience as well as by the majority of the critics who reviewed *The Hollywood Connection*: 'Reactions – both audience and critics' – were great. The play ran for about a year. One reviewer called me "a great actor" – I'm serious. Me, with no formal training. *The Connection*, that was my pass-mark.'

And it was his success in *The Hollywood Connection* which provided the prime motivation for Cannonball Adderley journeying west in order to bring Dexter Gordon back inside a recording studio. Both Dolo Coker and Lawrence Marable, who comprised two-thirds of the rhythm section, had, of course, worked onstage at Le Grand Comedy Theatre with Dexter in the Gelber play.

Local gigs, though, were still available only on an irregular basis. During the years 1959 and 1960, Gordon's tenor was heard wailing out-front of the hard-swinging, blues-based big band fronted by Onzy Matthews, in and around LA.

It was towards the end of 1960 that Dexter started to revisit New York, renewing old acquaintanceships, checking out the local scene and playing the odd job. But merely returning to the Big Apple didn't mean an automatic change in fortunes, gig-wise. Because of his criminal record, Gordon could not obtain the all-important cabaret card. Doled out by the local licence bureau, this vital document was the passport to full-time employment; without it, he was not permitted to work more than once a week in clubs serving alcohol (which more or less meant every club which might welcome his services). Instead, he would have to make do with the once-a-week club situation and, if he were very lucky, a one-off concert appearance – scarcely a real opportunity to earn anything like a full-time living. This was something which Dexter, released once again on parole, needed.

Despite the limited gigs situation, help was at hand. Early in 1961, Alfred Lion, the always perceptive founder/producer of the esteemed Blue Note label, approached the welcome visitor, with a view to signing Dexter Gordon to a contract. Naturally, Gordon was delighted. With such a contract, he would be recording on a fairly regular basis for the first time since 1947.

The immediate results of his signing with one of the most celebrated of all jazz labels were two album dates in May, the second taking place only three days after Gordon's Blue Note debut session. Freddie Hubbard, one of the most promising trumpet players of the period and a most positive performer, was selected as Dexter's front-line partner for the first Blue Note date, while a strong rhythm section of Horace Parlan, George Tucker and Al Harewood drew no complaints from the tenorist. Then it was Gordon, with just a rhythm section, for the follow-up recording. Once again, Lion came up with a trio which, if anything, was even better than the first: Kenny Drew (who had worked with Dexter many times in Los Angeles, between 1953 and 1956), and Paul Chambers and Philly Joe Jones, the last twosome with strong Miles Davis connections (bassist Chambers, present; drummer Jones, recent past).

The ideal selection of musical associates, plus the kind of relaxed yet freewheeling atmosphere actively encouraged for such occasions by Lion and his partner Francis Wolff, no doubt made Blue Note's latest signing feel more than welcome. Certainly, his playing at both sessions gave no indication of just how infrequent his visits to recording studios had been in so long, and what a lengthy term of imprisonment might have done to both his general health and his playing ability. That great magisterial quality of Dexter Gordon's tenor-saxophone playing remained. It is not fanciful to say that there was also a sense of maturity about it, in practically every area, and an almost triumphant aura pervaded both sessions, providing a positive statement-of-intent for the future. It was as if Dexter himself was proclaiming, to all and sundry, his intention to re-establish himself on the jazz scene.

In terms of in-person performances, there were two occasions which remain in the memories of those who were present. The first was when he sat in with trumpeter Kenny Dorham, at the Jazz Gallery, NYC, and stunned everyone with a pulverizing display of hard-hitting tenor playing. Even more heart-warming – especially for the man himself – was an October 1961 reunion with his old Eckstine section-mate Gene Ammons, in the latter's home town of Chicago. The locals, who adored their local man's big-toned, emotional tenor playing, were so enamoured of the visitor's performance – in tandem with 'Jug' Ammons – that some of them hung a sign on the club window which proclaimed: DEXTER, WE LOVE YOU! Dexter, obviously moved by his reception in the Windy City, and the banner-hanging dedication, told Brooks Johnson: 'Since I've been here, nearly everyone I talk to tells me how much they've missed me. It's a very good feeling, knowing that you have been missed. It's inspiring. It touches you where people like to get touched.'

One year after finishing *Dexter Calling*, his second Blue Note album, Gordon found himself in the studios four times during a single month. Three of these dates were for Blue Note. The first of these was under his name, but only half the material was deemed worthy of release. The second found him working as a sideman in an impressive eight-piece band assembled in the Epic studios in support of altoist/sopranoist Norwood 'Pony' Poindexter. The third – co-starring Dexter with altoist/tenorist Sonny Stitt, plus an unknown rhythm section – remains in all other ways a complete mystery. Two or three titles only were performed – all were rejected. Finally, at the end of May 1962, the rejuvenated Gordon recorded under pianist/composer Herbie Hancock, with Freddie Hubbard present once again. This extraordinarily productive period continued with no fewer than three further Blue Note album dates under his own name, each with superb piano support from Sonny Clark. The standard of Gordon's playing on all these occasions was first-class.

On the completion of the last of these – on 29 August 1962 – Dexter Gordon embarked on the longest trip he'd made so far in his thirty-nine years. Just hours after finishing a splendid quartet date at Rudy Van Gelder's studios in Englewood Cliffs, New Jersey, he boarded an airliner from New York to London. The journey itself proved uneventful (Dexter, predictably, slept like a bear in hibernation all the way). But the consequences of that trans-Atlantic flight to London were to be far-reaching, and of inestimable importance to Gordon: the lean years were over.

7

The Expatriate: Nights at the Montmartre

Dexter Gordon never intended to become an expatriate. In fact, he didn't realize he was beginning to put down roots in a foreign country, thousands of miles away from the United States, until he read an article in *Down Beat*, written by an old friend, Ira Gitler. The article, which tried to draw the attention of jazz-minded Americans to the fact that a great talent seemed to be disappearing from their midst, used, in connection with Gordon's prolonged absence, the word 'expatriate'.

> After seeing that article, referring to me as 'expatriate Dexter Gordon', I reacted. Because I had not thought of myself as being 'expatriate'. I didn't originally come over to stay – as some cats have. When I came, it was just to make a gig. It was very fascinating, all these new elements, and I enjoyed it very much. Musically, it wasn't *always* totally rewarding. In spite of that, it worked out quite well.

The gig which brought him to Europe for the first time took place at the Ronnie Scott Club, in London, at the beginning of September 1962. Indeed, Gordon's one-month season at Scott's started only two days after his flight from New York landed at London Airport.

Ronnie Scott, one of Europe's leading tenor saxophonists, had opened the club bearing his name in London's Soho, in 1959. Two years later, thanks to the perseverance of his partner and friend Pete King, the Scott club began importing a succession of top American soloists. That there was a distinct bias in favour of tenor players needs no further explanation.

Zoot Sims was the first to appear at the club, followed by
another great saxophonist, Lucky Thompson. Dexter Gordon
was third in line. Scott himself was responsible for asking
Gordon to make his London debut, and in a nicely informal
way. Gordon was relaxing in Charlie's Tavern, a favourite
place for jazz musicians to hang out in New York. Scott
introduced himself. They talked, and the tenor-playing club
owner invited Dexter to come to London for a month. The
American accepted at once.

The Scott's season proved to be the outstanding event in the
London jazz calendar for that year . . . even though towards the
end the distinguished visitor's playing wasn't as exciting and as
constantly uplifting as it had been for the first three-quarters of
his stay. This disappointing tail-off was due to what one local
musician later described as 'Dexter being extremely well looked
after by certain people in London who knew of his offstage
preferences'.

One British musician who had a close-quarters opportunity
to witness the onstage developments during September is Stan
Tracey, a hugely gifted composer/instrumentalist, who had
fronted the house rhythm section at Scott's since 1960.
Musically, Tracey enjoyed working with Gordon – even though
he agrees that the last portion of the engagement did result in
problems which caused some tension between Dexter and his
accompanists.

> Good to work with, yes. He's a very relaxed player – nice
> long lines. Socially, though, I don't know, because Dexter
> had his own scene going . . . But it's very unfair of me to
> make any judgements or remarks about him because he got
> well hung-up on heroin while he was here. And that turns
> you into another sort of person. So, certain of his actions and
> words came from a situation that isn't normal. Because he
> *did* get fucked-up, and he *did* get shitty about things; like a
> junkie would get shitty about . . . unimportant, trivial,
> things.

Certainly, from the non-playing visitors to the club – critics as well as punters – reactions were uniformly laudatory. Dexter's commanding presence, his friendly rapport with audiences and, most memorable of all, his often electrifying performances, drew near-rapturous applause nightly. His warm, deeply-felt ballad work, too, registered consistently throughout his first-time appearance at Scott's. Most of all, though, it was his almost overwhelming sound (especially on the medium- and up-tempo numbers) which remained longest in the memory.

Despite any moments of tension or awkwardness generated towards the end of the month by the visitor's extra-curricular extravagances, Gordon and the Tracey trio did establish (and sustain) a fine rapport during the first three weeks. Dexter was happy with the pianist's powerful contributions and intrigued that a British jazz pianist could be so deeply influenced by Monk, yet still obtain a completely individual approach of his own. He had no complaints either with the bass-playing consistency of twenty-four-year-old Jeff Clyne, whose impeccable time, clean articulation and satisfying tone made him an excellent accompanist. Jazz drumming, particularly in the modern field, was on the threshold of rising above its general level of ordinariness at the time of the initial importation of top American talent to Scott's. Its development, not surprisingly, continued to improve with a non-stop stream of other importees, as well as the return of most of the early guests, during the rest of the decade.

On the face of it, the appearance during the month of September of no fewer than *eleven* of either the very best local drummers, or others whose skills were not too far behind, would seem to indicate that Dexter, for one, didn't believe in the all-round improvement in British jazz drumming . . . or that he was undoubtedly jazz's most unholy prima donna of all time. In reality, the bewildering change of drummers has a most innocent, and understandable, explanation. Gordon, who had never been confronted with such a musical-chairs situation – before or since – often relates this story, and its reason, with friendly amusement:

Ronnie and I were alternating and using the same rhythm section, which was Stan, Jeff and Jackie Dougan. About the third or fourth night, Ronnie and Dougan had an argument. They got a little hysterical, so Dougan wound up being fired. So, for the next two weeks we had eleven drummers – including Jackie Dougan. These guys *all* had other commitments, other gigs ... they could make *this* night, but they couldn't make it after that. So, every night there was a new drummer! Tony Crombie ... Phil Seamen, a couple of nights ... Phil was great ... Ronnie Stephenson ... Tony Kinsey ... then, we wound up with Benny Goodman, he finished out the gig. How d'you adjust? You just do. That kinda situation ... it's a different thing, and if you dwell on it, you just get bugged.

Overall, critical reaction to the Dexter Gordon month at Ronnie Scott's (plus a couple of single dates outside London) was favourable. Drawing attention to 'a big brilliant tone without the acidulousness of much contemporary music', plus the warmth and unforced humour in his playing, Alan Beckett's *Jazz Journal* review could find little to fault in Gordon as a soloist. But, for Beckett, 'one could perhaps mention the comparative lack of variation in his emotional range, though this probably reflects more upon the listener's precociousness than upon the musician's playing ...' And club manager King – again, with qualifications about the final part of the month – offered what was for most people who heard him in London on that first occasion as fine an epitaph as any: 'Musically, the chance of having Dex with us was something we wouldn't have missed ...'

It was through King's good offices that Gordon was able to fly to Paris at the conclusion of his Scott's debut to undertake another month-long season, this time at the Blue Note Club. Infinitely more so than in London, his very presence in the French capital attracted the kind of buzz and excitement created by a major musical performer – especially the kind with a flamboyant personality. The Blue Note season drew consistently turn-away crowds and, in every way, was an outstanding success. Dexter himself blew with renewed power and admirable invention. And from all accounts, he enjoyed the social amenities – amply available – to the full.

But his next European experience was to have the most far-reaching consequences for Dexter Gordon. This was a trip to Scandinavia, to accept yet another comprehensive engagement, this time at the Montmartre Jazzhus, in Copenhagen. The reception, once again, was extraordinary. For the next two years, this latest American jazz musician to find unexpected recognition and respect in Europe was more or less to divide his time between Denmark and France, working with a regularity he must have found to be almost unnatural. These gigs were interspersed with periods of self-imposed inactivity, when the need to rid himself of the pressures and pain of his inescapable habit resurfaced. There was always someone to provide that magical (but never permanent) trip to euphoria. But, then, some things cannot change, or be changed, overnight.

It was probably only after rereading Ira Gitler's *Down Beat* feature that Dexter Gordon realized just how long ago he had made that initial journey to London, just how much time had passed – and so quickly – since he had seen his ex-wife and two daughters, still living in Los Angeles. Suddenly, it seemed ages since he had performed in any North American jazz joint, had met and blown with his musical friends; the old ones and the newer, younger lions.

> I went back to the States, for about six months. I was in New York for a couple of months. Then, I went out to LA for two or three months. I wanted to see my daughters and check out the domestic scene. But there were still sort of 'holes' – and I wasn't happy. At any rate, I had my return ticket.

In his heart, Gordon realized that if he used that return ticket it would be to resecure his European foothold. Periodic Stateside visits notwithstanding, he had a feeling it would be a long time before he would leave his new friends and security in

Europe. There were several reasons for using that return ticket. One was the insecurity of his own family set-up. Another was the constant flow of work which had been coming his way since his European experience began.

> I always had been able to work. The only time I didn't was because of *me*. There was nothing, really, to hold me in the States. And, in two years in Europe I had gotten a taste for the life. And there was so much more to absorb and learn about. Just knowing that I could work – regularly. All these things were waiting for me. And getting the chance to work – not every day, of course – with Byas, Bud and such was part of the main ingredients. No, I never regretted going back.

Not that Gordon was to cut himself off completely from his homeland. Certainly, he kept in contact with what was happening on the jazz scene back home, as far as he could. He continued to check out the new arrivals as well as the older, established artists – including, of course, news of any latest 'new star' junior tenor threat. And although it was to be the exception rather than the rule, he did indeed make further trips Stateside – in 1965, 1969, 1970, 1972 – when he would play selected dates: in New York, or California, or maybe Chicago. (There was a particularly memorable reunion with Gene Ammons, as well as a guest appearance at a Charlie Parker Memorial Concert, both in the Windy City, in 1970.) On the occasion of each of these homeward journeys there was one specific reason, at least, to justify the undertaking. In 1965, Gordon completed a splendid series of Blue Note recordings (the previous two had taken place in Paris). And between 1969 and 1972, he was to add a further six studio-made albums to his discography, this time for Prestige, another major jazz label. (There was also a shared live date, with Ammons, *et al*, in 1970; plus three other Prestige recordings, these involving location dates in Europe.)

Not that there was any shortage of recording activities on the European scene, especially with regard to SteepleChase – almost on his front doorstep – based in Copenhagen. The perceptive SteepleChase owner, Nils Winther, had long admired Gordon's playing. Starting in 1971, Winther recorded the Montmartre's star attraction – both in studio and live settings – up to November 1976, at regular intervals. And there were dates for other labels, including Black Lion, MPS, Storyville and Sonet.

So there was no lack of action: clubs and concerts, almost always on schedule; an ever-increasing number of appearances at a variety of European jazz festivals; recordings, radio, TV. And something with which Gordon was pleased to be associated: summer jazz clinics at the high schools, at Valle-kilde and Magleaas, with either television or radio documenta-tion of the occasions.

But even before his first trip back home, the Europeanization of Dexter Gordon had begun. The adopted citizen of Copenhagen (and Valby, his suburban home) was to experience a myriad of mostly enlightening events – personally and professionally – before he would, once again, start life in the land of his birth – this time with no return ticket in his pocket.

When thoughts of spending some unspecified time in Europe had at first crossed his mind, Dexter had big eyes for a temporary home in Paris. Certainly, he'd fallen in love with the French capital on his very first visit. Not surprising, then, that the near-three-year period in which he lived and worked there was mostly a happy one. Musically, much was happening in Paris, of course, and the frequent on-the-spot reunions with old buddies such as Kenny Clarke, Bud Powell and Art Taylor – all resident in Paris – and others like Johnny Griffin, Ben Webster, Kenny Drew, Idrees Sulieman and Don Byas – who flew in periodically from other European countries of their choice – gave Gordon ample reason for dropping anchor. Outside of purely musical considerations, the facilities in Paris were also plentiful. And as temperamental as they could be, he liked the locals, especially their *comme-çi, comme ça* attitude to life. He dug their free-and-easy approach, especially their (to him) almost unbelievable lack of racial prejudice. And, of course, how could he not be thrilled by their genuine love for his kind of music?

Yet, in that first period of readjustment, he had been just as impressed by the warmth of his welcome in Denmark. The Danes, much more laid-back and undemonstrative than their French counterparts, had made a lasting impact on Gordon, right from that first gig at the Montmartre Jazzhus. As in Paris, he had been treated with the kind of civility, good manners and all-round friendliness which had been all too rare back home during the first four decades of his life. In retrospect, Dexter called it, simply, 'love at first sight'.

During that all-important first year of absence from the States, Dexter wielded his axe, to wild acclaim, in other Scandinavian countries – Norway, Sweden, Finland – as well as France, Britain and Denmark. But he knew that, to begin with at least, he would return to Denmark. He had taken an immediate liking to Copenhagen, a city of quiet beauty with its simple yet elegant architecture. He had soon responded to the way the Danes conducted their lives: the local musicians with whom he worked, the patrons of the Montmartre, and even those people he came in contact with on a day-to-day, or a meet-by-chance basis only.

In addition to their basic courtesy and friendly disposition, the Danish people – particularly the residents of Copenhagen – seemed only too happy to accord Dexter Gordon his rightful status as a major contributor to one of this century's most vital musical forms. And, as in France, he found there a refreshing absence of racial prejudice. From a professional standpoint, Gordon's personal rating soared even higher than in Paris. Throughout what was to be the period of over ten years he was to live in Denmark, he remained as a cross between a cult figure and an adopted cultural hero.

As in Paris, Dexter responded, both personally and musically. Performance-wise, his debut season at the Montmartre tended to be erratic. Some nights, he would fully justify his legendary status; on others, he would ramble, sound unsure of himself, lose his flow of ideas. One of the local musicians who appeared with the illustrious visitor at various times during the initial month-long season remembers the disappointment felt by himself and his colleagues about the 'off' nights.

> To start with, he missed one air flight several times, so he came in four or five days late. Actually, he didn't play that well for most of that [first] time. I'm sorry to say so. He was in bad shape. I think there were so many problems at that time, they rather overshadowed what he did. Once he'd really got settled in Denmark – this would be the next summer – it was much different . . .

When he had completed his first Montmartre booking, had found the right kind of accommodation in which to relax and sort out his personal problems, and take some kind of interim stock of his life – the present anyway – Gordon really appreciated the collective hand of friendship being extended to him in this small country.

Apart from the unaccustomed security he was to experience in Denmark, prior to his move to Paris and at much more length on his return to Copenhagen, Gordon was happy to find that neighbouring countries would call, asking him to bring his horn and play in fresh pastures.

To begin with, his appearances outside Denmark were sparse, probably due as much as anything to Dexter's urgent need, once again, to bring some real order into his life. Certainly, though, by the time he had become ensconced in Paris, the situation began to change. Having returned to Denmark, the pages of his passport were being stamped and restamped on a regular basis. These 'overseas' visits weren't confined solely to playing club engagements, at an ever-increasing number of cities and towns; there were also one-off concerts, and a mushrooming jazz-festival circuit in Europe. In addition, there were frequent invitations to appear on both TV and radio programmes, mostly in Denmark.

In fact, Dexter Gordon's work-rate improved in a way he can scarcely have dreamed of, particularly if he related this to the years of inactivity and neglect which had preceded that fateful flight across the Atlantic. Like practically every North

American jazz musician who visits Europe – for a brief period only, or to stay for much longer – he was astonished by the extent of knowledge of European fans, on the subject of jazz in general and about Dexter Keith Gordon in particular.

> I had no idea of the European love for jazz – and jazz fans . . . I'd heard that it was beautiful. All the cats that came over spoke about it. But I really had no idea of *how* much it was appreciated. It was such a great revelation. And to feel all this respect, as a musician, as an artist . . . It was quite a new thing for me and, I would say, for most American musicians. Because at that time *jazz* musicians were, in America, just horn-blowers: 'Oh, you're one of them *horn-blowers*!' A kind of musical weirdo? Yes. Unless you were Duke Ellington – you had to be on that kind of pedestal to get any kind of respect. But I found it, in England and in Europe. And I found this very heartwarming. As for the knowledge . . . you meet these guys and they know *everything* about you. They've got what you did . . . when . . . the whole thing . . . at their fingertips. And it wasn't uncommon to run into people like this all over Europe – Sweden, Denmark, Italy, England, Belgium. Everywhere.

Wherever he turned up, Dexter Gordon's sunny personality matched his playing. And his playing, even in a few years as an American expatriate, began to equal the splendid consistency of his first peak period of the second half of the forties. Indeed, well before the end of the sixties, it had taken on an all-round maturity that often was awesome in its projection, yet retaining the fire and power of his youth. He had very few complaints about his personal situation, and musically that was more or less the same.

There was, however, one problem which presented itself in his early years in Denmark. True, he had the good fortune to work with top performers from back home who had made a similar journey to Europe, to stay. Yet only those as gifted as Kenny Drew (who arrived in 1963), and drummer Albert 'Tootie' Heath (resident just over two years), were working and living permanently in the Danish capital. And much-in-demand as they soon became, both Drew and Heath would often be touring elsewhere on the Continent.

Which left the basic problem for Dexter in that, with a few notable exceptions, the standard of jazz players generally in Denmark was rather less than he had been accustomed to, virtually at any time, in the States. As sympathetic as he tried to appear, it was indeed a problem – and it was not a problem he found only in Denmark. There were excellent pianists, drummers and bassists in Britain and occasionally elsewhere, but these players, he discovered, were at a premium. In Denmark, for instance, it was rare to find a jazz musician who played for a living – almost impossible to come across one who even attempted to played jazz full-time.

> It just wasn't possible to live from playing music professionally. Consequently, I was playing with all types of people. Doctors. Dentists. Architects. Salesmen. Students. They played because they loved it. But, experience-wise, they hadn't paid their dues. So, it was always a thing of you being cast in the role of a teacher. Because all they knew was what they'd learned from the records. Which is considerable, but not enough ... And with jazz, you've gotta come up by playing with other musicians – older musicians – who would explain and tell you about this and that. In the way we all came up in the States.

Still, even without the comfort of even the minimal number of home-grown talents, Gordon concedes there were some rhythm-section players – particularly pianists – with whom he was happy. Gifted keyboard practitioners like Atli Bjørn, Ole Kock Hansen, Bent Axen. Superb bass players of the calibre of Benny Nielsen, Bo Stief and Niels-Henning Ørsted Pedersen (something of a boy wonder, and already on the way to becoming a Danish legend when Dexter arrived on the scene). And if he could be persuaded to leave his native Spain, Gordon seemed always inspired by the presence, at the Montmartre (and indeed elsewhere), of the immensely gifted blind pianist Tete Montoliu.

Of all the local Danish jazzmen, Ørsted Pedersen, his first-choice bass player always, was to work with Dexter Gordon more than anyone during the latter's European residence. Pedersen, with his awesome technique, huge tone and impeccable time, had been playing with local combos since just after his fourteenth birthday. A perfect anchorman for any rhythm section, and a soloist of exceptional ability, he was, even in the early sixties, very much on a par with the finest bassists in the States. As obviously talented as he was before Dexter Gordon's arrival in Denmark, the quiet-spoken, always modest Pedersen is the first to agree that working alongside a jazz musician of Gordon's stature helped in his own growth. For Pedersen, his first real appreciation of Gordon's true abilities as a saxophonist of real stature came during the American's second, three-month season at the Montmartre, in 1963.

Because of the unusual length of Gordon's stay at the club, Pedersen and his two rhythm-section associates got to know him better personally than was normally the case with other American guests. And, of course, they were able to understand his music, and answer his requirements more easily.

Dexter was – is – of a much more communicative nature than most people. From the playing point of view? Well you got your openings from Dexter. With Bud [Powell], I played out of necessity. When he didn't want to play any more, I had to play solo. But with Dexter, it was like an opening – it was in the tune. It was like there should be a good long piano solo. Where you would hopefully get into something. And there should be a bass solo – if I wanted it. There should be extended eights with the drums – all that sort of thing. In other words, he wasn't looking at the rhythm section and saying: 'Well, let's get this over with!' Not to say a lot of people thought like that. But he had a positive attitude towards us, really trying to make this a groove: make this sound like something . . . once he got himself settled, he got to like everybody so much, and you could sort of feel the warmness around the person. He's still like that . . . the main feeling was that you just felt comfortable around him. Very comfortable. I think that was the first time we established any kind of musical *and* personal relationship with one of the Americans.

Pedersen's memories of the cult figure Gordon was to become at the Montmartre Jazzhus are plentiful. Many jazz musicians from the States visited the club over the years when Pedersen's bass was one of its most regular sights (and sounds). But no other performer appeared so often at the Montmartre, and no other performer endeared himself as closely – and lastingly – to the committed fans to whom the club became something of a shrine. Their admiration and respect for Dexter – the man as well as the great soloist – soon became deep-rooted. Indeed, unofficial though it might have been, their hero had a hard core of perhaps thirty followers – mostly students, but also covering a variety of professional people – which became something of a Dexter Gordon Fan Club.

The kind of genuine love and respect he received from some of the fans was often unconcealed . . . yet never embarrassing. As Pedersen remembers:

People would literally come and kiss him. Bring him gifts. And say: 'Hey, Dexter's back in town!' And I remember the years when he went back to the States . . . then he'd return to the Montmartre. Opening 1 June, carrying on through August. And the people would turn up, yet again. You'd have to be stone-hard not to be literally crying. Because they'd just be sitting there, and they'd cheer and cheer when he came onstage.

The friendship extended to more than one person arranging for Gordon to see a doctor, perhaps loan him their summer-house, for him once more to take a rest from drugs. When he'd become an established citizen – at his own home in Valby, a suburb of Copenhagen – and had married again, this time to a local girl, it was not uncommon to find his picture on the front page of a Danish Sunday newspaper, seated on a bicycle, having a joke outside a pub, or just hanging out.

Just how fiercely supportive his most loyal fans could be was demonstrated by the fact that when he was playing one of his long seasons at the Montmartre, some Gordonites would be present nearly every other night. Even more dramatic evidence of the esteem in which he was held by many came in 1966 when Dexter was arrested in Paris on drugs charges and was forced to spend a couple of months in jail. As a result of this, the Danish Home Office took the decision to ban him from re-entering the country.

Johnny Griffin, who was working in Paris at the time, was able to see for himself, courtesy of French television, just what some of his great friend's activist-admirers thought of this, and to what lengths they were prepared to go to help him gain re-entry to Denmark.

These people had a big rally in the Town Hall Square, in Copenhagen. Students, mostly, but older people too. Carried big signs, saying: '*We want Dexter – we don't want NATO.*' And this was nothing to do with socialism or communism or such. They got him back into Denmark too. Once he was back, they took very good care of him. That's the way these people are.

In Denmark, there were to be more delightful surprises in the shape of fresh outlets for his talents; for Dexter, these were maybe unexpected new outlets, in some ways at least. In November 1962, he had probably his first ever full-length broadcast, beamed direct from the Montmartre by Danish Radio, during actual performance. Less than two years later, at the start of another three-month season at the club and continuing through until the third week in August, he was afforded the same generous facility. One hour of the Dexter Gordon Quartet, live at the Montmartre, each Thursday, lasting one hour per show, starting an hour before midnight, with the leader free to select repertoire, act as an amiable, articulate master of ceremonies and, if he felt like it, even indulge in a little highly personalized vocalizing. There also seem to have been few or no restrictions on the length of each of the numbers performed.

As his previous opportunities to broadcast on radio back home were negligible, one can reasonably suppose Gordon's reactions to such freedom to have combined a mixture of deep gratitude with genuine puzzlement. The hour-long shows continued in a similar vein at appropriate times during the next few years. Television, too, came Dexter's way. Not surprisingly perhaps, his appearances in this medium weren't as plentiful as on radio, but when they occurred, they provided even greater exposure.

One out-of-the-ordinary event which took place in 1964 should have increased his popularity as a multi-media artist. Unfortunately, a first-time production of *The Connection* proved to be rather less than successful. Hardly noted for its adventurous spirit, and hitherto apparently not interested in any form of experimentation, the Danish theatre world was surprised when Stig Lommer, a noted local producer, announced he had acquired the rights to stage the Gelber play in Copenhagen. Its prospects seemed considerably enhanced when Lommer proclaimed that Dexter Gordon had accepted a leading role. As in Los Angeles, he would also be responsible for the music which, in the event, was mostly the score he'd written for and performed in *The Hollywood Connection*.

However, the brave venture, even with Dexter's commanding presence, his powerful playing and his acting, failed abysmally, due primarily to the fact that the rest of the cast had absolutely no idea how drug addicts behaved (hard drugs were not commonplace in Denmark at this time). Today, Dexter Gordon can speak of the Danish *Connection* with amusement, but it was indeed a personal disappointment in 1964.

The actors, when they were supposed to be 'getting high', they played it as if they were *drunk*. Staggering around . . . drunkenly . . . I tried to offer my 'technical expertise', but they wouldn't listen to me. They wouldn't play it any other way. Not even the director listened. Consequently, it didn't make sense. Critical reaction was terrible. It actually lasted five days. My critiques were all very good – for acting and playing – I knew what I was doing. As to the manner born, so to speak! All this heavy self-analysis they were giving out . . . why they'd become addicts and da-da-da . . . they'd go offstage to meet their Cowboy – their connection – and come back onstage acting as if they'd drunk a bottle of stout. And nobody understood what the essence of the play was about. Sad . . .

This was one of the four projects with which he was involved which could be deemed an absolute failure – although Dexter himself was the only ingredient which received any kind of critical applause. Little wonder, though, that the Danish *Connection* was taken off after only five performances.

Gordon's lengthy European residence was comprehensively a happy and fulfilling period in his life; in many ways, the peace of mind, tranquillity and all-round acceptance he discovered wherever his travels took him, combined to make the years 1962 to 1976 as rewarding as any other previous portion of an already eventful life.

In fact, the only real black spot of those fourteen years concerned the aforementioned occasion of his arrest and imprisonment in Paris in 1966. He was charged, together with two other males, and a Danish woman, with using drugs. Although his committal to the Santé prison no doubt bothered Gordon – not least by forcing him to spend some of his sentence in a cell with five or six other prisoners – what angered him above all was a brief, two-paragraph report in the Paris edition of the *New York Herald Tribune*, datelined five days after his arrest. The report stated he was being held by Paris police 'on charges of peddling drugs in a jazz cellars of the student quarter'. For, however philosophical he might have been over the years about using narcotics, Gordon is adamant that at no time has he trafficked in drugs.

After learning of Gordon's arrest, a concerned Mike Hennessey, in his usual caring way for jazz musicians, tried to help in whatever ways he could. Before his release, Hennessey filed his 'Drugs – and Dexter Gordon' story – published by the *Melody*

Maker 23 July – which drew attention to what the writer called 'the primitive and hideously prejudiced attitude society has towards the problem of drug addiction'. It was based not only on Hennessey's personal observations, but on a candid, revealing interview he undertook with Gordon, just a few days after his release on bail of $2,000. Hennessey says, of his drugs-and-Dexter article: 'I just felt compelled to write the piece. *Somebody* had to write it. Dex, I know, approved. He wrote me, from prison, to tell me so, after I'd sent him a copy, for his perusal and approval.'

It wasn't only the *New York Herald Tribune* which picked up the story of the 'American Negro jazzman, a Danish blonde and two other Americans' being arrested. It made all the Danish papers, which is how Dexter would have been prevented from re-entering Copenhagen ... if it hadn't been for the fierce loyalty and determined action of his unofficial Dexter Gordon Fan Club, who, for the next ten years, would continue to demonstrate their affection and admiration – personally and professionally – at his favourite European jazz *pied-à-terre*.

8

Goin' Home . . . and the Big Treatment

Came the middle of the 1970s and Dexter Gordon was thinking more of home than he had in many years: not the pleasant home in Valby, but home in the United States of America. Not necessarily Los Angeles – although he retains an imperishable affection for his native city. Not necessarily New York – although this location, too, was constantly in his thoughts.

It wasn't as if he was unhappy in Denmark. Personally and professionally, the situation remained as it had been for years: no real complaints, or at least nothing tangible.

It was just a gut feeling that his long spell as an adoptive European was about to end. As an added incentive, the situation – jazzwise – in the States seemed to be improving since the end of the previous decade. He had really enjoyed his two-month trip to New York in 1972, when he'd recorded twice for Prestige in June, and had participated at a couple of all-star jam sessions at the Newport in New York Jazz Festival the following month – plus a guest appearance in a roaring Lionel Hampton Reunion Band set at the same event. Clubwise, too, New York seemed to be really *happening*.

Fate decreed it would be October, 1976 when Dexter would return, yet again, to New York. This was a visit which would set into motion a train of events that would make his presence take on a sense of permanency; ultimately, it was to mean the end of his decade and a half in Europe. A fine LP date for Don Schlitten's Xanadu label more or less started off a remarkable final three months of 1976. Gordon sounded relaxed and involved, in company with fellow-tenorist Al Cohn, trumpeters Blue Mitchell and Sam Noto, and a particularly propulsive rhythm section: Barry Harris, Sam Jones, Louis Hayes.

But it was when Gordon was booked at the Storyville Club, that the real momentum began. This was a short engagement, but one which Gordon remembers vividly today. The ovation he received on opening night stunned him (one critic reported he had to plead exhaustion, at 3 a.m., to avoid a further encore). It was the same the next evening, with a packed Storyville roaring its collective approval.

During the Storyville stay, Gordon rehearsed diligently for a week at the Village Vanguard (a favourite club of his). The preparations obviously worked, because his playing throughout a wholly memorable week remained at optimum level. And, for Dexter, his personal triumph was confirmed by the nightly crowds who packed the Vanguard and reacted at least as strongly as the Storyville audiences. And on each evening, crowds stretched far out into the street.

Always happy to accommodate an obvious demand for any of the artists to play his club, the pocket-sized Max Gordon, the Vanguard's guiding light, fixed a further booking for Dexter, for December. First, though, Gordon had to undertake a tour, in the company of trumpeter Woody Shaw, pianist Ronnie Mathews, bassist Stafford James and drummer Louis Hayes (which included a date at the Village Gate that was broadcast).

The tour was hugely successful, and by the time the quintet returned to the Vanguard it had become, in all the more important aspects, a superb working band. The return Vanguard gig of December 1976 is remembered with a joy and affection by those fortunate enough to have been present at any of the evenings of memorable music which filled the club. Both individually and collectively, each member of the band was heard on top form, with Gordon's contributions magnificent at all times.

Concomitant with the tremendous reception from the various club audiences came a most important event, one, of course, which would help in any serious attempt to re-establish himself in the country of his birth. During the second of the initial two evenings at George Wein's Storyville Club, Dexter accepted warm congratulations from a smartly-dressed member of the audience who identified himself as Bruce Lundvall, an executive of Columbia Records. Lundvall, who also confessed to being something of a tenor-sax freak (and an avowed admirer of Gordon's work since the forties), offered a record contract. And so, apart from the contract-signing formalities, and much to his amazement, Gordon found himself a member of the roster of a major US record company for the first time in his professional life. Lundvall rang him the very next day. After hearing of Gordon's projected schedule of appearances, he suggested an obvious way to begin their association would be to fix to record – in live performance – during a couple of the evenings of the return engagement at the Vanguard.

With Michael Cuscuna appointed to produce the location recording (a position he has retained ever since), Gordon, Shaw, Mathews & Co were taped on consecutive nights, 11 and 12 December. So much good music emanated from the recording project that Columbia (thanks to Lundvall's personal push) made Dexter Gordon's debut LP a two-disc affair, entitled, appropriately, *Homecoming*.

General reaction to its appearance in 1977 was positive: sales nationally were good enough to indicate that not only those who had applauded his end-of-'76 appearances were purchasing *Homecoming*. The reviews, too, were uniformly excellent. In a lengthy, and particularly affirmative write-up, Chuck Berg, in *Down Beat*,* forecast that *Homecoming* would 'stand as one of the landmark albums of the '70s'. And in conclusion, Berg described it as 'a celebration of the roots of a giant. It stands as a new plateau in Dex's career and, for us, an opportunity to share in the workings of one of the great hearts and minds of improvised music.'

The icing on the cake was still to come. At the beginning of 1977, Gordon returned to Denmark. But he was back in New York – and the Village Vanguard – by May. The difference, though, was that, for the first time in his entire career, Dexter Gordon was leading his *own* band. That first Gordon combo comprised Rufus Reid (who had first played bass with Dexter, and Gene Ammons, in Chicago in 1970), George Cables (one of

*21/4/77.

the most promising of the younger pianists) and drummer Victor Lewis (another young player of great potential). The Dexter Gordon Quartet gelled from its outset. And even when Lewis, on loan from Woody Shaw's group, returned to his previous employer, Gordon was fortunate in acquiring the services of Eddie Gladden, another gifted drummer.

The latter line-up, which stayed together for two years, has been described by Michael Cuscuna as 'one of the finest-sounding quartets in jazz history'. Certainly, this superbly integrated trio seemed to inspire its leader to produce optimum performances for most of the quartet's all-too-short lifetime. The leader was especially forthcoming about how his first ever group was working out when he and the trio returned to Ronnie Scott's in February 1978. He was happy to report, first, that he and the trio had hit it off, musically and personally, right from their opening gig.

> This is a very special happenstance – that this group gelled so well together from the beginning. It wasn't that the guys had all been playing together before, on a regular basis. They knew each other, and had some contact . . . but not to that degree. It was just a natural osmosis . . . very fortunately. And it's just been like that all the time. From the first note. Unbelievable. It just keeps building and expanding. These guys – I don't mean they're kids, they're in their early thirties – they've all had good foundations and are knowledgeable about jazz, its different forms and styles. It's all gelled very well. And I'm very, very pleased and thrilled that, at last, I have this kind of group.

Just as it was obviously stimulating for Gordon to find a band – his own band – as good as the Cables–Reid–Gladden line-up, it was a fundamental learning experience for his sidemen. Like pianist Cables, who is happy at any time to recall his three-year (1977–9) association with the Gordon quartet:

> Dexter has been a real experience. Put it this way. Somebody once asked Salvador Dali whether he took drugs, or whether

he used hallucinogenics. Dali replied: 'Dali takes drugs? Dali *is* drugs!' I feel that way about Dexter. Dexter *is* jazz. He plays jazz – but he *is* jazz. I learned a lot from Dexter. Playing with him really brought me back to the acoustic piano. And I was able to play with an immense amount of space. I started playing solo piano with Dexter, including ballads. I tell you, the thing I learned mostly from him was the history of the music. The roots. He would tell me about territorial bands . . . his experiences . . . and that meant a lot to me, because it gave me a little perspective and insight on where it's coming from.

Between 1976 and 1980, Dexter Gordon was to cut five albums under his own name for Columbia (CBS). In contrast to the triumphant *Homecoming* came *Sophisticated Giant* (recorded at two sessions in June 1977), which finds him showcased handsomely within the framework of a splendid ten-piece ensemble, assembled by Michael Cuscuna and Slide Hampton, the latter playing trombone and supplying a series of first-class arrangements. *Manhattan Symphonie*, a consistently rewarding Gordon quartet date, with Gladden making his first appearances on record with Dexter, was completed over three sessions in May 1978. *Great Encounters* was taped in two parts, with one title, 'Ruby, My Dear' (an out-track from the *Manhattan Symphonie* project) added. The first part celebrates the quartet's Carnegie Hall concert appearance in September of the same year, with Johnny Griffin added as special guest. The second main part, a studio date, has the quartet augmented by Woody Shaw, trombonist Curtis Fuller and, most interesting of all, Eddie Jefferson, the master of jazz vocalese. Jefferson's inimitable singing of 'Diggin' In' and 'It's Only a Paper Moon' is a fitting epitaph, on record, to his noble art: he was killed in Detroit six months after this, his last studio date. In all, the quintet of LPs demonstrate an impressive consistency in performance by Gordon – and his various sidemen.

In term of live performances, Gordon and his regular working bands covered a lot of ground – literally as well as metaphorically – following that initial trail-blazing end-of-'76 period. There seems to have been a regular itinerary throughout the States for the remainder of the seventies and into the eighties, not too sizeable, however, to prevent Dexter from coming back to Europe at very regular intervals. In fact, following the journey to Copenhagen in 1977, he was back in Europe the next year – twice, returning, again, for the next five years (including two separate trips in 1980).

During his London visit in June 1981 – for two further weeks at the Scott club – Gordon was happy to take time out to give an interim resumé of his manifold activities – at home and away – since 1976, and to explain his feelings about trying to come to terms with being a re-emerging North American. Certainly, he was unequivocal about the fact that, increasingly, life was becoming extra-busy.

> Chaotic – but *beautiful*! Because so much has been happening in these past few years. Being on another level, as a performer, a musician. Consequently, there has been more exposure and attention. Et cetera, et cetera. I can understand now when you see Sammy Davis or Frank Sinatra, or somebody like these, they've got six or seven guys with them, leading the way . . . 'Who is it? What do you want?' . . . I'm not in *that* category, that level. But even so, for myself the pressure is so much. People wanting to interview me. It's the pressure thing that really gets to you. I can dig these tennis kids, like McEnroe and Borg – he's *cool* . . . Me, during these last few years, I've been doing three or four interviews a day, morning and night. Finally, I've learned how to say: 'See my manager.' And, of course, that takes a lot of pressure off.

Even by 1982, Gordon had not completely severed his basic connections with Europe, although the idea of bringing his Danish wife, Fenja and his young son Benji to the States to start a new life there had not worked out. He had recently obtained a divorce, and his now ex-wife, together with his son, had returned to their Valby home. And in a more general way, Gordon was still finding it difficult to make the readjustment necessary to become, as it were, re-Americanized.

It's still strange. Because my mentality has been stretched – expanded – by living over here, in Europe, and for so long. Learning all the different cultures, some of the languages – some bits and pieces. Whatever. But my outlook is much different. I just don't think like an American . . . You know: America first – God's country. I don't think like that. When there is a catastrophe, or an incident of the moment, at home, I think about it. But not just from an American viewpoint. I know Danes, Swedes, Norwegians . . . British, French, Belgians, Germans, Spaniards, Israelis, Arabs, Africans. I kinda think in much broader terms than I would imagine the average American would. Even in daily life and so forth, I'm not really American.

Two out-of-the-ordinary events in Dexter Gordon's life which had taken place since his all-conquering venture back to old pastures provided vividly contrasting experiences for an already worldly-wise jazzman who had passed his fiftieth birthday long before the idea of resettling 'back home' must have crossed his mind.

The widespread acclamation from the American jazz world at large, plus TV, radio and news coverage (including a *Newsweek* salutation), had delighted its recipient, who was learning to cope with all the mass attention. But an invitation from President Carter, to participate in a 'Jazz at the White House Lawn' event, on 17 June 1978, must have been almost unreal. Gordon found himself in stellar company, too, rubbing shoulders with the likes of Dizzy Gillespie, Lionel Hampton, Stan Getz, George Benson, Roy Eldridge . . . and even the utterly contrasting pianistic offerings of ragtime-influenced nonagenarian Eubie Blake, and Cecil Taylor, the epitome of the avant-garde in jazz. For Gordon anyway, the White House extravaganza was memorable for more than one reason, outside of the fact of actually being present. For example, there had not been any kind of jazz celebration at the presidential headquarters pior to this time. 'This made a deep impression. Because never in my life did I think I would be invited to the White House. And for the guy himself to say: "Hey, Dex!"

And for me to say: "Hello, Jimmy!" Can you believe it?'

Gordon, like his illustrious jazz colleagues, warmed to Carter's obvious affection for the music, which stretched back to his student days and continued during his Coast Guard days with visits to Greenwich Village. The President and Rosaline Carter, and his family and staff, put on an impressive spread for their guests ('. . . lots of New Orleans-type food flown in . . . red beans and rice . . . and they had a beer concession . . . wine . . . it was beautiful'). And Gordon recalls that Secret Service agents, predictably, were around, but kept a low-profile presence throughout. Much to remember on his first visit to the White House, then, but one incident, above all others, remains in his memory:

> The one person that Jimmy Carter dug the most – you'd never guess – was Cecil Taylor. Cecil Taylor *killed* him – wowed him! When he finished playing solo, man, Carter jumped up and ran on to the stage, hugged him and said: 'Oh, man, I wish I could play piano like that!' I mean . . . Maybe if it were Roy Eldridge, he'd say: 'I wish I could play trumpet like that.' Or Getz, or me. Or Mary Lou. Or even Herbie Hancock, he was there. But Cecil Taylor . . . *dig it*! Life full of surprises? Yeah. You never know . . .

Purely as a performance, Dexter Gordon thoroughly enjoyed the White House soirée. In an obviously happy and relaxed atmosphere, he was featured within the context of an all-star sextet, working alongside Dizzy Gillespie, George Benson, Herbie Hancock, Ron Carter and Tony Williams. Two numbers by the group ('I'll Remember April', 'Caravan') were recorded by, and broadcast over, National Public Radio.

There can scarcely have been a more starkly contrasting location (or setting) than that at which Dexter and his own quartet found themselves, just over two years after the jam session on the lawns of the White House. Certainly, though, Gordon himself was rather more familiar with the establishment which opened its less-than-welcoming doors in 1980.

Rikers Island Penitentiary – sited on New York's East River,

Lionel Hampton Orchestra, 1940. L-R: Milt Buckner (p); Vernon Alley (b); Hampton (vib); Irving Ashby (g); Shadow Wilson (d); Illinois Jacquet (ts); Marshall Royal (clt); Ernie Royal (t); Sonny Graven (tb); Dexter Gordon (ts); Karl George (t); Fred Beckett (tb); Joe Newman (t); Ray Perry (as); Henry Sloan (tb); Jack McVea (bs) (Peter Vacher Collection)

Gene Norman Presents 'Just Jazz', California, 2 February 1952. L-R: Billy Eckstine, Conte Candoli, Gene Norman, Don Lamond (partly obscured), Wardell Gray, Dexter Gordon (Roy Carr Archive)

Louis Armstrong (John Antill)

Lionel Hampton, Capital Jazz Festival, Knebworth, 1982 (Brian O'Connor)

Billy Eckstine (Stan Britt Collection)

Charlie Parker (Stan Britt Collection)

Lester Young (Stan Britt Collection)

Art Pepper (Brian O'Connor)

Benny Golson, Capital Jazz Festival,
Knebworth, 1982 (Brian O'Connor)

Freddie Hubbard (Brian O'Connor)

Chico Hamilton, London, 1973 (Brian O'Connor)

Illinois Jacquet, London, 1982 (Brian O'Connor)

Tony Scott (Brian O'Connor)

Helen Humes (Brian O'Connor)

Kenny Drew, Pendley Jazz Festival, 1985 (Brian O'Connor)

Dexter Gordon (Brian O'Connor)

Rufus Reid (Brian O'Connor)

Niels-Henning Ørsted Pedersen
(Brian O'Connor)

George Cables (Brian O'Connor)

Sonny Rollins (Brian O'Connor)

Johnny Griffin, Pendley Jazz Festival,
1985 (Brian O'Connor)

stable mable   Dexter Gordon quartet

Dexter Gordon Trio
Lullaby for a Monster

SteepleChase covers, 1975–81

Dexter Gordon (Brian O'Connor)

Billy Higgins, London, 1976 (Brian O'Connor)

Herbie Hancock, Royal Festival Hall,
1986 (Brian O'Connor)

Dexter Gordon, Capital Jazz Festival, Knebworth, 1981 (Brian O'Connor

Dexter Gordon, Capital Jazz Festival, Knebworth, 1981 (Brian O'Connor)

Dexter Gordon and Art Pepper (Brian O'Connor)

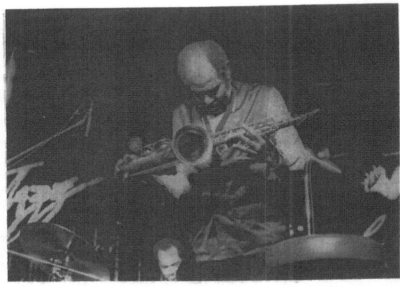

Dexter Gordon, leader of the 'Round Midnight All Stars,
Montreux Jazz Festival, 1988 (Roy Carr)

in between La Guardia Airport and the Bronx – remains one of America's most feared prisons. In 1980, Dexter Gordon and his three associates came to Rikers to provide their own brand of musical entertainment for at least some of its inmates. It was a salutary experience for the band's leader, for Gordon had served time there during a period in time when his addiction was making alarming inroads into his very existence. For the prisoners who attended the concert, the event appears to have been a success; their collective reactions were enthusiastic – sometimes near-hysterically so – throughout. As regards how the inmates might have benefited from listening to the music of the Dexter Gordon Quartet – during the concert itself, or indeed thereafter – there can never be a wholly satisfactory answer. Leading British jazz writer Brian Case, who accompanied the four musicians into the penitentiary for the occasion, offered the best summation, in his subsequent *Melody Maker* report: 'It is impossible to say whether the music has broken down barriers, or merely provides a free period, and it doesn't much matter.'

The pianist who appeared at the Rikers Island gig with Dexter was Kirk Lightsey. A native of Detroit, Lightsey had been playing for many years before replacing Albert Dailey (who, in turn, had succeeded George Cables), around the spring of 1979. But to a jazz audience at large, Lightsey's was not a household name, explained principally by the fact that fifteen years of his career had been spent as personal accompanist to singers Damita Jo, Ocie Smith and Lovelace Watkins, in that order. In all, he was to remain with Dexter Gordon for more than five years.

The first time Kirk Lightsey had seen and heard Gordon in live performance came when he was touring Europe with Ocie Smith. He sat in with the tenorist at a Stockholm jazz club. Lightsey remembers being 'rather nervous', due to a combination of being in awe of someone as legendary as Gordon, and the fact that the man he was accompanying was very drunk ('that was really a bit of a challenge'). It was to be several years before Lightsey was, once again, to sit in with the man who was to become his full-time employer not too long afterwards. This was at the Lighthouse, at Hermosa Beach, California, which is where and when he struck up a lasting friendship with bassist Rufus Reid. It was when George Cables intimated he would be leaving the Gordon quartet that Reid more or less offered Lightsey the chance to replace him. Lightsey's commitments with Lovelace Watkins precluded the chance of his accepting such a tempting invitation. Later still, on a visit to the Village Vanguard, Gordon offered him the job, to take over immediately from Albert Dailey. This time, Lightsey accepted.

Kirk Lightsey retains many and varied memories of his five-year stint with Dexter Gordon. Some of the memories are less than fulfilling; some indeed have elements of sadness and deep concern (these are confined to the final year and a half of their association). Mostly, though, Lightsey's time spent in the company of someone for whom he has such an obviously lasting and genuine affection was something he has not experienced during his entire career, before or since.

Being with Dexter was probably *the* greatest lesson – one-to-one – that I've had in playing jazz. But it wasn't easy to get this lesson because Dexter doesn't say things simply. He doesn't tell you in words – you have to read totally between the lines. And sometimes he'll tell you something very important in just one word, one phrase. Like, one night, at some big concert in Europe – someplace – I had played what I considered [to be] a brilliant solo on this ballad. Everything was just perfect, and it had reached the maximum . . . I was amazed with myself. And very seldom does that happen with me. When the solo finished, nobody moved a muscle. There was no applause. There was *nothing*. No reaction. I was stunned. I was almost in tears, because I didn't know why . . . I struggled through the rest of the set – which was probably just one more tune – and walked off the stage, almost crying. Desolate. Of course, Dexter saw the whole thing. He watched me the whole time. Came over and said: 'They didn't clap 'cos they were *mes-mer-ized*!' And walked away. I said to myself: 'Wow! Never thought of that!'

Lightsey's five years with Dexter Gordon contained many moments of musical magic, experiences he is scarcely likely to forget. Like concerts at Carnegie Hall (1979) and Munich (1981) – both featuring Woody Shaw's trumpet added to the regular Gordon quartet – and, especially, an unforgettable appearance at the Auditorium Maurice Ravel, in Lyon, France. Lightsey enthuses, of the last-named:

> That was amazing – at least as good as that at the Munich Sports Arena. We followed Woody's group, who had really burned it down. We had to go on, after that, and do our stuff. Dexter, with his infinite magic, just went out and captured 'em . . . just by walking out onstage. From that point on, it was just captivating. The Maurice Ravel Theatre is a lovely place to play – to be inside. All of that helped make it a magic, magic concert.

The rhythm section to which Kirk Lightsey became such an important contributor showed only one change during its lifetime. The redoubtable Rufus Reid, who had anchored the George Cables-led trio, stayed until 1980. His replacement, for about six months, was John Heard. Then, in August, a slim young bassist called David Eubanks succeeded Heard. And it was to be Lightsey, Eubanks and Eddie Gladden who would work together with Gordon until the middle of 1984. This Dexter Gordon Quartet was to produce the kind of all-round superlative jazz that was at least as fine as its predecessors; on its own, or when Johnny Griffin was added for various gigs – both in Europe and the States – between 1980 and 1982.

Yet, as great as were so many of the musical experiences for Lightsey and his colleagues, there were times when it looked as if the quartet's very future might be in jeopardy. The problem concerned its leader, whose health deteriorated from around 1980, due, in no small part, to his ever-increasing consumption of alcohol. Accordingly, there were times when his playing, in person at least, tended to become rather less than consistent. A near-lifetime of self-abuse was beginning to take its effect, even on someone as obviously teak-tough as Dexter Gordon.

The inevitable took place during the latter part of 1984 when, after collapsing in his Manhattan flat, he was rushed in a comatose condition to hospital, where he spent some time in intensive care. It was only Dexter's cast-iron constitution which pulled him through. When eventually discharged, he rested in his apartment, cared for by Maxine Gregg, who had become his personal manager since his return to the States.

For the members of his pre-hospital quartet, the omens had been signposted for several years. Kirk Lightsey remembers that Gordon had been taken ill in Finland, early in 1984, after being invited to make a guest solo appearance with the local radio orchestra. On returning home, he was attended by a doctor who advised, in the strongest terms, a period of non-playing recuperation. Then came a small handful of gigs, including a projected trip to Morocco.

That he had in no way recovered completely was evidenced by the fact that Gordon was too ill to make the same journey by air as his three colleagues.

His arrival in North Africa was so delayed as to make it impossible for him to appear at the opening concerts of what was, to all intents and purposes, a first-time tour by Dexter Gordon. Lightsey, Eubanks and Gladden undertook the engagements, working as a unit in their own right.

That he should never have made the journey anyway was instantly obvious on his very arrival. He could remain on his feet for only short periods. It was hardly conceivable he could actually complete one set.

The local promoters, however, were not at all sympathetic. They refused to pay over the money due him. They threatened, at one stage, to imprison Maxine Gregg. They ignored requests that a doctor be called. In the end, no one was paid. In fact, Lightsey, Gladden and Eubanks had to dig into their own pockets so that Gordon and Gregg could pay their hotel bill.

A potentially ugly situation still had not resolved itself. The promoters succeeded in holding up the outward flights which would take the party back to the States. No satisfactory reason was given. The five were allotted rooms, but all other amenities were disallowed. Finally, after four days, the officials relented and allowed them to leave. It surprised his musical colleagues not at all when, after their arrival back home, Gordon decided, for the time being anyway, to disband the quartet. Then came the news of the collapse and hospitalization. Again, as sad and as worried for him as they were, Kirk Lightsey and the other two now ex-members of the quartet were in no way surprised.

> We felt – we could see – it coming on. We could tell it by the way he was playing; like, the amount of time he gave *us*. He was not moving about as well. He would make little comments like: 'I'm getting too old for this shit.' But he was still making the gigs – until, of course, such time as he *wasn't* making them . . . It was just the culmination of forty years in the business, and not being so kind to himself . . . much later, I used to go up to his house, in Manhattan. To put it mildly, he's in much better condition these days than he was then.

Following Gordon's discharge, very little news was forthcoming for some time. For his many British fans there was little or no information emanating from across the Atlantic, except very strong rumours that his illness had left him suffering from emphysema, diabetes and some kind of liver and/or kidney problems. When his friend Johnny Griffin played London in November 1984, he was able to report that although he hadn't actually seen Dexter at any time during the past eight months, he understood the patient was recovering . . . slowly: 'He's been very weak. He's had respiratory problems, and a touch of emphysema. Todd Barkan, of Keystone Korner, called me . . . he'd just come from New York and said he'd seen Dexter. Said that he's looking healthier. He's gained some weight. And he was noodling on his horn, at home . . .'

Sporadic though they were, odd items of news continued to trickle through during the next several months. Reports suggested he was undergoing a lengthy period of rehabilitation in Cuernavaca, Mexico, where he was said to be 'recovering slowly . . . regaining his strength'.

Naturally, of prime importance was Gordon's recovery and a return to good health. After what he'd been through, and in the context of the alarming deterioration in his general health for several years before his collapse, it was likely to be a slow process. Even with his cast-iron constitution, nothing was absolutely certain. As for thoughts of a resumption in his playing career, that was something not even his closest medical advisers could (or would) predict with any reasonable accuracy.

If an indeterminate period of convalescence brought back his strength and stamina, just how much the various ailments might have taken from his playing abilities – bearing in mind, of course, that his was a blowing instrument – was equally impossible to forecast. And after his debilitating experiences, just how much enthusiasm would Dexter muster in actually *wanting* to continue his playing career, whether on a full-time or part-time basis? With regard to his future as a professional jazz musician, something quite out of the ordinary would have to materialize.

Something of that order was not too far away, something so unexpected, that not even the eternally optimistic tenor player himself could have imagined it. It was something which was to transform his whole life during the next two or three eventful years.

9

Was I Good? A Star is Reborn

When running through a film of Dexter Gordon, Bertrand Tavernier knew instinctively he had found the leading character for the movie about jazz and jazz musicians he and producer Irwin Winkler were keen to undertake. The trouble was, the French director didn't know how to contact the man he wished to play the part of Dale Turner, a fictitious character based on Lester Young and Bud Powell. No one in France seemed to know either. One report he received said Gordon had disappeared from the scene – he might even have died. Eventually, thanks to the help of Henri Renaud, a record-company executive and sometime jazz pianist, he was informed that Dexter had just returned to New York. Meeting Gordon on that first occasion proved to be a salutary, as well as something of a startling experience for Tavernier. Even the way the saxophonist walked deeply affected the director. As he said later: 'Watching him come into the room, I had the impression that he was going to fall down and die on the spot. I don't know who else could project that.' Tavernier knew in a second that provided Dexter was interested – and, of course, provided he was sufficiently recovered to participate – he was talking to Dale Turner. Tavernier outlined his project. Gordon seemed rather sceptical, only marginally interested. Tavernier left, but kept in touch, and came to see the American on several occasions. Eventually, Gordon agreed to take the principal role in the Tavernier–Winkler movie 'Round Midnight.

Tavernier knew that once he had persuaded Warners to take his film, the involvement of Dexter Gordon and a string of other jazz musicians – some would also have small speaking parts in addition to their playing roles – would bring to 'Round

Midnight the kind of authenticity he felt was an absolutely basic requirement for success. Gordon's was, of course, the key role, but after that first meeting he knew that no other jazz personality would do. For Tavernier, there was no question of an actor, as opposed to a jazz musician, playing Dale Turner. As he told Ira Gitler in 1986:

> I always choose people when I see them in life. I saw him walking. And I saw his hands. And what I liked in him, I saw something that no actor will give me. Everything in him is musical. Even when he doesn't play music. The way he sits, the way he moves. He is bebop in walking. You don't find that in Paul Newman or Sidney Poitier. They are good actors but they approach one millionth of the truth Dexter is bringing. And I knew that . . .

Hollywood's record with regard to movies purporting to involve the subject of jazz and at least some of its leading personalities had been, to put it euphemistically, embarrassing. The mere mention of titles such as *The Benny Goodman Story* (1955), *The Gene Krupa Story* (1959), *The Five Pennies* (1959) and *Lady Sings the Blues* (1972) is sufficient to send any self-respecting jazz buff racing for the hills. As for jazz musicians themselves . . .

This kind of *débâcle* had remained in the memory of Bertrand Tavernier. For *'Round Midnight* both he and his colleague Winkler were determined that credibility should be of the essence. To this end, attention to fine detail was of paramount importance throughout. This is why, for instance, the Blue Note club was re-created, to exact specifications, and resited at the rue de Buci–rue de Seine intersection, on the Left Bank. The Blue Note's actual location, on the rue d'Artois, was considered visually unattractive.

Wisely, the advice and experience of the musicians was constantly sought, particularly that of Dexter. It was Dexter who suggested that although Billy Higgins and Herbie Hancock were ideal choices for the rhythm section which would accompany him during the live musical performances at the reconstructed Blue Note, it was invariably a local French musician who would play bass at the kind of European jazz-club session at the time the Paris section of *'Round Midnight* was trying to recapture (1959). It was Dexter who suggested that Hancock simplify a far too sophisticated arrangement he had penned for 'As Time Goes By': 'It's my first night with those musicians. I've never played with them before, so I wouldn't do that kind of arrangement. Later on maybe, but not the first night. On the first night I would play the melody. When musicians come to a new club it takes them two or three nights to get it together.'

Even more important, Gordon's advice on the script was absolutely vital. During the four months he spent at the Eclair studio, located in Epiamy-sur-Seine outside Paris, he was constantly questioning the dialogue co-written by David Rayfiel and Tavernier. As he related to *Rolling Stone*'s Neil Tesser:

> The script was really, I tell you, less than swell. I don't want to put anybody down, but the writer – his conception was that the musicians thought and spoke like they were down on the levee. 'Dese, dose' – it was degrading. And I told this guy I was infuriated with this script, because – hey, this film is about *geniuses*. In their field, in their way, they were intellectuals. Modern. I mean, in their music, everything was progress. And he had all this dialogue in there, and I told him: 'Listen, man, if I got on the screen and spoke like that, you know what? I would lose my lifetime calling card in the NAACP.' It was terrible. It took me time to understand that they were really serious about doing this film. Right?'

Slowly and painstakingly, the technical problems were overcome, including that encountered by the sound men in faithfully recording Gordon's battle-scarred bass-baritone speaking voice. But there was also the ever-present factor of Gordon's slow recovery from a major illness. He could work only a few hours a day before retiring to his hotel, exhausted. Quite apart from the fact that he is on screen for most of the film, there was the additional burden of performing as a musician. Dexter and the four different combos with which he appeared during the film taped the music at four different dates, between the beginning of July and the end of August 1985.

Tavernier was ever-conscious of the fact that his leading man was still, to all intents and purposes, a sick man. As he was to admit, well after the film's completion, with a well-developed sense of the dramatic:

> He found it very tiring. He's an old sixty-two and an enigma for all the doctors. He has no liver, a case of diabetes, and the percentage of alcohol in his blood is absolutely confounding . . . Yet he never had any problem remembering his lines. He was aware of everything, including lights and camera angles – in fact, much more than some actors I know!

Even before they had made the final print, Tavernier and his colleagues must have been aware that 'Round Midnight was no ordinary movie, and that Dexter Gordon was no run-of-the-mill actor.

Even if 'Round Midnight had turned out to be rather less than the artistic triumph that most of those who have seen it believe it to be, there is no doubt that its star performer had, overnight, become a film actor of considerable ability. In every way, he dominates the film, with an utterly personal, delightfully idiosyncratic performance which gives a whole new meaning to the term 'laid-back'. Some cynics have suggested that what he achieved was really nothing more than playing himself. There is, of course, much truth in that allegation. But his is nevertheless a comprehensive piece of acting that goes far beyond just acting like Dexter Keith Gordon. Where the personal touch is manifestly obvious is in some of the dialogue – the dialogue which Dexter himself rewrote, or ad-libbed. Odd phrases, like 'Was I good?' or 'Happiness is a nice, wet reed', come straight from the highly personal Gordon vocabulary. Visually too, his impact is often devastating. His sheer physical size casts a giant shadow over everything and everyone in 'Round Midnight. His unique splay-legged walk is even more compelling, visually, than the long, expressive hands, or the expression of deep melancholia he wears for much of the opening third of the film. His permanently crumbling speaking voice seems to be operating at half-speed, with sometimes near-painful pauses in a halting speech pattern that remains beyond parody. Even the use of the Lester-patented 'Lady', when Dale Turner addresses his friends, comes out as pure Gordon.

The long and serious illness had succeeded in ageing him in a way that must have shocked even his closest friends. For his portrayal of the dissolute drunk Dale Turner had become, that dramatic physical deterioration was, in purest irony, ideal. Not even the most skilled of make-up specialists could have given Turner the kind of facial decline which stared from the screen. Even though Dale Turner has apparently seen better times, and Dexter plays him that way, there is also a certain touching dignity in his performance. The developing relationship between Turner and Francis Borier (played by young Gene Kelly look-alike François Cluzet), who hero-worships the visiting American, is handled with intelligence. The Borier character is based more than loosely on Francis Paudras, who cared lovingly for Bud Powell during the great pianist's own sojourn in Paris between 1959 and 1964. And thanks to Tavernier's skilful direction, the interplay between Gordon and Gabrielle Haker (who plays Berangère, Borier's daughter) is completely free from the kind of sickly sentimentality Hollywood usually considers obligatory.

For the serious-minded jazz fan, a most important factor in the film's success must be, surely, that the musical characters are allowed to speak and behave as real-live jazz musicians speak and behave. For the uninitiated, it might seem strange, perhaps, that Dale Turner should have spent practically all of his offstage time on his arrival in the French capital inside his hotel room. But Dexter Gordon, for one, invariably *has* spent most of his non-playing periods, when touring at home and abroad, inside hotel rooms . . . or at least he did before *'Round Midnight*.

From a purely musical standpoint, there is much to enjoy in

the movie. Dexter gets ample opportunity to play – using both tenor and soprano saxophones – and even though his solos, quite obviously, can hardly be said to rank with his best in previous years, the fact that he is actually blowing can be considered something of a bonus. And on the slower tunes, particularly 'Body and Soul' and 'As Times Goes By', he combines a basic soundness of technique with an emotional depth undiminished even by a lengthy illness and near-death.

The reaction among the international critics at the 1986 Venice Film Festival was unanimous: *'Round Midnight* was the best movie of the year. As such, it became firm favourite to carry off the coveted Golden Lion award; and the star of *'Round Midnight* was strongly tipped for the individual actor's accolade. In the event, the top-film prize was given to Eric Rohmer's *Le Rayon Vert*; an Italian garnered the actor's award. The majority of the critics were astonished – and outraged. Together, they composed a note of protest, which was handed to the head of the festival jury. All, of course, to no avail . . .

Nevertheless, Dexter himself thoroughly enjoyed his unaccustomed fêting. He also enjoyed the new experience of several internationally renowned movie stars, including Peter Ustinov, requesting his autograph.

The enthusiasm of the Venice critics was soon repeated elsewhere. The reviews which followed the film's opening, both in and out of the States, were astonishingly – and uniformly – excellent. Unsurprisingly, all but a small handful of jazz critics loved *'Round Midnight* ('. . . the first jazz fiction film that *listens*', was Howard Mandel's reaction in *Down Beat*). But it was the overall response by the critical community in various parts of the film world which was the real eye-opener. In Britain, for instance, there was general approval both for the film and Gordon's performance. The London *Standard*'s Alexander Walker, one of the most respected of local film commentators, elevated the movie to being 'the kind of film we might have expected to come from Kazan or Ray or Huston in that fifties era. I mean to pay Bertrand Tavernier a compliment when I say he has made the best American film this year.' The *Daily Express*'s Ian Christie, himself a jazz clarinettist, called the film 'unique in that its depiction of the jazz life – or one aspect of it – has total credibility'. Gabriele Annan (*Sunday Telegraph*) unequivocally averred that it was a *jazz* film – '. . . down to its seemingly improvised rhythm and monumental unpretentiousness – a contradiction in terms which nevertheless describes its impact. And only a jazz fan could like it as much as it deserves.'

Of Dexter Gordon, the UK critics were positively eulogistic. Richard Barkley (*Sunday Express*) spoke glowingly of Dexter's 'extraordinary presence' living on in the memory. Ian Christie thought he was a formidable actor – 'I doubt that he would make much of a success as King Lear or Hamlet, but playing himself – which is what the part amounts to – he is quite superb.' For Jonathan Fenby (*Independent*), Dexter had taken his role by the scruff of the neck 'and buttresses the film's slim storyline with a characterization that would rank as a fine piece of imagination if it was not so close to the bumpy reality he has lived with for four decades'. Tim Pulleine (*Guardian*) spoke of 'a wonderfully detailed performance by a real jazz musician'.

Three jazz-loathing writers liked both film and its principal actor. Victoria Mather (*Daily Telegraph*) felt that the film belonged to Dexter Gordon, who 'speaks like a bass drum, his voice marinated in *le vieux vin rouge*. His walk is so loose-limbed as to be utterly disconnected: this is a man in severe danger of falling apart . . .' Iain Johnstone (*The Sunday Times*), referring to his slow-motion movements ('like an astronaut in a vacuum'), spoke of 'an ineradical performance that lingers like a tune lodged in the memory'. And Gordon's 'husky chivalry', opined the *Financial Times*'s Nigel Andrews, 'is rhymed with a carriage and gestural eloquence that are positively baroque'. Probably the most persuasive description of Dexter's comprehensively dominating performance came from Alexander Walker. Likening that dominance to that of Jean Gabin, Walker declared: 'Like many big men who move with a child's gentleness, Gordon has also an unsettling tension

– you feel this big barrel might have gunpowder in him . . . His voice is like a great vintage full-bodied wine, glug-glugging into the vessel of silence he seems to occupy – Gordon always looks as if he's listening to sounds we can't hear.'

During the first week of the British showing of *'Round Midnight*, Warner Brothers brought Dexter to London, to undertake a handful of interviews with selected national newspapers. Obviously still far from well and easily exhausted, he nevertheless proved to be as fascinating an *off*screen orator as in previous visits.

For the *Daily Mail*'s Shaun Usher he philosophized about the Jazz Life: 'Why does jazz have such a high mortality rate? Look, you were working in dives and bars, harmful stuff was all around and in the air . . . a little *difficult* to remain Mr Clean in such circumstances, you follow?'

And about his perhaps one-chance-only to get it right, where the making of a *real* movie about *real* jazz people was concerned:

> This film has been a heavy responsibility because I was intent that it shouldn't be Hollywood jazz, Mickey Mouse jazz. Its success pleases me, not for myself but because it tells a story of friendship, and that way opens minds to what musicians' lives are like and what the music is about. Previous films never made the point that the musicians are dedicated; everything else is marginal, good or bad alike. A lot of good men self-destructed out of frustration, you know. I understand that.

To the *Observer*'s Dave Gelly (another jazz-playing critic, but one who is a music columnist/reviewer), he summarized his personal involvement in *'Round Midnight*, reiterating an obligation to try – maybe just once – to ennoble jazz and its practitioners, in an area where previously both had suffered untold indignities and humiliation:

> So much of my life is in this film, so many of my peers and

heroes. It's not just acting, it's ... uh ... reliving a lot of lives, a whole generation. I didn't realize it when I started, but I came to see that this was the chance to tell the story straight. You only get one shot. It had to be right.

For the obvious – and best – reasons, it was not at all startling to find Dexter Gordon's name listed among the final selection of names for the Best Actor trophy at the Academy Award presentation the following April. He had every right to be rubbing shoulders with such as Paul Newman (the eventual winner, and one of the safest odds-on favourites in years), Bob Hoskins and Michael Caine. But the shock of finding Dexter in such an elevated and extraordinary situation had little to do with his obvious abilities as a natural-born Thespian; but more with the fact that such a fairytale happening had actually taken place at all. Exactly how much behind-the-scenes hustling took place, between the opening and closing period for the 1986–7 Oscar nominations will probably never be known. Ultimately, though, that a black American jazz musician, starring in his first 'authentic' full-length movie, should be elevated to the pantheon of the motion-picture industry, Hollywood-style, represents something of a minor miracle. Before Dexter's nomination, such an event would have been considered by the film pundits as the height of absurdity bordering on the realms of fantasy.

One can only wonder what thoughts were going through Dexter's mind as he sat quietly, with his wife, in the packed auditorium on the day of the Oscar celebrations. He remained impassive at the final announcement as an obviously flustered Bette Davis seemed to lose her place in identifying, on cue cards, the Best Actor finalists, and ran her introduction of Dexter and *'Round Midnight* into the brief piece of dialogue from the film. Dexter, no doubt, would have found apt comments both on his presence at the presentation ceremony, and Ms Davis's unfortunate goof. No doubt, too, he would have delivered his own brand of *sang-froid* combined with homespun philosophy, suffused with his inimitable humour. For the latter, his succinct comment might have been something simple and straight-ahead: 'A rather unfortunate . . . huh . . . happenstance . . .'

Neither Dexter Gordon, nor *'Round Midnight* itself, won an Oscar in 1987. Herbie Hancock, to the surprise of many, won the movie's only Academy Award, for his straight-ahead film score. But for Dexter – rescued from near-oblivion, and as close to death as he could have been less than three years before – his very involvement with such a remarkable project remains as important an event in an eventful lifetime as any other. In terms of his threatened career as a full-time working jazz musician, *'Round Midnight* represents more than just a well-publicized, wholly successful diversion from the norm. Because of the seriousness of his health's deterioration, and the lasting effects of the various afflictions which resulted from his collapse and subsequent diagnoses, it was far from being an impossibility that as Dexter Gordon, influential and historically important jazz tenor saxophonist, he had little future. The general response to his *acting*, much more than his *playing*, in *'Round Midnight*, made it more than a mere possibility that, even if his career as a musician were to be at an end, a whole new career had suddenly opened up before him.

Most significant of all, perhaps, *'Round Midnight* represents for Dexter Gordon a *symbol*. With regard to that one-off chance, in making sure that jazz and its participants – past as well as present – were for once presented with dignity as well as truth it is, of course, indisputable that through *'Round Midnight*, Gordon, Hancock, Hutcherson, Tavernier, Winkler *et al*, did indeed get it *right*.

10

Blow, Mr Dexter: The Sound and the Style

The first, and certainly most arresting, aspect of Dexter Gordon's playing of the tenor saxophone is that huge, forward-propelling, wall-to-wall sound, completely individual, both in terms of strength and timbre, with the accent firmly on the rhythmic pulse. In medium- to up-tempo performances, the tough, unsentimental tone, complemented by a distinctive vibrato, is augmented by a comprehensive, often unrelenting commitment to swing. The legacy of Lester Young can be seen in Dexter's own adaptation of Pres's classic laid-back approach, except that the younger man has taken this latter quality to its limits: he sometimes appears to be lagging so far behind the beat that he cannot possibly catch up. But – of course – he always does. Gordon's harmonic acuity is his own, though traceable to the message of Parker. His main influence, however, remains Lester Young.

It is in his ballad playing that the tender side of the man is revealed, invariably in a most fetching and poignant manner. In fact, in terms of honest self-revelation, it is with ballads that much of the soul of Dexter is manifest. His heart-on-the-sleeve solos in this genre are every bit as important in his overall vocabulary as, say, his massively swinging 'up' statements on classic bebop numbers, standards or originals alike, or his marvellously authentic excursions into the blues. As distinctive as any great tenor, living or deceased, there is no trace of maudlin sentimentality in Gordon's ballad stylings. Here, too, are traces of his formative years. The classic thirties/forties ballad styles of figures such as Hawkins, Webster and Byas are strongly evoked – but, again, Gordon's individualism is always omnipotent. His essentially straightforward approach adds a lyrical touch to his ballad playing, while simultaneously allowing the emotional intensity of his work in this vein to remain its most potent attribute. Of course, the kind of legendary stamina he possessed in the halcyon days of the forties and the sixties (in particular), which allowed him to play chorus after chorus of steaming, massively swinging tenor, more or less died with his near-fatal illness; it had been apparent for some time that his failing health was taking its toll in the years leading up to his dramatic collapse. But in those earlier times – especially in live performance – he was capable of sustaining some of the most exhilarating and impact-full playing on his principal instrument to have been perpetrated at any time in jazz's history.

Humour, too, has remained a basic element in the art of Dexter Gordon. In lesser hands, the frequent use of quotes can soon prove to be both tiresome and non-creative. Gordon's repeated recourse to brief excerpts from cornball pop standards, and even an occasional snatch of a classic, has been for the most part judicious in execution, and genuinely funny in impact. Even 'Alice Blue Gown', in the middle of 'Sonnymoon for Two', or the 'Habanera', from *Carmen*, inserted towards the conclusion of 'Second Balcony Jump', can sound delightful, uncontrived, and – in the best sense – hilarious.

For the majority of those who have caught a live appearance by Dexter for the first time, the general consensus seems to be that it is the profound impact of that almost overwhelming, exclamatory tenor sound which registers first and remains longest in the memory. Seated in the front row of some small (or fairly small) jazz club, that first-time exposure to Gordon blowing at full throttle is something of an awesome experience.

For Dexter Gordon's many British fans, his debut at Ronnie Scott's in 1962 proved to be unforgettable. Visual interest was, of course, provided by the huge frame, which seriously threatened the ceiling of the first basement club in Soho's Gerrard Street, London. That deep, friendly, bass-baritone speaking voice which extended a warm greeting to the audiences at Scott's also helped establish an immediate rapport with the receptive audiences which packed the club nightly during his month-long season. Naturally, though, it was the sound of his tenor sax that was to be the instant attention-grabber, and it was the sheer volume of sound which emanated from the bell of his horn that astonished the Scott habitués and casual visitors alike. When its perpetrator was in full stride, careering mightily through some up-tempo bebop blues, at sixty bars a minute, the combined sight-and-sound impact was unlike anything the local jazz scene had experienced, individually and collectively. Gordon's total commitment was likewise something to behold, his jaw muscles standing out like short tree roots as he seemed intent on biting his way completely through his Otto Link mouthpiece. Often, too, he would bear down on the beat with venom.

Apart from experiencing the thrill of hearing Dexter in live performance, British music journalist Roy Carr remembers another stunning reminder of just how voluminous Gordon's tenor-sax sound could be, in a strictly non-gig context. It is a personal memory which stays with Carr, every bit as lasting as any one of the innumerable occasions he has been present at a variety of Gordon gigs, both in London and elsewhere.

I went to Ronnie's, one afternoon during that first season at the club, to take some photographs of Dexter. It was almost like a scene out of some movie. The tables were covered by the chairs stacked, two at a time, one on top of the other. There was just a chink of light coming in from some place. Dexter was there when I arrived. I remember he had on a light-grey suit. He was just walking up and down, just playing some basic bebop. I'd never heard anything like it in my life. Just Dexter and me in the club. And I actually felt I was right in the middle of the sound – *that* sound just sort of envelops you, hugs you. It filled every corner of the room. I've heard a lot of tenor players. But the only other player I heard do this was Coleman Hawkins, when he was warming up backstage at the Free Trade Hall, Manchester, during a Jazz at the Phil concert . . . The sound that Dexter got – there wasn't one corner of that club, whether it be in the ceiling, or a mousehole – which wasn't filled by that sound. It was just uncanny.

For Carr, an architectural analogy was found in going from a small church hall and hearing a choir there, and then experiencing the same inside an edifice as cavernous as, say, St Paul's Cathedral or Notre Dame: 'It was majestic. It was inviting – very seductive. It made you want to go out and buy all Dexter's albums and say: 'But why don't they sound like that which I've just heard!' Even though, of course, they do indeed sound wonderful.'

As to how Dexter Gordon manages to produce that all-enveloping sound, there seems to be, if not a conflict of opinion, a variety of suggestions, each providing a basically common-sense – sometimes obvious – explanation. From a purely physical standpoint, there are those tenor players who prefer to think that Gordon's hugeness of sound is primarily achieved through his giant frame containing probably larger-than-normal lungs. Both Johnny Griffin and Jimmy Heath tend to favour this explanation. As the diminutive Heath puts it: 'Usually, the man that gets a really big sound has a huge, barrelled chest, he's a big guy . . . Yusef Lateef, Gene Ammons, as well as Dex. Even shorter guys, with big chests, such as Griff, Coleman Hawkins and James Moody.'

For George Coleman (another big-sound tenorist with an ample frame), possibly the principal reason is down to the kind of mouthpiece Dexter uses: 'There are a lot of things which relate to sound – certainly, the equipment you use and, in particular, the bigness of the mouthpiece. Of course, it's an individual thing too – what the player himself wants – but that "largeness" that is Dex's probably has a lot to do with his mouthpiece . . . plus, of course, his choice of reed.'

For Junior Cook, though, it is probably Dexter's thinking process, as much as his superior lung-power, which enables him and the other big-sound tenormen to project so powerfully: 'I think it's an inner projection, 'cos it doesn't seem to depend solely on size. Take Don Byas. He was a short man, and he had a large sound. It's just an individual thing that each musician projects. I believe it's what they hear inside, or something like that.'

Benny Golson's interpretation of this he calls 'The Thinking Process'.

Anything you are going to do as a way of life begins – always – with thoughts. So, you think *big*, first of all. And when you put the mouthpiece into your mouth, you're still thinking big. Unconsciously, you make adjustments in the mouth . . . the palate, and in the throat. Anything like that which would enhance whatever sound's gonna come out of that horn, and to make it big.

But Golson is sure that it is equally important to blow through the correct mouthpiece set-up, including the size of aperture that is right for the individual player. These are the premier considerations, he says. But there are other important factors which can dominate the size of sound and its production:

With some players, it's also the stiffness or the softness of the reed. Even the neck of the saxophone – for a while, many saxophone players were trying out ɹifferent kinds of necks to put on the sax. Now, obviously, you just don't pick it up and get a big sound because you're [just] thinking big, you have to spend time on it. Practise, hard. Really, it's a pot-pourri of many different things that go into producing a big sound.

Zoot Sims's explanation was as personal and as straight-ahead as his own brand of superb tenor-sax playing:

It's all within you, what you wanna sound like. Because why would you sound like something you wouldn't wanna sound like? These saxophone players who fool with mouthpieces and reeds all the time – it never changes 'em, really. Everybody gets the sound that they hear, that they want. That's all there is. Dexter always had that big sound, from the early days. He's a big man. Stands to reason he's gotta lot of lungs . . .

With a refreshing lack of false modesty, Illinois Jacquet takes credit and an obviously genuine pleasure in having helped Dexter Gordon in developing both a satisfying tonal quality as well as a sound of ample proportions:

> He developed that sound sitting beside me every night. And, of course, he'd heard Byas and Hawkins too ... and *my* sound was getting bigger all the time. The thing that did it, finally, happened on the bandstand. We decided we'd try each other's mouthpiece. He was interested in my sound, so he said: 'Let me try your mouthpiece, Baptiste, and you try mine.' And we never did change back. That, for Dexter, was it.

As for Gordon himself, the acquisition of a large sound was always a personal requirement, well before he joined Hampton. At the latter time, he was fully aware it was something he obviously lacked: 'My concept of sound was that it should be powerful. The heavyweight kind. And the sound comes from what you hear in your mind. Obviously, if that *is* what you hear, that's what's gonna come out, eventually. For me, the sound just developed.'

By the end of the forties, Dexter Gordon's reputation had made him something of a hero for the up-and-coming tenor players who were emerging at this period. Among those tenor saxists who were influenced directly by Gordon's exciting, hard-blowing style were Yusef Lateef, Frank Foster, Jimmy Heath, Billy Smith (a long-forgotten performer who recorded with Thelonious Monk at the latter's first own record date), Bill Barron and John Coltrane – this last an especially significant follower. Two other aspiring tenors, who for a brief period in the mid-forties were under Dexter's spell: Stan Getz and Allen Eager. (Documented proof for the two last-named can be found on record, at the first dates under their own names – both for the Savoy label.)

One other tenorist who, like Coltrane, later exercised a profound influence on his chosen instrument, is Sonny Rollins. Rollins's name has often been cited as a man whose own sound

owed much to Gordon's. Rollins, however, while he acknowledges the other man's greatness, is far from being in total
agreement with the pundits who for many years have consistently spoken of his debt to the Angeleno. Coleman Hawkins
and Charlie Parker were – and are – his only significant
inspirations.

> Being a working musician, I kind of listened to everybody
> and kind of took things I could use . . . Dexter, being before
> me, I'm sure I got some things from him. But Dexter is not
> the sort of person who would be my direct lineage. I thought
> he was sort of in the Lester Young mould . . . that he was sort
> of a progression in that way of playing – but with his own
> sound. Maybe some other people can draw a line between us,
> but I can't. Dexter is another guy that I've listened to,
> certainly. For me, he's continued the tradition and added to
> it. He's been part of that great tradition, which came down
> from Coleman and all those people.

For Frank Foster, himself a gifted performer, and an
arranger/composer of real distinction, Dexter Gordon is a
figurehead, and a definite inspiration – particularly in his own
formative years, and after he'd switched, like so many other
saxists, from alto to the bigger horn. Apart from the cavernous
sound, Foster's interest in Dexter Gordon's approach to the
tenor sax also included the virility he brought to his work in the
upper register: 'Most of us "modern" tenor players don't stay
in the lower register so much as Don and Ben and the Bean did.
We make use of the upper register quite a bit. My last influence,
I would say, is John Coltrane. We both came out of that school,
so Dexter gave us a direction.'

It wasn't exclusively tenor saxophonists who responded to
Gordon's declamatory approach. Jackie McLean, an authoritative and distinctive *alto* saxophonist, gives, as his joint principal
influences, Charlie Parker and Dexter Gordon. McLean's own
powerful sound is the result of his admiration for both men –
and he heard Dexter first.

That was when I was still in my tenor phase. Apart from that sound, I dug the way he handled the metre, and the way he played chord changes. One of my favourite early solos of his was 'Dexter's Deck', because it's such a grand solo. Grand saxophone playing. Like he is. He's a grand image of a man, and that's just how he plays. He's just fabulous and grand.

11

Dexter Calling: Just for the Record

In spite of the periodic gaps in his not inconsiderable discography – in particular, during the fifties, due to his long absences from the jazz scene – the sound of Dexter Gordon has been a familiar part of the history and growth of recorded jazz for the past forty-five years.

Not all of his recordings can in truth be said to rank as masterpieces, or to be of vital importance. There have been times when he has tended to disappoint, due no doubt to a variety of personal and other reasons. But overall, Dexter has managed to contribute handsomely and significantly towards jazz's evolution; and there is an enviable list of Gordon solo statements on record which can be called, without fear of contradiction, classics.

It is regrettable that so little of Dexter's big-band work has been documented on record. At the time of writing, the one example of his soloing with the Hampton band exists only in private-tape form. This dates from a public broadcast datelined 26 September 1941, and the solitary item ('Train Time') was originally recorded by the legendary location recording 'engineer' Jerry Newman. In terms of actual commercial recordings, Gordon made only one session with Hampton and, predictably, he received no solo allocation. However, Gordon's brief association with Fletcher Henderson has been part-documented by the contents of two AFRS Jubilee Series broadcasts being made available on long-playing record. These were still early days for the young tenorman, but not even the poor sound reproduction on the numbers in which he is featured can disguise the fact that his premier influence is Lester Young (with overtones of Jacquet), or that he has a positive commitment to a basically rhythmic approach. A declamatory style is also apparent on 'I Got Rhythm', and a Lestorian easygoing relaxation informs his thirty-two-bar chorus during 'Stompin' at the Savoy'. There are definite hints of what he is seeking in terms of a personal sound both here and during 'Bugle Blues', but his contribution to 'Jeep Rhythm' is pure Lester.

A second, and shorter, recording ban, imposed once again by the American Federation of Musicians, principally through its feisty president, James C. Petrillo, meant that, in retrospect, it is in no way possible to ascertain whether or not Dexter Gordon made any significant progress during his time on the road with Louis Armstrong. As with Hampton, he made just one record date (also with Decca) which yielded little or no opportunity to express himself on his own. And as with the Hampton period, the only documented evidence of his progress is to be found on the precious few individual statements which emanate from poor-quality airshots. Still, it is possible to perceive from these rare outings that he is growing in confidence. His solo work on, for instance, 'Perdido' (broadcast live from Camp Reynolds, Philadelphia, 12 September 1944) is both muscular and laid-back, although still reveals very little individualism. 'Ain't Misbehavin'', from the same transmission, is similarly promising. After delivering one of his inimitable vocals, Louis cues in his youthful tenor soloist ('Brother Dexter!') And Gordon responds with another Pres-styled offering that is commendable for its completely unhurried mode of despatch. Another Gordon solo on the same number, from a few months prior to this, is perhaps even more relaxed.

Of course, it was Gordon's last involvement with the big-band genre which was most exciting and fulfilling. It was also responsible for bringing his name to the attention of the general public, as well as the critics and fellow musicians. Certainly, for many up-and-coming young performers, it was Dexter's showcase features with the trailblazing Billy Eckstine Orchestra which made him both an individual hero and, for the budding tenor stars, someone to follow closely. Record-wise, though, Gordon didn't stay long enough to produce a string of memorable solos. In any case, he had to share tenor-sax solo duties with Gene Ammons; indeed, it was with Ammons that Gordon had to share his most famous Eckstine showcase. 'Blowing the Blues Away' is almost certainly the first of the really famous two-tenor features, with both men in top form, spurring each other on to the series of exciting exchanges which follow the leader's brave attempts at a convincing blues vocal – and his enthusiastic invitation to 'Blow, Mr Gene! Blow, Mr Dexter, too!' Ammons's softer tone makes a contrast with Gordon's tougher sound, and it is the Chicagoan who leads off the exchanges. With Art Blakey's magnificent drumming uplifting both band and soloists, 'Blowing the Blues Away' remains the Eckstine outfit's most pulsating, best-remembered studio creation, despite the all too obvious recording inadequacies. Thankfully, it has been made available in two takes. There is little to choose between them in terms either of overall standard of performance or genuine excitement.

Not too long before his exit from the band, Dexter was present at its 2 May 1945 date for National. He is heard on two of the titles cut on that date. On the ballad 'Last Night', he establishes a suitably reflective mood for Eckstine's vocal, his sound evidencing much of Lester Young's poignancy. For 'Lonesome Lover Blues' he follows Eckstine with a contribution that combines power and relaxation – and more than a hint of Young – in equal proportions. There is more of the laid-back quality which would soon be recognized as a Gordon trademark. On 'Lonesome Lover Blues', too, he uses a couple of phrases which were to be incorporated as the foundation of his own blues, 'Long Tall Dexter'.

Gordon's first small-combo date – also his debut as a session leader – had taken place towards the end of 1943, in Los Angeles. Harry Edison's trumpet complements Gordon's Lestorian tenor, bringing a definite Basie flavour to the proceedings. The group is rounded out by Nat Cole, Johnny Miller (the pianist's bassist in the King Cole Trio), and a drummer who might be the little-known Juicy Owens. The Young influence on Gordon is probably most pronounced on a loosely swinging 'I Found a New Baby' and 'Rosetta', but the results of the time he had been spending alongside Illinois Jacquet also manifest themselves, during a flowing contribution to 'Rosetta'. The one ballad performance of the session ('Sweet Lorraine') finds him combining a Hawkins/Webster approach with Young's deceptive nonchalance.

By far the most important record date to which Dexter Gordon made positive contributions took place in the New York studios of the small independent label Guild on 9 February 1945. It found Gordon working under the leadership of Dizzy Gillespie as part of a sextet which also included guitarist Chuck Wayne and pianist/composer Frank Paparelli. Paparelli, who collaborated with Gillespie on the celebrated 'A Night in Tunisia', is likewise co-credited with the creation of 'Blue 'n' Boogie', one of the two numbers recorded for Guild. At his absolute peak in '45, it is not at all surprising that Gillespie dominates the solo work on both cuts. Gordon, though, is in no way pushed into the background. His contribution to 'Blue 'n' Boogie' is positive, basically rhythmic, and its concept still leans heavily on the Lester Young style. Much can be said about his opening solo on 'Groovin' High', during which he lays back on the beat to splendid effect. And there is little doubt that he sounds completely at home in what is, to all intents and purposes, a bebop situation.

Eight months following the Gillespie/Guild date, Gordon was able to record with his new idol and current boss, Charlie Parker, an unrepeated combination. On 4 September, both men, together with trumpeter Buck Clayton (employed at the time by the US army), comprised the front line of a seven-piece group fronted by 'Sir' Charles Thompson, a fine pianist/composer who had been invited by Apollo, another independent, to make his debut as leader at his own record date. Danny Barker, the ex-Cab Calloway guitarist from New Orleans; drummer J.C. Heard and bassist Jimmy Butts completed the Thompson All Stars – the kind of stylistically varied line-up common at this time which usually contrived to make superior music. Thompson was responsible for three of the compositions and arrangements. Gordon solos on all but one of the quartet

('20th Century Blues' is dominated by an idiomatically superlative Parker).

Following Clayton's warm solo, Gordon sounds reasonably happy and relaxed on 'Street Beat', a straight-ahead swing piece with a hint of bop in its staccato introduction. He is much more confident as he opens the solo sequence for Thompson's Basie-like 'Takin' Off'. And on the only non-Thompson piece – the 1928-published Ted Shapiro–Jimmy Campbell–Reg Connelly ballad, 'If I Had You' – he mixes the big-sound approach of Hawkins with the kind of delicacy which Lester Young seemed always to reserve for his post-Basie work in this context.

Despite his ever-increasing jazz experience, Dexter was still only twenty-two when he made his first important record date under his own name. It was the first of four separate occasions on which he would take a quartet or quintet into the New York studios of Savoy, one of the most famous of all the post-war jazz/R&B labels, between 1945 and 1947.

The four different groups were certainly much more homogeneous than the Thompson All Stars, and all but the first were cast in the classic bebop mould. The 30 October 1945 session found Gordon leading pianist Sadik Hakim (aka Argonne Thornton), a somewhat shadowy figure of the mid-forties period, and non-boppers Gene Ramey (a colleague of Parker's in the Jay McShann band), and drummer Eddie Nicholson. All the four titles make specific references to the leader's Christian name – as do the majority of the Gordon originals which originate from the Savoy dates. Hardly noted as a prolific composer, at any stage of his career, Dexter was obviously a busy man when recording for the label, composing, running through each new number, then going for a take. Recording in those days was usually a bit frantic, with little time for such luxuries as rehearsal time. Dexter recalls:

Rehearsal time? No, I don't remember any. It was all done there. But, of course, with most of the guys we were playing together every night anyway. Jamming, or working – whatever. Of course, where you could, you'd try to get something ready, maybe even work it in the club, ready for the date. But you had to be ready. Those things were done in three-hour sessions. All that means it was very spontaneous. Wasn't much preparation, as such. I mean, you'd come in the studio and decide: 'What we gonna do . . . da-da-de-da . . .?' And then do it. And go on to the next one. In those days, most people were basically acoustically attuned. But I don't recall there being any much more difficulty than today.

That first Savoy session was a most impressive affair, especially for Dexter. That he had really come of age is amply demonstrated on each of the four titles mastered that October afternoon – 'Blow Mr Dexter' (made available in two different, but equally splendid takes), 'Dexter's Deck' (thereafter a favourite Gordon recording for several fellow musicians, including Jackie McLean), 'Dexter's Cuttin' Out' and 'Dexter's Minor Mad'. Even though there is still plenty of Young/Jacquet influence, the Parker message, harmonically at least, is insinuating itself into his overall solo structure. The Gordon sound is, above all, large; the drive, powerful and unrelenting (particularly on the second take of 'Blow'), and there is some delicious honking ('Dexter's Deck') – yet another legacy from Lester. 'Minor Mad' (based on the chords of 'I Found a New Baby'), is probably the most exciting performance of the date, with Gordon driving powerfully throughout.

The second Savoy date took place on 29 January 1946 – just three weeks after Dexter had recorded as a member of an all-star orchestra led by Benny Carter. This time he was accompanied by an authentic bebop rhythm section whose credentials were beyond dispute: Bud Powell, Curley Russell, Max Roach. The difference in the leader's playing is apparent from his work throughout. He sounds more relaxed than at the previous Savoy session and, if anything, his tone is even bigger. The little-known, averagely talented Leonard Hawkins's trumpet provides an opportunity for some unison horn during three of the titles – 'Long Tall Dexter' (two takes mastered), 'Dexter Rides Again', and 'Dexter Digs In' (another two-take effort). 'I Can't Escape from You', a standard pop tune written by Leo

Robin and Richard Whiting, is a warm, straight-ahead ballad performance (on both takes) which reflects both the Hawkins/ Webster school and the more restrained beauty of Young. The up-tempo numbers contain blistering tenor choruses of magisterial quality, with both takes of 'Long Tall Dexter' ranking with his greatest recordings of this period. Bud Powell, however, is in scintillating form, and his contributions vie with Dexter's for quality and inspiration. Roach, of course, is masterful and uplifting throughout.

It was to be almost two years before a different Dexter Gordon Quintet recorded again for Savoy. Gordon and Russell apart, the rest of the combo lined up as: Leo Parker, baritone sax; pianist Tadd Dameron, Dexter's all-time favourite jazz composer; Nelson Boyd, bass; and the redoubtable Art Blakey on drums. Only three Gordon originals were mastered at this 11 December 1947 session, with only one Dexterian allusion in the list of titles. Gordon himself disclaims ownership of the Dexter-type titles, giving that dubious honour to Savoy's Teddy Reig, who produced most of the sides. This time, too, three takes apiece were made, although some remain unissued.

The extrovert baritone of Leo Parker was a splendid choice. His fascinating synthesis of bebop and rugged R&B sometimes found him disfavour with some jazz critics, who either couldn't take the heady mixture, or were unable to find a suitable category for the apparently aptly nicknamed Mad Lad. Gordon and his former section-mate with Eckstine are in cracking form throughout. 'Settin' the Pace' is a long and exciting 'chase' performance – it covered both sides of a 78-r.p.m. disc (Savoy 913) on its initial release – with both protagonists spurring each other on to produce ever more exciting solos. There is much honking from both horns during Takes One and Two of 'Dexter's Riff'. Even so, Parker is on his best behaviour – he even tends to sound laid-back on Take One. There is plenty of Pres and Bird during both Dexter's solos on 'So Easy', a relaxed blues, which also encourages Parker towards restraint. The musical (and no doubt personal) compatibility between the pair probably had something to do with the fact that Gordon appeared at Leo Parker's own next record date – just over a week later, also for Savoy. This time, the front line sounds even more power-packed, with the addition of Joe Newman's trumpet and J.J. Johnson's trombone. Gordon solos on only two of the four titles – Johnson's bop classic 'Wee Dot' and his own fast blues 'Lion Roars', each producing four releaseable takes. Here, his stylistic influence throughout tends to be Lester.

Three days after the Parker All Stars date, Gordon was completing his own final session for Savoy. For this, he welcomed back the pianist and bassist from his own previous studio encounter with Leo Parker, with Art Mardigan replacing Blakey and the baritonist's place taken by Fats Navarro. Navarro – together with Gillespie, *the* trumpet genius of the bop era – makes a first-rate partner for Gordon, who responds accordingly. The composer produces an emotive statement on 'Dextrose' (a 'Fine and Dandy' line), but Navarro's beautifully articulated, marvellously felt solo which follows is even better. The trumpeter repeats the process during 'Index', but Gordon (sounding, tonally and harmonically, out of Byas) is in no mood to take second place during the sprightly 'Dextivity'. With Navarro laying out, the tenorist has his and Dameron's 'Dexter's Mood' virtually to himself. In his most effective ballad style, and with further reference to Byas's influence, he produces a solo that is as authoritative as it is emotionally satisfying.

By dint of his making a periodic trip back to his home town, much of Dexter's recording activity between the second and third Savoy dates took place in Los Angeles. The September blues-based date, as a member of Russell Jacquet's Yellow Jackets and featuring singer Numa Lee Davis, proved to be the last time he would work inside a recording studio during 1946. Apart from a small handful of sessions (with singers Mary Ann McCall, Jessie Price and Wynonie Harris, and vibist Red Norvo), plus the two aforementioned Savoy dates, the rest of Gordon's recording dates – all on the West Coast – involved Ross Russell's Dial label. Among the numerous other musicians who also recorded for Dial around the same time were Erroll Garner, Howard McGhee, Charlie Parker (including his cataclysmic 'Lover Man' date), Fats Navarro, Earl Coleman, Dodo Marmarosa, Teddy Edwards and Wardell Gray.

It was the highly combustible two-tenor partnership of Gordon and Gray which would produce the most popular of all Dial releases – more popular even than any of the sides Bird cut for Russell. The thirty-two-bar 'The Chase' – with Gordon borrowing its main theme from the immortal Alphonse Picou clarinet obbligato to 'High Society' – covered both sides of a 78 r.p.m. disc. It remains not only a wholly successful attempt to re-create the kind of genuine excitement in performance heard nightly at the Bird in the Basket on Central Avenue, but also a superbly creative, consummately swinging, two-part performance. The popularity of 'The Chase' – not to mention the duo which created it – undoubtedly provided the inspiration for the birth of similar twin-tenor partnerships which flourished in later years, those of Al Cohn–Zoot Sims, Johnny Griffin–Eddie 'Lockjaw' Davis, Gene Ammons–Sonny Stitt, and Ronnie Scott–Tubby Hayes being among the most memorable.

Gray is absent for the rest of the Dial session on 12 June, which enabled Gordon and the same rhythm section: pianist Jimmy Bunn, bassist Red Callender, drummer Chuck Thompson, to complete a further three sides. Two of these were Gordon originals, the minor-key 'Blues Bikini' and the interestingly structured 'Chromatic Aberration' (Take C of this is known alternatively as 'Iridescence'). Both elicit fine all-round blowing from Dexter. With his usual combination of wit and worldly awareness, he subtitled 'Bikini' 'All Men are Cremated Equal', a personal comment on the sequestration by the US Government of the tiny Pacific atoll of the same name in order to detonate a succession of atomic weapons. To complete the session, Gordon – in Hawklike mood – left his imprimatur on the standard ballad 'It's the Talk of the Town' (two mastered takes).

Gordon's first Dial date had taken place exactly a week before 'The Chase'. His colleagues on that occasion were Callender, Thompson, Charles Fox (in place of Bunn), and a youthful trombonist/arranger, Melba Liston. Just two numbers were completed on 5 June, at the same C.P. MacGregor Studios in Hollywood: 'Mischievous Lady' (a dedication to Liston from Gordon) and the standard 'Lullaby in Rhythm'. Apart from some sprightly keyboard work from Fox, the solos are dominated by Dexter. That which informs Take F of 'Lullaby' is as perfect an example of his work on record at this period as any.

The final Dial session, on 4 December – just prior to the studio clampdown imposed by a telling American Federation of Musicians ban, and Dexter's return to New York – was a four-number affair. A fine Jimmy Rowles–Red Callender–Roy Porter rhythm team supported Dexter during the making of two superior ballad performances, with Dexter cast once more in the Great Tradition. The second of two issued takes of 'Ghost of a Chance' is finest of all, after which he is joined by fellow tenorman Teddy Edwards in an attempt by Russell to repeat the success of 'The Chase'. Edwards, a native of Jackson, Mississippi, had been a resident of Los Angeles since 1944. In Gordon's absence from the local scene, on a full-time basis, he had become the best bebop tenorist in the area. The new Gordon–Edwards team completed two titles – 'Hornin' In' and 'The Duel'. Very seldom do attempts at repeating a successful formula come off. While neither performance can be said to emulate the spontaneous excitement of the Gray–Gordon masterpiece, there is much to commend the efforts of the replacement duo. Edwards by no means takes a secondary role. In terms of powerful drive and keen sense of dynamics, he matches Gordon, stride for stride. Less laid-back than Wardell Gray, and indeed more forthright in his approach, Edwards proves a splendid substitute for Dexter's close friend and regular sparring partner. Certainly, his is a style that is totally committed to the bebop idiom – much more so than either Gordon or Gray. Of the brace of Gordon-originated tunes, 'The Duel' probably registers more convincingly, with some frenzied exchanges during the final two choruses, and plenty of ripe honks thrown in by the combatants.

The Gordon–Gray team continued to prove a popular booking on the Los Angeles scene for several years, right up until Dexter's first incarceration, in 1953. Luckily, some documented evidence of their post-Dial recording exists, in the form of further joint appearances involving both commercial studio and live performances. Thanks to producer/engineer Ralph Bass, several notev̶   .   examples of the latter have found their way on to variou̶ ̶ ̶ng-playing records. Each gives a first-hand illustration of Dexter and Wardell in the context of the Central Avenue jam sessions of the forties. As such, they are of extreme importance, both musically as well as historically.

These unique, mostly unabridged location recordings were made on two portable disc-cutters. Considering the primitive mode of recording, and thanks to modern technological expertise (especially from the extraordinary Rudy Van Gelder, in respect of the most recent reissues), much of the vibrancy and spontaneity of the music remains. The two tenors apart, a fascinating mixture of musicians participates in the lengthy, Bass-recorded jam series, held at the Elk's Auditorium, on the night of 6 July 1947. Younger players, such as Hampton Hawes, Barney Kessel, Sonny Criss and Harry Babasin, worked naturally alongside older men like Trummy Young (a noted catalyst of the period in Central Avenue circles), Red Callender and Howard McGhee. Musical generation gaps were non-existent in these kind of levelling situations.

Gordon's playing throughout is confirmation in itself that he had come of age. On 'After Hours Bop', for instance, he follows a remarkably mature, two-fisted blues statement by Hawes (not yet nineteen) with a masterful contribution of his own. Unhurried, understated, it too shows his ability as a blues player. A subtly inserted quote from 'My Kinda Love' sounds not at all unnatural, or out of place. Gray is absent from this number, but he is at his finest, rhythmically and creatively, during 'Cherokee'. So too is altoist Criss, whose searing effort acts as a real inspiration to Wardell. Interesting, here, is the fact that Gordon's own solo follows immediately after Gray's. In fact, his appearance is the signal for one of their customary duels. The same happens during the final portion of 'The Hunt' (more than a trifle reminiscent of 'Stompin' at the Savoy'). The contrast between Dexter's sinewy, large sound and Gray's smoother, even sensuous, tonal quality is manifestly obvious.

On Hawkins's 'Disorder at the Border', the horns are separated by two superb contributions from McGhee and Criss. Lester's lasting influence is readily apparent as Gordon takes over from Criss, augmented by elements of Jacquet's declaratory style. The impact of Parker is also present, including the use of double time late in his solo.

More fine music was recorded, live, three years after the Elk's date, this time emanating from the Hula Hut Club, once a popular blowing spot on Sunset Boulevard. Unfortunately, Gordon, who had just returned from New York, appears alongside nominal leader Gray on just two items: a whirlwind version of 'Move' and, in obbligato only, during Damita Jo's 'I Can't Give You Anything but Love'.

The crowd-pleasing abilities of the Gray–Gordon team were documented for posterity during the aforementioned Gene Norman Just Jazz concert in February 1952. There is real excitement to be found on the Decca-released versions of 'The Chase' and 'Steeplechase', even though the playing by both on each of these overlong performances doesn't sustain after the opening choruses. There is an air of tiredness about the playing of both, particularly towards the conclusion of 'The Chase'. Still, this is the only known live recording of their *pièce de résistance*; as such, it retains its historical interest. Although a private recording is known to exist of Gray and Gordon locking horns on 'Stompin' at the Savoy' at a club appearance in March 1952, the last known 'official' recording featuring the pair was made for the Californian independent label Swingtime, in June of the same year. While nothing startling happens at any time, both Wardell and Dexter sound suitably happy and relaxed throughout both released takes of 'The Rubaiyat' and the one-take-only 'Citizen's Bop'. The saxes are used in a purely supportive role during a wretched 'Jingle Jangle Jump', a feature for the inept vocalizing of Gladys Bentley. For 'My Kinda Love', Gray takes five, while Dexter gets the chance to blow a big-toned yet tender ballad. There were not to be too many further collaborations between them. Gray died before Gordon left Chino ... their idol, Charlie Parker, also self-destructed before his release.

These few studio/live dates with Wardell Gray apart, opportunities for Dexter to record – post-forties and up to his admission to Chino – were practically non-existent. In fact, the only other dates on which he was recorded during this time involved singers, and his involvement was strictly supportive. The best of these undoubtedly involved Helen Humes.

First, on 20 November 1950, it was Gordon who fronted the accompanying six-piece unit that recorded with Humes for Discovery. The former Basie vocalist had been living in LA since around 1947, and her career had been completely revitalized by a switch in style, from basically straight swing to a more biting R&B delivery. There is not one of the four sides she cut with the Gordon-led band which can be described as anything but delightful. Certainly, the subsequent coupling of 'Helen's Advice' and 'Airplane Blues', both from the session, gave Helen a smash R&B hit record. And it was Dexter Gordon, who had played so splendidly on the Discovery date, who appeared in the small band which wailed behind Humes at the same Gene Norman concert at which he and Wardell had performed 'The Chase' and 'Steeplechase'. Finally, Gordon was present at a Swingtime session, featuring bluesman Lowell Fulson, although only one item ('Christmas Party Shuffle') has been released.

For the rest of the fifties, Dexter Gordon was to record on only three subsequent occasions – all in the space of a three-month period towards the end of 1955, the first two in September.

Although there are some tell-tale signs of his inactivity, his playing at two Bethlehem dates – both cut within a period of a fortnight – is generally first-rate. 'Daddy Plays the Horn' – the title tune from the first, which also celebrates his initial involvement with the long-playing record – contains several marvellously uplifting original blues choruses by Dexter, accompanied with tremendous collective skills by the superior rhythm team of Leroy Vinnegar, Lawrence Marable and Kenny Drew, who himself contributes a masterful solo, suffused with real blues. Elsewhere, there are rewarding interpretations of Parker's 'Confirmation' and 'You Can Depend on Me', and some deeply-felt ballad work ('Darn that Dream', 'Autumn in New York').

Just over a week later, Gordon took his place in a second Bethlehem date, this one fronted by his old 52nd Street buddy, Stan Levey. Again, it is a blues which brings out the best in Gordon, his own basic twelve-bar, 'Stanley the Steamer'. There is an almost calculated logicality about the lengthy tenor solo, but in every way it is expressive and profoundly emotive. 'The Steamer' is indeed a showcase for Gordon, who wastes not one note throughout a magnificent performance which runs for over six and a half minutes. The rhythm section, of Levey, Vinnegar and Lou Levy, is every bit as good as that which backed Dexter on his own Bethlehem date, and he and the trio coalesce wonderfully during a similarly heated rendition of the Bloom–Mercer standard 'Day in, Day out', with Gordon's slashing attack and booming sound an exciting twin asset. And he even manages to sound unperturbed by the murderous tempo established by Levey for his own showcase outing, 'Max is Making Wax' (retitled here as 'This Time the Drum's on Me').

Both the Bethlehems hoisted a warning to his fellow tenorists that Dexter was back – and he'd not only proved his chops had been largely undiminished by any personal troubles but, at thirty-two, that his playing had reached full maturity. This was confirmed by a third recording project that same year, a quartet/quintet date for Dootone, another of the numerous West Coast 'indies' which proliferated in the region during the fifties and the preceding decade. Dootone was the brainchild of Dootsie Williams, a black jazz fan, who recorded his favourite music, plus R&B, gospel and comedian Redd Foxx, the label's best-seller. As with the Bethlehem recordings, *Dexter Blows Hot and Cool* contains sufficient boss tenor playing to convince even the severest doubters that Gordon was very much back in charge. With the superbly idiosyncratic pianist Carl Perkins adding his own sparkling comments, Gordon is in trenchant mood on the up-tempo selections, rhythmically rampant on 'Blowin' for Dootsie', 'I Hear Music' and the appropriately-named Gordon piece, 'Rhythm Mad'. Complementing the powerful blowing, the ballads are projected with a touching tenderness: 'Cry Me a River' retains its poignancy over thirty years later.

That sudden, almost unnatural, rush of recordings seemed likely to presage what would amount to Dexter's 'comeback'. But still further dues remained to be paid. It would take another five years before he would re-enter a recording studio. That event occurred in October 1960, for Jazzland, a Riverside subsidiary. It was produced by Cannonball Adderley. The LP which resulted was perhaps too ambitiously titled: *The Resurgence of Dexter Gordon*, for the music produced by a five-piece group under Gordon's leadership was of only average quality, hardly likely to challenge the recorded output of the top jazz combos of the day. Gordon himself is rather less than fluent throughout, and only on 'Jodi', an appealing ballad, does he sound completely involved. Years later, in an interview with Jean-Louis Ginibre and Jean Wagner of the French *Jazz* magazine, Dexter was to admit that 'it's a mediocre album: the session suffered from a clear lack of preparation . . .' He was right.

At least, though, a new decade had opened with one new recording. By the following year matters had improved significantly. Concurrent with his return to New York, and the need for a cabaret card, came the contract-signing with Blue Note. With one of the most famous of all jazz labels, starting in May 1961, Gordon was able to put together a remarkably consistent series of albums, most of which are the equal of any Dexter Gordon recording, at any stage of his career.

The first – *Doin' Allright* – set that standard of consistency. Indeed, it is probably the finest of all the Blue Notes, and his most impressive date thus far. His longish, deceptively casual solo on the opening 'I was Doing All Right' is a perfect example of his sixties renaissance, utterly relaxed, with the kind of loping swing which informs his best work, and a comforting warmth which communicates at once to the listener. With pianist Horace Parlan and bassist George Tucker producing a unison 'Highland vamp', Dexter states the theme to 'It's You or No One', then positively leaps into a pungent solo which swings unrestrainedly. 'You've Changed', the album's only ballad, contains the kind of basic emotive power that helps rank Gordon with the greatest in this area of saxophone playing. Dexter's entry alone, on his own persuasive 'For Regulars Only', is dramatically superb, and the following improvisations are delivered with a growing power which has reached white heat before its conclusion. 'Society Red', another Gordon opus, has further extemporization of pulsating quality. Certainly, Gordon sounds happy in the company of a typical Blue Note rhythm section which carries no passengers. It was particularly perceptive of Alfred Lion to select Freddie Hubbard as Gordon's front-line colleague. Hubbard, at that time one of the most promising of the younger trumpet men, plays with all the power and all-round impact Blue Note aficionados had come to expect of him, even at this early stage. Working with Dexter, Hubbard modified some aspects of a dazzling technique, and his playing sounds the better for it. Hubbard himself is grateful for the few chances he was given to record with the older man for the label – and acknowledges how much this improved his own playing . . . and thinking:

> He helped me learn how to phrase. You see, playing with Coltrane and Sonny, and those guys, I found out that they'd gotten a lot of ideas from Dexter. Because, of course, he came before them. You know, with Dexter he'll play that same stuff – hip, quiet, laid-back, but still with humour in it. He's in no rush, but he just takes off. He and Sonny Stitt started that stuff . . . I sounded so young, then. Like a babe in the woods! He taught me how to blow-out when you played parts. You see, some cats don't blow-out – I mean, play with a full sound, even when you're playing with the ensemble. He had me playing in a way that would almost sound to me a little lazy. And it was funky with it. I always like to play on top, but I learned how to lay back, behind the beat just a little bit. Not play slower, but just lay back with the notes . . .

Gordon's old friend from the West Coast days, Kenny Drew, was present at his next Blue Note date – just three days later –

and he got to record with both Paul Chambers and Philly Joe
Jones for the first time (with regard to the bassist, it was to be
the *only* occasion they recorded together). Once again, Dexter's
playing stayed at a consistently high level. Of particular interest
is the use of three numbers Gordon had written for and been
featuring in *The Hollywood Connection* – 'Soul Sister', 'I Want
More' and the yearning 'Ernie's Tune'.

Gordon's next album date took place almost exactly a year
later, and during 1962 he appeared at three further sessions
under his own name, the last of these (*A Swingin' Affair*)
completed the day before he left for his first European visit. The
best of the 1962 sessions took place two days before his
pre-Europe LP. *Go!* reunites Gordon with Sonny Clark (who
had recorded with the tenorist two months before) in a quartet
setting, which also benefited immensely from the additional
presence of the superlative drumming of Billy Higgins. (Higgins, too, had first recorded with Dexter in 1962, as a member
of a splendid quintet led by Herbie Hancock, at a 28 May date
which produced, among other fine performances, the first
studio version of Hancock's 'Watermelon Man'.) That Gordon
had more than regained a fading reputation – and indeed that
he had developed into an even greater player – is perfectly
obvious from even casual inspection of any one of the six tracks
which comprise the contents of *Go!* He is devastatingly
rhythmic on 'Love for Sale', and imparts his own brand of
poignancy to two Sinatra-associated ballads: 'Where are You?'
and 'Guess I'll Hang My Tears out to Dry'.

A Swingin' Affair is not far behind in terms of overall
consistency. The same Clark–Higgins–Butch Warren team
reprises the empathy with Gordon which helped make *Go!* such
an outstanding project. Although it is rarely cited in analyses of
Dexter Gordon's work on record for its uniqueness, *Go!* should
be considered one of his most important issues if only for the
deeply moving, eminently understated reading of Billie Holiday's touching 'Don't Explain'. Never straying too far away
from the lovely melody line, and concentrating on an admirable
simplicity in approach, Gordon's takes second place to no other
as the finest instrumental recording of the song. Like other

great saxophonists (Lester Young, Ben Webster, Stan Getz), Gordon listens as closely to the lyrics of great ballads as to the melody. Certainly, with regard to 'Don't Explain', he both knew the lyric and understood its message. On checking out a song's lyric Gordon becomes serious:

> This is something, sadly, that very few young musicians know or understand or appreciate. How can you play a tune like 'Don't Explain', or 'You've Changed', and *not* know the lyrics? . . . but still play it: the lyric is so much of the song, its storyline. There's so much to music. You have to know these things to do them justice – to even attempt to play them.

Gordon's Blue Note period extended into his European sojourn: the final album for the label (*Gettin' Around*) was cut at Rudy Van Gelder's studios on 28 May 1965, on one of the expatriate's rare trips home. (The penultimate Blue Note – *Clubhouse* – was completed the previous day.) Before these, he had taped two albums in Paris, one in 1963, the second just over a year later.

There is much good music to be heard on both the Paris-made LPs. *Our Man in Paris*, the first, might well have become Gordon's finest Blue Note recording, for his colleagues included – local bassist Pierre Michelot aside – two of the greatest names from bebop's halcyon days: Bud Powell and Kenny Clarke. Even though the pianist's health had become rather more stabilized in the French capital by 1963, and his playing tended to be rather less erratic than for some time after his arrival, he remained an unpredictable genius. For the Gordon date, his playing is perhaps better than could be expected. Much more unlikely, though, is the unrelaxed playing at times of Kenny Clarke, usually a drummer of peerless ability. Dexter himself plays generally well, if not outstandingly so, throughout. On the debit side, he uses some strange-sounding honks and screams on both 'Broadway' and 'Scrapple from the Apple', which seem out of place, and foreign to his long-established style.

For *One Flight Up* (recorded 2 June 1964), he is in

consistently fine fettle, assisted splendidly by three fellow Americans (Donald Byrd, Kenny Drew, Art Taylor) and a phenomenal eighteen-year-old Dane, Niels-Henning Ørsted Pedersen, destined to become Gordon's premier bass player during his lengthy stay in Europe. The album's most interesting track is an eighteen-minutes-plus version of Byrd's 'Tanya', which contains, among other good things, a long and thoughtful tenor excursion that could hardly be bettered.

The next important phase in Gordon's recording career concerns his involvement, between 1964 and late 1976, with a variety of labels, most importantly SteepleChase, based in his adopted home of Denmark, and the American Prestige, another leading US jazz company. Chronologically, the association with the latter had begun with an electrifying two-tenor recording which took place in Munich, West Germany, in October 1965. Leader for the date was Booker Ervin, a former Mingus sideman, with a blistering, highly individual sound and a style completely his own. In company with a continuously inspiring rhythm section, led by the ubiquitous Jaki Byard, the Ervin–Gordon team roar through just two long titles. Although both 'Setting the Pace' and 'Dexter's Deck' are probably too protracted, both men are seldom lacking in inspiration, and if the intention of the date was to effect an excitement-packed jam session, then it can be considered a positive success.

Chronologically, Dexter's next appearance on Prestige relates to a session in Copenhagen in March 1969, at which he shares top billing with trombonist Slide Hampton. The recording, for the West German MPS label, was subsequently issued in America on Prestige. Nothing startling happens at any time, but the presence of Hampton, as arranger as well as trombonist, is a bonus. Gordon's showcase is a yearning 'The Shadow of Your Smile', performed with just the rhythm section.

His first Prestige date proper took place in New York, just under one month after the aptly titled *A Day in Copenhagen*'s completion. This provided Dexter with an opportunity to record with fellow tenorist James Moody for the first time; it was also a reunion for Gordon and the Bud Powell-influenced

Barry Harris, with whom he had twice recorded for Blue Note in 1965. Gordon and Moody sound eminently compatible throughout three longish titles cut on 2 April. Moody's softer, smaller tone contrasts beautifully with Dexter's. A ten-and-a-half-minute version of 'Lady Bird' – by Gordon's favourite jazz writer Tadd Dameron – perhaps best illustrates the friendly combative nature of their encounter. Two days later, *sans* Moody, Gordon and the same rhythm section completed a further seven titles – each running at over six minutes – of which only one has not been deemed suitable for release. Once again, there is an admirable consistency in his playing which gives the lie to any criticism which might have prevailed at the time to the effect that his long absence from the US jazz scene had in any way diminished his capabilities. A reworking of 'Stanley the Steamer' compares favourably with the Bethlehem recording, and he exudes confidence throughout a long solo which motors with Rolls-Royce-like precision. The lyrical side of Dexter is contained within a tender but strong outing on Jobim's 'Meditation'. The rather trite 'Those were the Days' seems an improbable choice, but in fact he is at his most relaxed on this cut, and this laid-back stance communicates to his colleagues, particularly Harris.

Prestige's next two dates with Gordon (both in 1970) are suitably contrasted, both in terms of geographical locations and contexts. The first is a live recording, at the Montreux Jazz Festival. It is a puzzle indeed as to why a uniformly superb set such as Dexter Gordon with Junior Mance at Montreux should have had to wait until the mid-1980s before its initial release. From the opening bars of his own 'Fried Bananas' (one of the items he'd recorded for Prestige at the second date in April 1969), Gordon is in total command, and his playing has a magisterial quality throughout this and the remaining four selections. Of the latter, there is a stunning interpretation of 'Sophisticated Lady' – his hugeness of sound in no way obliterates the heart-on-sleeve emotional content – and a personal contribution to 'Blue Monk' which demonstrates his awareness of the harmonic/rhythmic uniqueness of its composer's work – and, in this particular instance, its oblique humour.

Pianist Mance, in his only appearance on record with Gordon, must take credit for providing stimulating accompaniments behind the tenor solos, as well as making his own hard-swinging solo contributions to what must have been one of the finest sets seen and heard at the Swiss festival in 1970.

Prestige was on hand during another of Gordon's trips back home, recording him at its New York studios on 7 July. Another quartet session, it presented him with the opportunity to record for the first time with another top jazz keyboardist of the day: Tommy Flanagan. Flanagan, whose impeccable taste, distinctive touch and elegant style had long since made him a popular accompanist, had a special gift for working behind the finest singers. Flanagan's skills are amply evidenced throughout the session with Gordon, nowhere more sensitively employed than for 'Body and Soul' (which Gordon also had taped at Montreux in June). This version remains Dexter's finest on record, a magnificent performance in every way. Never a note wasted, deeply felt, and covering practically the entire range of his skills as a ballad player, his interpretation is a masterpiece, an assessment with which Dan Morgenstern agreed, in his *Down Beat* review, adding: 'From a non-historical perspective, it is simply one of the loveliest ballad performances you'll ever hear.' 'Body and Soul' apart, there is much trenchant, full-blooded blowing on the non-ballad numbers (e.g. 'The Blues Walk', and the minor blues, 'The Panther').

Following a well-received appearance at the Newport Jazz Festival – where he was presented in another quartet setting, this one featuring Kenny Burrell – Gordon paid a visit to Chicago, as part of a cross-country tour. Here, Prestige reunited him with his old buddy from Eckstine days, Gene Ammons. The venue was the North Park Hotel, and Prestige recorded Ammons's resident quartet, on its own and with Dexter guesting on some numbers. Much of the music recorded at both the afternoon and evening sets has never been issued, but the highlights of the occasion have appeared on one album at least and are, not surprisingly, classic 'duels' between Dexter and Gene. Of obvious interest is the pair's ten-minute revival of 'The Chase', during which both men appear to be enjoying every moment of each other's company. There are all the classic ingredients of a 'Chase'-type performance: the huge swing, the crowd-pleasing devices (the honks and squeals, and the outrageous quotes), and the sheer joy of playing together, with nothing at all to prove. 'Lonesome Lover Blues', with Vi Redd adding some basic vocal blues, is less extrovert than 'The Chase', but no less compelling. 'Wee Dot' has blistering Gordon tenor, and 'Polka Dots and Moonbeams' has fine ballad playing, but no Ammons.

Before his departure to Europe, Prestige booked Dexter for yet another date, this one in New York. Another quartet setting, it afforded him the chance to work with Wynton Kelly, a pianist he had long admired from afar, and for the one and only occasion. This was another brainwave by Prestige, for Kelly and Gordon sound at all times as if they have been working regularly together for years. Dexter imbues Dameron's 'If You Could See Me Now' with an intensely yearning quality, presents his rhythmic credentials in a most logical manner for 'Straight, No Chaser', and dominates 'The Jumpin' Blues' with a statement of awesome impact. The influence of Coltrane makes itself felt from time to time at the session, most notably during his own blues 'Evergreenish', as well as the standard 'For Sentimental Reasons'.

A further visit, in 1972, coincided with Gordon's two final studio dates for Prestige. The first (22 June) finds him reacting joyfully to the catalytic presence of Freddie Hubbard, and the collective contributions of another superior rhythm trio (Cedar Walton, Buster Williams, Billy Higgins). All the participants are on best form, with Gordon and Hubbard striking sparks off each other during each of the four numbers on which they appear (including an intriguing arrangement of Dory Previn's 'Scared to be Alone', which is double-timed throughout). Nevertheless, probably the single most memorable solo high-light is Dexter's soulful reading of 'Days of Wine and Roses', the only time Hubbard isn't present.

Thad Jones, another of the finest post-war trumpet players, took Hubbard's place for 28 June, with yet another stellar rhythm section: Hank Jones, Stanley Clarke and Louis Hayes.

The standard of performance throughout this date remains as high as its predecessor's. It is regrettable that Gordon and Thad Jones did not record together, this one occasion aside, because, as the results of this session prove conclusively, despite their supremely individual qualities – Jones, with his distinctive tone, his highly original use of intervals – they are *en rapport*, in every way. The partnership is particularly rewarding during two Gordon blues originals: 'August Blues' and 'What It was'. But Dexter, with just piano, bass and drums, takes charge of 'The First Time Ever I Saw Your Face': he really gets inside Ewan McColl's moving lyric, projecting an aching tenderness which few other tenorists could achieve. The song provided Roberta Flack with a chart-topping hit record in 1972.

Gordon's final Prestige recording found him, once again, at the Montreux Jazz Festival, this time in 1973. It was the occasion for a warm and friendly reunion with one of his friends from Central Avenue days, who was himself touring Europe. Hampton Hawes led a typical Montreux pick-up rhythm section, including the great Kenny Clarke, and although the music which Prestige taped on 7 July doesn't represent the best of either Dexter or the gifted pianist, there is an undisguised empathy between them that brings to a performance such as 'Some Other Spring' an air of truth and dignity.

The Prestige recordings were obviously important for keeping his reputation on a high plane back in the States, even though his home base continued to remain Copenhagen, and even though the periodic trips back home seldom resulted in his figuring prominently in either of the *Down Beat* polls (except for a sudden third placing among the top tenors in the '69 Critics' Poll).

Certainly, though, Gordon's fame rarely dipped in Europe, thanks in no small part to the many recordings he made for a variety of local labels, under his own name as well as with other artists. Of the European companies, his most prolific recordings were made for the Danish-based SteepleChase outfit, run with care and efficiency by Nils Winther. With SteepleChase, he was able to perform alongside the very best of both the local jazz talent, as well as fellow expatriates, and occasionally other visiting top Americans. The overall quality of Gordon's work for SteepleChase, in a series of recordings made between May 1974 and November 1976, is a tribute not only to Winther's astuteness in providing the right kind of settings and assembling the ideal players but also to Dexter's own continued excellence. The first of these – started in May 1974 and completed the following September – finds him in the congenial company of three musicians who had by then become regular associates. Kenny Drew, Niels-Henning Ørsted Pedersen and Albert 'Tootie' Heath are very much a working band, and the trio, plus Gordon, coalesce beautifully. Each of the six issued titles has something to commend it, but perhaps the most memorable performance is a deeply-felt 'Old Folks', with Gordon accompanied only by Pedersen's responsive bass.

The quartet setting proved the most popular for the SteepleChase series. A uniformly fine session in March 1975, with Horace Parlan taking over from Drew and with another American, Tony Inzalaco, relieving Heath of drum duties, produced further musical excellence at another Copenhagen get-together. Both 'Just Friends' and 'Stablemates' find Dexter in a dominant mood. Just for one number ('In a Sentimental Mood') he forsakes the Selmer tenor passed on to him by Ben Webster to produce a sensitive, beseeching solo on soprano. Another quartet date, in September, has Pedersen and Gordon assisted this time by Tete Montoliu and Billy Higgins. As with the Parlan–Inzalaco session, there is much superb blowing from Dexter and his cohorts. 'Billie's Bounce' is taken for a blistering ride – as indeed is Dexter's own 'Benji's Bounce' (a dedication to the then newly-born Benjamin Gordon, Jr). 'Easy Living' is, simply, a classic piece of Gordon balladeering.

Quite apart from the customary tenor–piano–bass–drums format, Nils Winther also took the opportunity to present Dexter within a context that was not only different but which he hoped would inspire the great tenor player. Certainly, it was something approaching pure inspiration when the Danish producer invited him into his Copenhagen studios, along with Pedersen and Higgins, in September 1975. This time, the Gordon tenor would be juxtaposed with the guitar artistry of

London-born Philip Catherine, a resident of Belgium for many years. Catherine's presence has a restraining effect on Gordon, but he is in no way inhibited. Indeed, he positively revels in the freedom afforded him by such tunes as 'Winther's Calling' and 'Freddie Freeloader'.

For years, Dexter Gordon had nurtured a wish to record with a section of strings. The opportunity came, finally, in February 1975, when he recorded together with an orchestra comprising brass, reeds, woodwind, rhythm, *et al*, under the leadership of the talented Danish trumpeter/arranger/conductor Palle Mikkelborg. Mikkelborg's arrangements, complex as well as exquisite, bring out all the essential beauty in Dexter's playing, and he responds with a restrained passion that is as moving as it is beautiful. His playing of the title track – 'More than You Know' – is sumptuous, and his reading of 'Naima' (switching, appropriately, to soprano) is in itself a personal, respectful salute to its composer. ('The Girl with the Purple Eyes', recorded by a ten-piece outfit just over a month later, has much expressive tenor work, together with another elegant Mikkelborg arrangement.) Dexter Gordon himself remembers the origins of the *More than You Know* LP, with no little affection:

I told Nils Winther it had always been a particular dream to do something like that – with strings and full orchestra . . . like Bird and Clifford Brown did . . . Of course, the next thing was to think about who would be the writer, the arranger. I'd worked with Palle. He'd been working with the radio band in Copenhagen. I was familiar with his writing and his talent. So I suggested him. Actually, it was done in about a couple of months. The recording took a few days. It was done partly ensemble, partly by doubling . . . I knew how seriously dedicated Palle was. I thought he would be *the* guy. Which turned out to be quite true. Some people, though, didn't accept the album too well. They would tell me: 'Yes, it's a nice album. But I want to hear you blowing.'

Following the completion of the *More than You Know* album, and the completion of the *Stable Mate* LP, Nils Winther took along his recording equipment to the Nova Park, for the Zurich Jazz Festival, to record two consecutive nights of the appearance by the Dexter Gordon Quartet, on 23 and 24 August 1975. It was worth the trip, for Gordon, together with Drew, Pedersen and Alex Riel, were in tremendous form. The leader himself was virtually unstoppable, rampaging through chorus after chorus of 'Tenor Madness', 'Wave', 'There is no Greater Love' and 'Rhythm-A-Ning'. On the ballads, such as 'Didn't We', 'Sophisticated Lady', 'Darn that Dream' and 'You've Changed', he was both soulful and tender. And Dexter's natural exuberance extended to a rare vocal outing – on Eckstine's 'Jelly Jelly' – at one stage during the second day's proceedings.

Apart from a Gordon quartet session, in New York in November 1976, the Zurich Jazz Festival sessions represented the final SteepleChase recordings – except, of course, for the remarkable series of direct radio transmissions which Danish Radio broadcast from the Montmartre Jazzhus. Together, they represent a perfect testimony to the kind of impact which Dexter had made upon the local Copenhagen scene following his arrival there from London. Whatever personal problems he might have been experiencing at the time, his playing always sustains a tremendous authority. He performs with a kind of ruthless dynamism that brooks no argument.

Ranging from an exhilarating 'I'll Remember April' – and that storms along at a blistering rate of knots – to an anguished 'Cry Me a River', both dating from a live transmission from the Jazzhus, the series of broadcasts emanating from the Copenhagen club are never less than memorable. For the most part, Gordon's associates are Montoliu, Pedersen and Alex Riel. Just how much that particular trio grew in stature (Benny Nielsen replaces Pedersen for a 25 June transmission) can be gauged by its individual and collective contributions to 'Billie's Bounce', from the 20 August broadcast. Throughout, Gordon maintains a position of absolute pre-eminence. It is indicative of his personal involvement in proceedings that he acts as master of ceremonies with warmth, humour and a sense of the occasion. This was, after all, Dexter's own radio series – an hour-long show – and he took full advantage of the fact.

Recording Dexter Gordon in live performance – especially with regard to the kind of excitement he could engender in those post-1962 days – wasn't confined to SteepleChase Records during the sixties. British producer Alan Bates shrewdly taped three nights at the Jazzhus, in July 1967, with the redoubtable Drew–Pedersen–Heath team in close support. The results were fairly predictable, with Dexter steaming through the more forceful numbers such as 'There will Never be Another You', 'Doxy' and 'Sonnymoon for Two', and handling the ballads ('Body and Soul', 'For All We Know') with tender care. Two years later, Dutchmen Joop Visser and Hans Dulfer taped the two sets which Gordon performed at the Paradiso, Amsterdam, accompanied by an all-Dutch rhythm section. While not quite as stimulating as the Jazzhus dates, there is much superior Gordon to be heard, including a biting 'Scrapple from the Apple' and a wondrously compelling 'Willow, Weep for Me'.

A live recording was to become the focal point of Dexter Gordon's return to the United States. Titled, appropriately, *Homecoming*, it also celebrated the fact that Dexter had been signed to a major US record label for the first time, and his acceptance, finally, as an artist of real stature.

The reception of *Homecoming*, from both a critical as well as a record-buying standpoint was, to put it mildly, enthusiastic. It was a perfect way for the jazz prodigal to make an official return to his homeland, performing at a consistently high level, showcased within a regular working band (Woody Shaw's), with the leader's fine trumpet playing complementing Dexter admirably. Whatever problems Bruce Lundvall might have had to contend with in signing him to Columbia, *Homecoming* (a double album) did the trick – ensuring that Gordon would be recording for the major company for a few more albums at least – and both the contract and the success of the project, recorded live at the Village Vanguard, were the twin clinchers that gave Dexter the incentive to make his personal homecoming a reality.

For many of those who thronged the Vanguard during that

memorable season, as indeed for others not as fortunate, but who purchased the recording, it was a rich new experience. Although the audiences comprised a fascinating selection from various age-groups, they contained a healthy number of youngsters, new to the jazz scene and with little or no experience of observing Gordon at first hand. The impact he created at the Vanguard seems to have been attributable as much to Dexter's personal charisma as to the nightly tenor outpourings from the bandstand.

The success of *Homecoming* not only gave reassurance to any of Lundvall's doubting executive colleagues, but it also gave Dexter's new record producer Michael Cuscuna the chance to think of the next album project, a studio recording this time, and one which wouldn't be confined to being simply a tenor-with-rhythm blowing session. In fact, for the follow-up LP, he had Gordon fronting an eleven-piece outfit, with Slide Hampton not only playing solo trombone, but also writing a series of first-class arrangements.

Producer Michael Cuscuna remembers just how involved Dexter was in its preparation:

> Dexter was always willing to listen and consider any intelligent idea, but of course he always had a gentle, final deciding vote on everything. During this album, I realized that Dexter had made hundreds of sessions in his time. Like most highly intelligent people, he had a low boredom threshold. Something had to interest him before he would become actively involved and inspired in a project. This wonderful ensemble and arrangements and the first-class way in which it was done (with enough time and money to do it properly and pay everyone well) inspired Dexter to pick a beautifully varied selection of material and to make love to it in the studio. This is still his favourite (or at least one of his favourite) albums.

Different, of course, in concept from *Homecoming*, *Sophisticated Giant* is, if anything, even more of an artistic triumph than its predecessor. With Hampton supplying a splendid brass-based backdrop, Gordon is totally in command through-out the entire two-day proceedings (it was recorded 21, 22 June 1977). He is passionate, forthright, and hugely swinging on such as a bossa-tinged 'Red Top', Woody Shaw's dynamic 'Moontrane' and a torrid reprise of his own 'Fried Bananas' (with the composer's solo peppered with a string of some of his favourite quotes). Of the five LPs he would record for Columbia between 1976 and 1980, *Sophisticated Giant* prob-ably remains Dexter's own favourite.

For one thing, he had been encouraged by Cuscuna into embarking on an out-of-the-ordinary recording situation, and he obviously responded to the opportunity of making his own contribution to the album's concept.

> I wanted to do something different, even though I didn't know that it was going to build into such a colossus! I had an idea in mind, because the last several years in Europe I'd had occasion to work with Slide, doing occasional big-band things and playing his music. I fell in love with his writing – and his playing – and shortly before I went back to the States we did a couple of concerts with the Woody Shaw–Louis Hayes Quintet, plus Slide and myself . . . the concept of the sound was very beautiful. I loved it. And I heard the possibilities in that. So, when we started talking about doing this new album, this was more or less what I had in mind.

A lot of thought went into putting the Hampton-led band together, and Dexter was particularly careful about the rhythm section (George Cables, Rufus Reid, Victor Lewis). He also suggested that the sound of Bobby Hutcherson's vibes would add a further dimension to the ensemble sound – quite apart from the session benefiting from Hutcherson's consistently superb solo work. And it was Gordon who agreed with Hampton that Howard Johnson, doubling on tuba and baritone sax, should provide the 'bottom' to the band; it was also he who felt that flute, scored with vibes, could provide yet another piece of sound colour. ('Slide says, yes, we ought to have someone that doubled saxophone and flute, then you wouldn't have to be playing parts *all* the time. So, that's where Frank Wess came in. And his flute thing was just unbelievable . . .')

After picking the personnel, there was time to select the tunes, which would include, apart from the aforementioned items, two standards which would draw from Gordon two of his very finest latterday ballad statements: 'Laura' and 'You're Blasé'. In addition, Jobim's 'How Insensitive' became a showcase for some touching work on soprano, an instrument with which Gordon had been dabbling for a couple of years.

The advantages of recording with a giant company like Columbia were obvious: more money, more time to plan and execute such a project, and, as Dexter recalls with great satisfaction, the ability to make a firm request for a particular sideman – even if he lived several thousands of miles away in Europe. This is how he and Cuscuna managed to obtain the services of one of the great unsung heroes of the trumpet, to work alongside the already selected Woody Shaw, supplying the occasional brilliant solo and sterling lead.

> Well, this was *Columbia*. I said: 'I want Benny Bailey.' Because the other trumpet player had to be someone special to play with Woody. It had to be somebody strong, somebody positive, and yet sensitive. It had to be somebody that Woody dug. I knew he loved Benny. So when I said: 'Benny Bailey', that was it. We flew him in from Munich. I was very happy to be able to do that. A luxury for me? Yes. Everything was cool!

So satisfied was he with how the rhythm section performed during *Sophisticated Giant* that Dexter Gordon took them on the road on a permanent basis (even though Victor Lewis had to rejoin Woody Shaw, to be replaced by the equally excellent Eddie Gladden). The Cables–Reid–Gladden trio, alone, supported Dexter for the next Columbia album, taped on four consecutive dates at the beginning of May 1978. Again, the level of performance from all concerned is impressive. The leader responds to the opportunity of playing Coltrane's

'Moment's Notice' (suggested by Cuscuna), and he sounds absolutely irrepressible during both 'LTD' (a reworking of his own 'Long Tall Dexter'), and Cables's light, flowing 'I Told You So'. And the kind of world-weariness he injects into 'As Time Goes By' is, simply, magnificent.

A superior version of Monk's 'Ruby, My Dear', recorded at the first of the May dates, failed to gain inclusion on *Manhattan Symphonie*, but it did form part of *Great Encounters*, the following Columbia LP, the remainder of whose contents were cut either on 23 September 1978 or 26 January 1979. The two items from the first of these latter dates finds Gordon reunited with fellow tenorist Johnny Griffin, supported by the former's regular rhythm trio. It contains plenty of fine, roaring tenor chasing from both, with Dexter obviously relishing the friendly combative spirit of a live date, at New York's City Hall. The classic Ammons–Stitt feature 'Blues Up and Down', running for almost fifteen minutes, evokes memories of Dexter and Wardell and 'The Chase'.

Elsewhere, inside the CBS Recording Studios, New York, the Gordon quartet responds happily to the additional presence of trombonist Curtis Fuller, a temporarily returned Woody Shaw and, most intriguing of all, the late, great jazz vocalist Eddie Jefferson. It is Jefferson, more than any of the other participants, who makes 'It's Only a Paper Moon' such a delight.

It was to be another year and a half before Dexter Gordon would produce further recordings for Columbia that would actually be released. (The contents of two separate sessions – from 1 February 1979 and 30/31 May, 1 June 1980 – were deemed not suitable for release. However, he did record for Columbia, between 3 and 5 March 1979, as a member of the truly star-studded CBS Jazz All Stars, at the Karl Marx Theatre, in Havana Cuba.) The resultant album – *Gotham City* – was to be his last for the label. And, apart from two versions of 'Have Yourself a Merry Little Christmas', taped the following November – for promotional use only – it would remain his final recording for Columbia.

For the occasion, a brand-new rhythm section is on hand – Cedar Walton, Percy Heath, Art Blakey – and sharing front-line duties with Gordon are Shaw or George Benson. Neither Shaw nor Benson is present for 'A Nightingale Sang in Berkeley Square'. After a tender rubato thematic statement, Dexter uncorks yet another superb ballad performance. While nothing startling occurs elsewhere, there is never any lack of inspiration. Obviously, Dexter relishes the presence of Benson, at their one and only recording date thus far, and the pair provide mutual inspiration during an effervescent performance of Dexter's own fine, B-flat twelve-bar 'Gotham City'. And Shaw and Gordon are completely *en rapport* during a tensile version of Clifford Brown's 'The Blues Walk (Loose Walk)'.

During the Columbia period, Dexter's other recording activities had produced little of consequence. An overblown, star-studded, ill-conceived presentation at the 1977 Montreux Jazz Festival finds him coasting through his own solos in a not surprisingly uninterested manner. A guest appearance in November the same year, with an impressive seven-piece combo led by Lionel Hampton, is depressing for his listless solos throughout – using both tenor and soprano; and he is clearly not at his best during his two appearances at a Philly Joe Jones date, for Galaxy, less than a month later.

Of infinitely greater interest are a series of expressive Gordon solos, recorded by Todd Barkan at the Keystone Korner, in May 1978 and March 1979. Supported magnificently by his own trio, and with George Cables vying with the leader for solo honours, he is heard at or very near to his best. 'Come Rain or Come Shine' (from 16 May) and 'Easy Living' (24 March) both contain elements of Gordon's finest work of the past twenty years.

But the impending near-disaster is all too well illustrated throughout most of the two albums he cut for the Bruce Lundvall-instigated Elektra-Musician label, in 1982. Perhaps only 'Skylark' – itself overlong and never totally inspired – has Gordon playing anywhere near to his best form, and there is an aura of inconsistency about his playing on the issued numbers recorded at the Aurex Jazz Festival in September, which augurs not at all well for the future.

Since those '82 dates, the only recordings by Dexter Gordon

have been his contributions to the companion albums whose contents were taped for the soundtrack of *'Round Midnight*. That his playing is scarcely representative of his best is not at all surprising. Bearing in mind his near-death condition of the previous year, however, it was a miracle he could actually make any musical contributions whatsoever to the movie. Naturally, his solos are, of necessity, restricted in length, and it is no surprise that of the respective tunes featuring his tenor or soprano saxes, it is the ballads which are most successful. Best of all is his melancholy 'As Time Goes By', issued as part of the Grammy-winning Blue Note album, *The Other Side of 'Round Midnight*.

Dexter Gordon is presently a pacted Blue Note recording artist, but as yet he has not added to his *'Round Midnight* titles for the famous label. At the time of completing this book, there was no definite date for him to make his first post-*'Round Midnight* Blue Note date. Just how viable he is, at present anyway, as a recording artist in his own right, remains to be seen.

Even if he were never to make another recording date, Dexter's not inconsiderable personal discography is a uniformly impressive one. There are gaps at certain intervals during his sometimes troubled life – most notably during the fifties – and there have been times when his inspiration has temporarily deserted him; overall, though, his legacy, up to and including *'Round Midnight*, is in itself a testimony to his greatness.

12

Coda

Considering his near-to-death condition before the advent of *'Round Midnight*, Dexter Gordon's post-1986 status has been almost miraculous in its impact. Quite apart from being nominated as Best Actor, at the 59th Academy Awards, he has been continuing to recover in general health, has been painstakingly working himself back into some kind of regular work routine . . . and has been the regular recipient of a number of honours and commendations.

In terms of actual performing, he was chosen in 1987 to be featured soloist – his first gig since the Oscar nominations – with the New York Philharmonic Orchestra, for the world premiere of 'Ellingtones, a Fantasy for Saxophone and Orchestra', by composer David Baker. Before that, 2 December 1986 had been designated Dexter Gordon Day, in Washington, DC, when Dexter received the US Congressional Commendation, and was awarded a grant for Lifetime Achievement (by the National Endowment for the Arts). At the same time, a Frank Alexander Gordon Scholarship was established at the Howard University's College of Medicine – Dexter's father having been one of California's first black doctors.

Later, Gordon was the subject of a major tribute by the university's Department of Fine Arts. Over 2,000 fans packed its Cramton Auditorium as homage was paid by the Howard University Jazz Ensemble. After a star-studded concert, including Jon Faddis, Stanley Jordan, the Terence Blanchard–Donald Harrison Quintet and Nancy Wilson, a brief segment from *'Round Midnight* was shown, and the evening's honoree was called on stage. CBS's George Butler then read a celebratory missive from President Reagan. Ed Birdwell, the National

Endowment for the Arts' Director of Music, offered his congratulations to Gordon on his selection for a Jazz Masters Award. Washington's Dexter Gordon Day Proclamation was presented. So too were roses from the Duke Ellington School of Arts.

Elsewhere, at the 1987 Chicago Jazz Festival's Grant Park, Dexter played to a sympathetic audience. Later in the year, *Down Beat*'s Art Lange, reporting from the Umbria Jazz Festival, suggested that the 'evening belonged to Dex'.

Since putting down the music for the *'Round Midnight* soundtrack, Gordon has made no further visits to the recording studios. A projected date for June 1988, to have been produced by Michael Cuscuna, was subsequently cancelled. At this stage, it seems unlikely that further recording projects will materialize.

Just what the future means for Dexter is uncertain. The latest reports, filmwise, suggest he has been looking at another film script, nothing more. In September last, a Japanese tour, with Dexter reprising the 'Ellingtones' piece, has by all accounts been a triumph.

There seems little doubt that Dexter has been gradually building his strength, making sure he is able to pace himself for future gigs. But will it be enough? Is there going to be a playing future for Dexter Gordon? For those who have followed his fortunes over the years, there has to be an element of doubt. For Roy Carr, another lifelong admirer, it is a matter of consideration.

From what I've seen over the last year, he knows his limitations – his physical limitations, not musical. And he might say: 'I'm gonna put myself out to graze for a few years . . . I might play thirty days in a whole year. I might like to go back to Paris and play a concert. I might like to take three or four days to do an album . . . maybe leave it for a month and do a few tracks more. Build up my strength.' Maybe enjoy his new-found popularity. He's obviously realized he can't work full-time. He's probably been told that. If he looks after himself, Dexter could live to be a nice old and happy man. I think Dexter's probably got one good album left in him – he might have another. But I think what he'll do in future is something like he did on the Tony Bennett/Berlin album. I think he will do celebratory guest spots. 'Ladies and Gentlemen . . . playing "'Round Midnight", Dexter Gordon!' And he'll come on and play his four or five choruses . . . Anyway, I think he'll know when he's ready . . .

There can be no doubt that Dexter Gordon will indeed know when he's ready – to play on or call it a day. It's doubtful, though, whether he'll ever change as a person. He'll always be the same kind of amiable character who'll walk through life with the kind of cool that makes him the superstar he has been through the years. Old Central Avenue friend Red Callender remembers recognizing Dexter in Nice last year: 'I walked up behind him and said: "Hi, Movie Star!" He turned, recognized me, and smiled. And he said: *"I only hope I never wake up . . .!"*'

Bibliography

Books:

Gitler, Ira *Jazz Masters of the Forties* (1966: rpt New York: Collier, 1974; London: Collier-Macmillan, 1975)

Gitler, Ira *Swing to Bop* (New York, London: Oxford University Press, 1987)

Gordon, Robert *Jazz West Coast* (New York, London: Quartet Books, 1986)

Priestley, Brian *et al* *Jazz: The Essential Companion* (London: Grafton Books, 1987)

Shaw, Arnold *The Street that Never Slept* (New York: Coward, McCann, McGeoghegan, Inc., 1971)

Magazines:

Beckett, Alan 'Dexter Calling', *Jazz Journal*, October 1962

Berg, Chuck 'Making His Great Leap Forward', *Down Beat*, 10 February 1977

Burns, Jim 'Dexter Gordon 1942–52', *Jazz Journal*, April 1972

Case, Brian 'Dexter Digs In', *New Musical Express*, 18 December 1976

Case, Brian 'The Exile's Return', *Melody Maker*, 27 May 1978

Case, Brian 'Within These Walls', *Melody Maker*, 11 October 1980

Gerber, Alain 'Les Deux Naissances de Dexter', *Jazz Magazine* (No. 176), March 1970

Gitler, Ira 'Dexter Gordon: The Time for Recognition', *Down Beat*, 9 November 1961

Gitler, Ira   'Dexter Drops In', *Down Beat*, 29 May 1969

Hennessey, Mike   'Dexter Gordon: First of the Jazz Commuters', *Melody Maker*, 30 October 1965

Hennessey, Mike   'Drugs – and Dexter Gordon', *Melody Maker*, 23 July 1966

James, Michael   'Dexter Gordon – A Crucial Study', *Jazz Monthly*, March 1961

Mandel, Howard   ''Round Midnight', *Down Beat*, January 1987

Shera, Michael   'The Resurgence of Dexter Gordon', *Jazz Journal*, June 1966

Tesser, Neil   'Flash Gordon', *Rolling Stone*, 6 November 1986

Zwerin, Mike   'There is a Tavernier in the Town', *Wire*, August 1985

Discography
by Don Tarrant

The following discography of Dexter Gordon lists all known material issued on record, together with any significant appearances on film. Each title is given an original catalogue number, and in cases where there were both mono and stereo releases, the stereo issue is the one listed. These entries are cross-referenced to an index of catalogue numbers for currently available issues, where applicable, and in both discography and index those numbers marked with a single asterisk are compact discs.

Other than those released on record, airshots and private recordings are not included, and because of the lengthy period Gordon spent in Europe, there are many sessions which fall into these categories. For those readers interested in a more comprehensive listing, may I recommend *Long Tall Dexter – The Discography of Dexter Gordon* by Thorbjørn Sjøgren, published in Copenhagen in 1986, and available from jazz specialist dealers.

The following abbreviations have also been used:

AFRS: Armed Forces Radio Service
arr: arranger
as: alto saxophone
b: double bass
bcl: bass clarinet
bgo: bongo
bs: baritone saxophone
btb: bass trombone
cel: celeste
cga: conga

cl: clarinet
cnt: cornet
cond: conductor
D: Danish
d: drums
dir: director
Du: Dutch
E: English
eh: english horn
elb: electric bass

elp: electric piano	p: piano
Eu: European	perc: percussion
F: French	picc: piccolo
Fin: Finnish	S: Swedish
fl: flute	Sp: Spanish
flh: flugelhorn	ss: soprano saxophone
frh: french horn	str: stritch
G: Germany	synth: synthesizer
g: guitar	tb: trombone
hca: harmonica	timb: timbales
I: Italian	tp: trumpet
J: Japanese	ts: tenor saxophone
keyb: keyboards	tu: tuba
manz: manzello	vb: vibraphone
mar: marimba	vcl: vocal
n.c.: not complete	vln: violin
org: organ	vtb: valve trombone

1941:
December 24   LIONEL HAMPTON AND HIS ORCHESTRA
New York City   Karl George, Joe Newman, Ernie Royal (tp); Fred Beckett,
                     Sonny Craven, Harry Sloan (tb); Marshall Royal (as, cl); Ray
                     Perry (as, vln); Dexter Gordon, Illinois Jacquet (ts); Jack
                     McVea (bs); Lionel Hampton (vb, vcl–1); Milt Buckner (p);
                     Irving Ashby (g); Vernon Alley (b); George Jenkins (d); Rubel
                     Blakey (vcl–2)

70100-A	Just for You – 2	Decca 18265
70101-A	Southern Echoes – 1	Decca 18285
70101-?	Southern Echoes – 1	MCA(F) 510 140
70102-A	My Wish – 2	Decca 18265
70103-A	Nola	Decca 18285

1943:
late 1943   DEXTER GORDON QUINTET
Los Angeles   Harry Edison (tp); Dexter Gordon (ts); Nat Cole (p); Johnny
                   Miller (b); poss. Juicy Owens (d)

1892	I Found a New Baby	(1) Mercury/Clef 8900
1893	Rosetta	(1) —
1894	Sweet Lorraine	(1) Phoenix Jazz LP 5
1895	I Blowed and Gone	(1) —

Note: Phoenix Jazz LP 5 isued as by NAT KING COLE.

1944:
April 24   FLETCHER HENDERSON AND HIS ORCHESTRA
Broadcast,   Tony DiNardi, Jake Porter, Clint Waters, Leroy White (tp);
Hollywood   Allen Durham, George Washington (tb); Edmund Gregory
                   (Sahib Shihab), Emerson Harper (as); Dexter Gordon, Wood-
                   row Keys (ts); Herman Johnson (bs); Horace Henderson (p);

"Chief"? (b); Gene Shelton (d); Fletcher Henderson (cond)

One O'Clock Jump (Theme)	AFRS Jubilee 76
I Got Rhythm	—
Keep 'em Swinging	—
Stompin' at the Savoy	—
Bugle Blues	—
One O'Clock Jump (Theme)	—

May 1
Broadcast,
Hollywood

One O'Clock Jump (Theme)	AFRS Jubilee 77
Jeep Rhythm	—
Rose Room	—
Clap Hands, Here Comes Charlie	—
One O'Clock Jump (Theme)	—

May 19–20
Broadcast,
prob. New York

LOUIS ARMSTRONG AND HIS ORCHESTRA
Prob. personnel: Louis Armstrong (tp, vcl–1); Jesse Brown, Lester Currant, Andrew Ford, Thomas Grider (tp); Larry Anderson, Taswell Baird, Adam Martin (tb); John Brown, Willard Brown (as); Dexter Gordon, Teddy McRae (ts); Ernest Thompson (bs); Ed Swanston (p); Emmett Slay (g); Alfred Moore (b); James Harris (d); Velma Middleton (vcl–2); Jimmy Ross (vcl–3)

Ain't Misbehavin' – 1	AFRS One Night Stand 240
I Lost My Sugar in Salt Lake City – 1	—
Besame Mucho – 3	—
A Pretty Girl is Like a Melody – 1	—
Swanee River	—
Baby, Don't You Cry – 1	—
Don't Sweetheart Me – 2	—
Easy as You Go	AFRS One Night Stand 253
Blues in the Night – 1	—
I Couldn't Sleep a Wink Last Night – 1	—
I'll be Around – 2	—
Keep on Jumpin'	—

May 23
Broadcast,
unknown location

unknown titles	AFRS One Night Stand 267

May 26
Broadcast,
Trianon Ballroom,
South Gate,
California

No Love, No Nothin'	(2)	Swing House (E) SWH 44
Is My Baby Blue Tonight? – 2	(2)	—
Blues in the Night – 1	(2)	—
Keep on Jumpin' – n.c.	(2)	—

June 7
Broadcast,
Stockton,

King Porter Stomp	AFRS Spotlight Bands 382
It's Love, Love, Love – 1	—
Ain't Misbehavin' – 1	—

California	When It's Sleepy Time Down South – 1	—

August 9		
Los Angeles	Add Dorothy Dandridge (vcl–4)	
DLA 3500-A	Groovin'	Decca DL 9225
DLA 3501-A	Baby, Don't You Cry – 1	Rare Records (F) LP 6
DLA 3502-A	Whatcha Say – 1,4	MCA Coral (G) 82055

August 18	Louise – 1	AFRS Spotlight Bands 444
Broadcast,	Going My Way – 1	—
Fort Wachuka,	Sweet and Lovely – 3	—
Arizona	Groovin'	—
	Is You is or is You Ain't My Baby – 1,2	—

September 12	Perdido	(3) AFRS Spotlight Bands 465
Broadcast,	Brother Bill – 1	(3) —
Camp Reynolds,	Time Alone Will Tell – 3	—
Philadelphia	Is You is or is You Ain't My Baby – 1,2	—
	Ain't Misbehavin' – 1	(3) —
	Groovin'	(3) —
	King Porter Stomp – n.c.	—

October 5	Theme	(4) AFRS Spotlight Bands 486
Broadcast,	Keep on Jumpin'	(4) —
Tuskogee Airfield,	Swingin' on a Star – 1	(4) —
Alabama	Sweet and Lovely – 3	(4) —
	I'm Confessin' – 1	(4) —
	It Had to be You – 2	(4) —

December 5
New York City

BILLY ECKSTINE AND HIS ORCHESTRA

Gail Brockman, Dizzy Gillespie, Marion Hazel, Shorty McConnell (tp); Taswell Baird, Chippy Outcalt, Howard Scott (tb); Gerald Valentine (tb, arr–1); Bill Frazier, John Jackson (as); Gene Ammons, Dexter Gordon (ts); Leo Parker (bs); John Malachi (p, arr–2); Connie Wainwright (g); Tommy Potter (b); Art Blakey (d); Billy Eckstine (vtb, vcl–3); Sarah Vaughan (vcl–4); Tadd Dameron (arr–5)

118-2	If That's the Way You Feel – 1,3	(4a) DeLuxe 2001
119-4	I Want to talk about You – 3,5	(4a) DeLuxe 2003
120-1	Blowing the Blues Away – 1,3	(4a) Audio Lab AL 1549
120-3	Blowing the Blues Away – 1, 3	(4a) DeLuxe 2001
121-2	Opus X – 2	(4a) DeLuxe 2002
122	I'll Wait and Pray – 4, 5	(4a) DeLuxe 2003
123	The Real Thing Happened to Me	(4a) DeLuxe 2002

1945:

February 9
New York City

DIZZY GILLESPIE SEXTET
Dizzy Gillespie (tp); Dexter Gordon (ts); Frank Paparelli (p); Chuck Wayne (g); Murray Shipinski (b); Irv Kluger *or* Shelly Manne (d)

554-A	**Groovin' High**	Phoenix Jazz LP 16
555-B	**Blue 'n' Boogie**	(5) Guild 1001

Note: A few copies of Guild 1001 were coupled with the above version of Groovin' High instead of the Gillespie recording of February 28, 1945 which does not include Gordon.
Phoenix Jazz LP 16 issued as PHOENIX JAZZ FIFTH ANNIVERSARY ALBUM.

May 2
New York City

BILLY ECKSTINE AND HIS ORCHESTRA
As for December 5, 1944 except Fats Navarro (tp); Budd Johnson, Sonny Stitt (as) replace Gillespie, Frazier and Jackson

NSC53-1	**Lonesome Lover Blues – 3**	(6) National 9015
NSC54-3	**A Cottage for Sale – 3**	(6) National 9014
NSC55-2	**I Love the Rhythm in a Riff – 3**	(6) —
NSC56	**Last Night – 3**	(6) National 9015

August 20
Unknown club,
New York City

JAM SESSION
Don Byas, Herbie Fields, Dexter Gordon, Ben Webster (ts); Stuff Smith (vln); Duke Ellington (p); unknown (g); Al Lucas (b); Eddie Nicholson (d)

Honeysuckle Rose – n.c.   Jazz Archives JA 35
Note: Issued as by BEN WEBSTER

September 4
New York City

SIR CHARLES THOMPSON AND HIS ALL STARS
Buck Clayton (tp); Charlie Parker (as); Dexter Gordon (ts); Sir Charles Thompson (p); Danny Barker (g); Jimmy Butts (b); J.C. Heard (d)

R1030	**Takin' off**	(7) Apollo 757
R1031	**If I Had You (CP out)**	(7) —
R1032	**20th Century Blues**	(7) Apollo 759
R1033-2	**The Street Beat**	(7) —

October 30
New York City

DEXTER GORDON'S ALL STARS
Dexter Gordon (ts); Argonne Thornton (Sadik Hakim) (p); Gene Ramey (b); Eddie Nicholson (d)

S5841-2	**Blow Mr. Dexter**	Savoy SJL 2211
S5841-3	**Blow Mr. Dexter**	(8) Savoy 576
S5842-1	**Dexter's Deck**	(8) —
S5843-1	**Dexter's Cuttin' out**	(8) Savoy 612
S5844-1	**Dexter's Minor Mad**	(8) —

1946:

January 8
New York City

BENNY CARTER AND HIS ORCHESTRA
Emmett Berry, Neal Hefti, Joe Newman, Shorty Rogers (tp); Al Grey, Alton Moore, Trummy Young, Sandy Williams (tb); Benny Carter (as, arr–1); Russell Procope (as); Willard Brown

(as, bs); Tony Scott (as, cl); Don Byas, Dexter Gordon (ts); Sonny White (p); Freddie Green (g); John Simmons (b); J.C. Heard (d); Maxine Sullivan (vcl–2); Frank Comstock (arr–3)

171	I'm the Caring Kind – 1,2	(9) DeLuxe 1012
172	Looking for a Boy – 1,2	(9) DeLuxe 1009
173	Rose Room – 3	(9) DeLuxe 1028

January 29
New York City

DEXTER GORDON QUINTET
Leonard Hawkins (tp); Dexter Gordon (ts); Bud Powell (p); Curley Russell (b); Max Roach (d)

S5878-1	Long Tall Dexter	Savoy SJL 2211
S5878-2	Long Tall Dexter	(8) Savoy 603
S5879-1	Dexter Rides Again	(8) Savoy 623
S5880-3	I Can't Escape from You (LH out)	Savoy SJL 2211
S5880-7	I Can't Escape from You (LH out)	Savoy 595
S5881-2	Dexter Digs in	Savoy SJL 2211
S5881-3	Dexter Digs in	(8) Savoy 595

Note: Some issues of Savoy 623 contained mx S5880-7 in error.

September 21
Los Angeles

NUMA LEE DAVIS WITH RUSSELL JACQUET AND HIS YELLOW JACKETS
Russell Jacquet (tp, vcl–1); Gus Evans (as); Dexter Gordon (ts); Arthur Dennis (bs); Jimmy Bunn (p); Leo Blevins (g); Herman Washington (b); Chico Hamilton (d); Numa Lee Davis (vcl–2)

JRC234-4	Just a Dream – 2	Jewel ON 2000
JRC235-2	Wake Up Old Maid – 2	Savoy SJL 2242
JRC235-5	Wake Up Old Maid – 2	—
JRC235-10	Wake Up Old Maid – 2	Jewel ON 2000
JRC236-5	Blues a la Russ – 1	Savoy SJL 2242
JRC236-7	Blues a la Russ – 1	—
JRC236-11	Blues a la Russ – 1	Jewel ON 2001
JRC237-3	Side Saddle Blues – 1	—

Note: Savoy SJL 2242 issued as BLACK CALIFORNIA VOLUME 2.

1947:
c.mid 1947
Broadcast,
Pasadena,
California

BENNY CARTER AND HIS ORCHESTRA
Exact personnel unknown but including Al Grey (tb); Benny Carter (as, tp); Dexter Gordon, Lucky Thompson (ts); Sonny White (p); Jimmy Cannady (g); Tom Moultrie (b); Percy Brice (d); The Pied Pipers (Clarke Gilben, Hal Hooper, Jane Hutton, Chuck Lowry) (vcl–1)

One O'Clock Jump (Theme)	(10)	AFRS Jubilee 246
Jump Call	(10)	—
My Gal Sal – 1	(10)	—
Prelude to a Kiss		—
Somebody Loves Me		—

June 5 *Hollywood*	DEXTER GORDON QUINTET		
	Melba Liston (tb); Dexter Gordon (ts); Charles Fox (p); Red Callender (b); Chuck Thompson (d)		
D1081-D	Mischievous Lady	(11) Dial 1018	
D1081-E	Mischievous Lady	(12) Dial LP 204	
D1082-C	Lullaby in Rhythm	(11) Dial 1038	
D1082-F	Lullaby in Rhythm	(12) Dial LP 204	

June 12 *Hollywood*	DEXTER GORDON AND WARDELL GRAY		
	Wardell Gray (ts); Jimmy Bunn (p) replace Liston and Fox		
D1083-C	The Chase – n.c.	(11) Dial LP 211	
D1083-D	The Chase part 1	(11) Dial 1017	
D1084-D	The Chase part 2	(11) —	

Same session	DEXTER GORDON QUARTET		
	Gray out		
D1085-B	Chromatic Aberration	(11) Dial LP 204	
D1085-C	Iridescence	(12) Jazztone J 1005	
D1086-A	It's the Talk of the Town	(11) Dial LP 210	
D1086-B	It's the Talk of the Town	(12) Dial 1038	
D1087-A	Blues Bikini	(11) Dial 1022	
	Note: D1086-A issued as On the Town and D1087-A as Bikini on Dial.		

June 19 *Los Angeles*	MARY ANN McCALL WITH RALPH BURNS ORCHESTRA		
	Howard McGhee (tp); Willie Smith (as); Dexter Gordon (ts); Jimmy Rowles (p); Barney Kessel (g); Red Callender (b); Jackie Mills (d); Mary Ann McCall (vcl); Ralph Burns (arr, cond)		
HCO2391-1	Money is Honey	Columbia 35790	
HCO2392-2	I Want a Big Butter and		
	Egg Man	Columbia 38131	
HCO2393-1	On Time	Columbia 35790	

July 6 *Elk's Auditorium,* *Los Angeles*	HOLLYWOOD JAZZ CONCERT		
	Howard McGhee (tp); Trummy Young (tb); Sonny Criss (as); Dexter Gordon, Wardell Gray (ts); Hampton Hawes (p); Barney Kessel (g); Harry Babasin (b); Connie Kay (d)		
BOP 3	The Hunt part 1	(13) Bop 104	
BOP 4	The Hunt part 2	(13) —	
BOP 5	The Hunt part 3	(1?) Bop 105	
BOP 6	The Hunt part 4	(13) —	
BOP 7	The Hunt part 5	(13) Bop 101	
BOP 8	The Hunt part 6	(13) —	
BOP 9	The Hunt part 7	(13) Bop 102	
BOP 10	The Hunt part 8	(13) —	
	Note: Some reissues as Rocks 'n' Shoals.		

	Ken Kennedy (d) replaces Kay		
BOP 15	Bopera part 1	(13) Bop 107	
BOP 16	Bopera part 2	(13) —	
BOP 17	Bopera part 3	(13) Bop 108	
BOP 18	Bopera part 4	(13) —	

BOP 19	Bopera part 5	(13) Bop 109
BOP 20	Bopera part 6	(13) —
BOP 21	Bopera part 7	(13) Bop 110

Note: Reissued as Disorder at the Border.

Criss out; Red Callender (b), Connie Kay (d) replace Babasin & Kennedy

BOP 36	Bopland part 1	(13) Savoy 962
BOP 37	Bopland part 2	(13) —
BOP 38	Bopland part 3	(13) Savoy 963
BOP 39	Bopland part 4	(13) —
BOP 40	Bopland part 5	(13) Savoy 964
BOP 41	Bopland part 6	(13) —

Note: Reissued as Byas-A-Drink.

Same concert — JAZZ CONCERT WEST COAST
Add Sonny Criss (as)

BOP 42	Jeronimo part 1	(13) Bop 111
BOP 43	Jeronimo part 2	(13) —
BOP 44	Jeronimo part 3	(13) Bop 112
BOP 45	Jeronimo part 4	(13) —
BOP 46	Jeronimo part 5	(13) Bop 113
BOP 47	Jeronimo part 6	(13) —
BOP 48	Jeronimo part 7	(13) Bop 114
BOP 49	Jeronimo part 8	(13) —

Note: Reissued as Cherry-Koke, or Cherokee.

Same concert — THE BOPLAND BOYS
Gray out

BOP 54	Bop After Hours part 1	Bop 115
BOP 55	Bop After Hours part 2	—
BOP 56	Bop After Hours part 3	Bop 116
BOP 57	Bop After Hours part 4	—
BOP 58	Bop After Hours part 5	Bop 117
BOP 59	Bop After Hours part 6	—

Note: Reissued as After Hours Bop; a long bass solo has been edited out of this performance.

November 28 — RED NORVO ENSEMBLE
Los Angeles — Ray Linn (tp); Jimmy Giuffre (as–1, ts–2); Dexter Gordon (ts); Red Norvo (vb, p–1); Barney Kessel (g); Red Callender (b); Jackie Mills (d); Shorty Rogers (arr–2)

2626-5D	I'll Follow You – 2	Capitol 15233

Same session — JESSE PRICE AND HIS BAND
Add Jesse Price (vcl)

2627-2D	Baby, Let's be Friends	
	– 1	(13a) Capitol 15138
2628-1D	My Baby Done Left Me	
	– 1 (BK out)	(13a) —

November 30	RED NORVO ENSEMBLE	
Los Angeles	Dodo Marmarosa (p) replaces Price	
2644-4D	Bop! – 2	Capitol 15233

December 4	DEXTER GORDON QUARTET	
Hollywood	Dexter Gordon (ts); Jimmy Rowles (p); Red Callender (b); Roy Porter (d)	
D1141-C	**Ghost of a Chance**	(12) Dial LP 204
D1141-E	**Ghost of a Chance**	(11) Dial 1018
D1142-A	**Sweet and Lovely**	(12) Dial LP 204
D1142-D	**Sweet and Lovely**	(11) Dial 1042

Same session	DEXTER GORDON AND TEDDY EDWARDS	
	Add Teddy Edwards (ts)	
D1143-C	**Hornin' In part 1**	(11) Dial LP 204
D1143-D	**The Duel part 1**	(11) Dial 1028
D1144-C	**Hornin' In part 2**	(11) Dial LP 204
D1144-D	**The Duel part 2**	(11) Dial 1028

December 11	DEXTER GORDON QUINTETTE	
New York City	Dexter Gordon (ts); Leo Parker (bs); Tadd Dameron (p); Curley Russell (b); Art Blakey (d)	
S3491-3	**Settin' the Pace part 1**	(8) Savoy 913
S3492-3	**Settin' the Pace part 2**	(8) —
S3493-2	**So Easy**	Savoy SJL 2211
S3493-3	**So Easy**	(8) Savoy 960
S3494-1	**Dexter's Riff**	Savoy SJL 2211
S3494-2	**Dexter's Riff**	(8) Savoy 960

December 16	WYNONIE HARRIS	
New York City	Bob Merrill (tp); Gerald Valentine (tb); Don Stovall (as); Dexter Gordon, William Parker (ts); Rene Hall (g); unknown (p); (b); (d); Wynonie Harris (vcl)	
K5318	**Snake Hearted Woman Blues**	unissued
K5319	**Wild Woman Blues**	—
K5320	**Baby, Shame on You**	rejected
K5321	**Your Money Don't Mean a Thing**	King 4217

December 19	LEO PARKER'S ALL STARS	
New York City	Joe Newman (tp); J.J. Johnson (tb); Dexter Gordon (ts); Leo Parker (bs); Hank Jones (p); Curley Russell (b); Shadow Wilson (d)	
S3495-1	**Wee Dot**	Savoy SJL 2211
S3495-2	**Wee Dot – n.c.**	(14) Savoy SJL 2225
S3495-3	**Wee Dot**	Savoy 950
S3495-4	**Wee Dot**	(14) Savoy SJL 2225
S3496-2	**Solitude**	(14) Savoy 929
S3497-1	**Lion Roars**	Savoy SJL 2211
S3497-2	**Lion Roars – n.c.**	(14) Savoy SJL 2225
S3497-3	**Lion Roars**	Savoy XP 8060
S3497-4	**Lion Roars**	(14) Savoy SJL 2225

| S3498-3 | **Mad Lad Boogie** | Savoy 929 |

Note: S3497–3 issued as Lion's Roar on Savoy XP 8060. Savoy SJL 2211 issued as by DEXTER GORDON; Savoy SJL 2225 issued as THE BEBOP BOYS.

December 22
New York City

DEXTER GORDON & HIS BOYS

Fats Navarro (tp); Dexter Gordon (ts); Tadd Dameron (p); Nelson Boyd (b); Art Mardigan (d)

S3511-2	**Dexter's Mood** (FN out)	(8) Savoy XP 8080
S3512-2	**Dextrose**	(8) Savoy 955
S3513-2	**Index**	(8) Savoy XP 8023
S3514-2	**Dextivity**	(8) Savoy XP 8022

1949:
January 18
New York City

TADD DAMERON AND HIS ORCHESTRA

Fats Navarro (tp); Kai Winding (tb); Sahib Shihab (Edmund Gregory) (as); Dexter Gordon (ts); Cecil Payne (bs); Tadd Dameron (p); Curley Russell (b); Kenny Clarke (d); Diego Iborra (bgo); Carlos Vidal Bolado (cga); Rae Pearl (vcl–1)

| 3391-3E | **Sid's Delight** | (15) Capitol 57-60006 |
| 3392-3E | **Casbah – 1** | (15)   — |

1950:
August 27
Hula Hut Club,
Sunset Boulevard,
Los Angeles

WARDELL GRAY ALL STARS

Clark Terry (tp); Sonny Criss (as); Dexter Gordon, Wardell Gray (ts); Jimmy Bunn (p); Billy Hadnott (b); Chuck Thompson (d); Damita Joe (vcl–1)

1231	**Jazz on Sunset parts 1 & 2**	Prestige 778
1232	**Jazz on Sunset parts 3 & 4**	Prestige 779
	I Can't Give You Anything	
	but Love – 1	(16) Xanadu 200

Note: Jazz on Sunset parts 1–4 reissued as Move. Gordon out on one other title from this session.

November 20
Los Angeles

HELEN HUMES WITH DEXTER GORDON'S ORCHESTRA

Vernon Smith (tp); Dexter Gordon (ts, dir); Maurice Simon (bs); Ernie Freeman (p, prob. arr); Red Callender (b); J.C. Heard (d); Helen Humes (vcl)

D418	**Ain't Gonna Quit You**	
	Baby	(17) Savoy SJL 2215
D419-4	**Helen's Advice**	(17)(18) Discovery 535
D420	**Knockin' Myself Out**	(17) Savoy SJL 2215
D421-4	**Airplane Blues**	(17)(18) Discovery 535

Note: Savoy SJL 2215 issued as BLACK CALIFORNIA.

1952:
February 2
Civic Auditorium,
Pasadena,
California

GENE NORMAN'S "JUST JAZZ" CONCERT

Conte Candoli (tp); Dexter Gordon, Wardell Gray (ts); Bobby Tucker (p); Don Bagley (b); Chico Hamilton (d)

	The Chase (CC out)	Decca DL 7025
	The Steeplechase	—
	unknown titles	unissued

Same concert	**LES THOMPSON**	
	Add Les Thompson (hca)	
	Take the 'A' Train	Victor LPM 3102
	Robbins' Nest	—
	Stardust	—

Same concert

HELEN HUMES
Unknown (tp); (as); Dexter Gordon (ts); unknown (bs); (p); (g); (b); (d); Helen Humes (vcl)

WL82473	**They Raided the Joint**	(18) Decca 28113
WL82474	**Loud Talkin' Woman**	(18) —
WL82475	**Mean Way of Lovin'**	(18a) Decca 28802
WL82476	**I Cried for You**	(18a) —

Note: Although Gordon is thought to be on this session, it is not entirely proven.

c.June 1952
Hollywood

LOWELL FULSON
Lowell Fulson (g); Dexter Gordon (ts); unknown (bs); (p); (b); (d)

320A+   **Good Party Shuffle**   Swing Time 320
Note: Reissued as Xmas Party Shuffle. Gordon may be present on other titles from this session.

June 9
Hollywood

DEXTER GORDON AND HIS ORCHESTRA
Dexter Gordon, Wardell Gray (ts); Gerry Wiggins (p, org–1, cel–2); Red Callender (b); Chuck Thompson (d); Gladys Bentley (vcl–2)

4120-2	**The Rubaiyat**	Fontana (E) FJL 907
4120-4	**The Rubaiyat**	Swing Time 321
4122	**My Kinda Love – 1 (WG out)**	Swing Time 323
4123-1	**Jingle Jangle Jump - 1,2**	Swing Time 321
4124-1	**Citizen's Bop**	Swing Time 323

Note: Gordon out on other titles from this session.

1955:
September 18
Hollywood

DEXTER GORDON QUARTET
Dexter Gordon (ts); Kenny Drew (p); Leroy Vinnegar (b); Lawrence Marable (d)

Daddy Plays the Horn	(19) Bethlehem BCP 36	
Confirmation	(19)	—
Darn That Dream	(19)	—
Number Four	(19)	—
Autumn in New York	(19)	—
You Can Depend on Me	(19)	—

September 27, 28
Los Angeles

STAN LEVEY SEXTET
Conte Candoli (tp); Frank Rosolino (tb); Dexter Gordon (ts); Lou Levy (p); Leroy Vinnegar (b); Stan Levey (d)

Diggin' for Diz	(20) Bethlehem BCP 37	
Ruby, My Dear	(20)	—
Tune Up	(20)	—
La Chaloupee	(20)	—

	Day in, Day out	(20)	—
	Stanley the Steamer	(20)	—
	This Time the Drum's on Me	(20)	—

November 11, 12
Los Angeles

DEXTER GORDON ALL-STARS
Jimmy Robinson (tp–1); Dexter Gordon (ts); Carl Perkins (p); Leroy Vinnegar (b); Chuck Thompson (d)

Silver Plated – 1	(21)	Dootone DLP 207
Rhythm Mad – 1	(21)	—
Bonna Rue – 1	(21)	—
Cry Me a River	(21)	—
Don't Worry 'bout Me	(21)	—
I Hear Music	(21)	—
I Should Care	(21)	—
Blowin' for Dootsie	(21)	—
Tenderly	(21)	—

1960:
October 13
Los Angeles

DEXTER GORDON SEXTET
Martin Banks (tp); Richard Boone (tb); Dexter Gordon (ts); Dolo Coker (p); Charles Green (b); Lawrence Marable (d)

Dolo (MB, RB out)	Jazzland JLPS 929
Home Run	—
Lovely Lisa	—
Jodi (MB, RB out)	—
Field Day	—
Affair in Havana	—

1961:
May 6
New Jersey

DEXTER GORDON
Freddie Hubbard (tp); Dexter Gordon (ts); Horace Parlan (p); George Tucker (b); Al Harewood (d)

	I was Doing All Right	(22)(22a)	Blue Note BST 84077
	You've Changed	(22)(22a)	—
take?	**For Regulars Only**	(22)(22a)	—
take?	**For Regulars Only**	(22a)	Blue Note CDP7 84077 2*
	Society Red	(22)(22a)	Blue Note BST 84077
	It's You or No One	(22)(22a)	—
	I Want More	(22a)	Blue Note CDP7 84077 2*

May 9
New Jersey

Dexter Gordon (ts); Kenny Drew (p); Paul Chambers (b); Philly Joe Jones (d)

Soul Sister	(23)	Blue Note BST 84083
Modal Mood	(23)	—
I Want More	(23)	—
The End of a Love Affair	(23)	—
Clear the Dex	(23)	—
Ernie's Tune	(23)	—
Smile	(23)	—
Landslide	(23)	Blue Note LT 1051

1962:
May 5
New Jersey

Tommy Turrentine (tp–1); Dexter Gordon (ts); Sir Charles
Thompson (p); Al Lucas (b); Willie Bobo (d)
Love Locked Out   Blue Note LT 1051
You Said It – 1   —
Serenade in Blue   —
Six Bits Jones   rejected
McSplivens   —
How Now   —

May 10
New York City

PONY POINDEXTER AND HIS ORCHESTRA
Pony Poindexter (as, ss); Gene Quill, Phil Woods (as); Dexter
Gordon, Billy Mitchell (ts); Pepper Adams (bs); Gildo
Mahones (p); Bill Yancey (b); Charlie Persip (d); Gene Kee
(arr–1)

C069689	Cattin' Latin – 1	Epic BA 17035
C075264	Pony's Express – 1	—
C075265	Artistry in Rhythm	—
C075266	Salt Peanuts – 1	—
C075267	Struttin' with Some	
	Barbecue – 1	—
	Rudolph, the Red-Nosed	
	Reindeer	Columbia CS 8693

Note: Columbia CS 8693 issued as JINGLE BELL JAZZ.

May 14
New Jersey

SONNY STITT
Sonny Stitt (as, ts); Dexter Gordon (ts); unknown (p); (b); (d)
unknown titles   Blue Note rejected

May 28
New Jersey

HERBIE HANCOCK
Freddie Hubbard (tp, flh); Dexter Gordon (ts); Herbie Han-
cock (p); Butch Warren (b); Billy Higgins (d)
Watermelon Man   (24) Blue Note BST 84109
Three Bags Full   (24)   —
Empty Pockets   (24)   —
The Maze   (24)   —
Driftin'   (24)   —
Alone and I   (24)   —

June 25
New Jersey

DEXTER GORDON
Dave Burns (tp); Dexter Gordon (ts); Sonny Clark (p); Ron
Carter (b); Philly Joe Jones (d)
Blue Gardenia   Blue Note LT 1051
Six Bits Jones   —
Second Balcony Jump   —
Three O'Clock in the Morning rejected
McSplivens   —
My Heart Stood Still   —

August 27 *New Jersey*	Dexter Gordon (ts); Sonny Clark (p); Butch Warren (b); Billy Higgins (d)		
	Cheese Cake	(25)	Blue Note BST 84112
	I Guess I'll Hang My		
	Tears out to Dry	(25)	—
	Second Balcony Jump	(25)	—
	Love for Sale	(25)	—
	Where are You?	(25)	—
	Three O'Clock in the		
	Morning	(25)	—

August 29 *New Jersey*	**Soy Califa**	(25a)	Blue Note BST 84133
	Don't Explain	(25a)	—
	You Stepped out of		
	a Dream	(25a)	—
	The Backbone	(25a)	—
	Until the Real Thing		
	Comes Along	(25a)	—
	McSplivens	(25a)	—

November 28 *Broadcast,* *Jazzhus Montmartre,* *Copenhagen*	DEXTER GORDON & ATLI BJORN TRIO		
	Dexter Gordon (ts); Atli Bjorn (p); Marcel Rigot (b); William Schiopffe (d)		
	I'll Remember April	(26)	SteepleChase (D) SCC 6004
	Cry Me a River	(26)	—

1963: *May 23* *Paris*	DEXTER GORDON		
	Dexter Gordon (ts); Bud Powell (p); Pierre Michelot (b); Kenny Clarke (d)		
	Scrapple from the		
	Apple	(27)(29)	Blue Note BST 84146
	Willow Weep for Me	(27)(29)	—
	Broadway	(27)(29)	—
	Stairway to the Stars	(27)(29)	—
	A Night in Tunisia	(27)(29)	—
	Our Love is Here to		
	Stay	(28)(29)	Blue Note BST 84430

Note: Gordon out on Like Someone in Love from this session.
Blue Note BST 84430 issued as by BUD POWELL.

1964: *June 2* *Paris*	Donald Byrd (tp); Dexter Gordon (ts); Kenny Drew (p); Niels-Henning Orsted Pedersen (b); Art Taylor (d)		
	Tanya	(30)	Blue Note BST 84176
	Coppin' the Haven	(30)	—
	Darn That Dream		
	(DB out)	(30)	—
	King Neptune		unissued

Note: All four titles will eventually be issued on Compact Disc.

June 11 *Broadcast,* *Jazzhus Montmartre,* *Copenhagen*	DEXTER GORDON QUARTET Dexter Gordon (ts, vcl–1); Tete Montoliu (p); Niels-Henning Orsted Pedersen (b); Alex Riel (d)		
	Cheese Cake	(31)	SteepleChase (D) SCC 6008
	Manha de Carnival	(31)	—
	Second Balcony Jump	(31)	—

June 25 *Broadcast,* *Jazzhus Montmartre,* *Copenhagen*	Benny Nielsen (b) replaces Orsted Pedersen		
	King Neptune	(32)	SteepleChase (D) SCC 6012
	Satin Doll	(32)	—
	Body and Soul	(32)	—
	I Want to Blow Now **– 1, n.c.**	(32)	—

July 9 *Broadcast,* *Jazzhus Montmartre,* *Copenhagen*	Orsted Pedersen (b); Rune Carlsson (d) replace Nielsen and Riel		
	I Want More	(33)	SteepleChase (D) SCC 6015
	Come Rain or Come Shine	(33)	—
	Where are You?	(33)	—
	I Want to Blow Now – 1	(33)	—
	Second Balcony Jump **– n.c.**	(33)	—

July 23 *Broadcast,* *Jazzhus Montmartre,* *Copenhagen*	Alex Riel (d) replaces Carlsson		
	Love for Sale	(34)	SteepleChase (D) SCC 6018
	I Guess I'll Hang My **Tears out to Dry**	(34)	—
	Big Fat Butterfly – 1	(34)	—
	Soul Sister	(34)	—
	Cherokee – n.c.	(34)	—

August 6 *Broadcast,* *Jazzhus Montmartre,* *Copenhagen*	**Just Friends**	(35)	SteepleChase (D) SCC 6022
	Three O'Clock in the **Morning**	(35)	—
	Where are You?	(35)	—
	It's You or No One	(35)	—

August 20 *Broadcast,* *Jazzhus Montmartre,* *Copenhagen*	**Billie's Bounce**	(36)	SteepleChase (D) SCC 6028
	Satin Doll	(36)	—
	Soul Sister	(36)	—
	A Night in Tunisia – n.c.	(36)	—

1965: *May 27* *New Jersey*	DEXTER GORDON Freddie Hubbard (tp); Dexter Gordon (ts); Barry Harris (p); Bob Cranshaw (b); Billy Higgins (d)	
	Hanky Panky	Blue Note LT 989
	I'm a Fool to Want You	—
	Devilette	—
	Clubhouse	—
	Jodi	—
	Lady Iris B	—

May 28 *New Jersey*	**Manha de Carnival**	(37)(38)	Blue Note BST 84204
	Everybody's Some- **body's Fool**	(37)(38)	—
	Le Coiffeur	(37)(38)	—
	Flick of a Trick	(38)	Blue Note CDP 7466812*

Bobby Hutcherson (vb) replaces Hubbard

May 29 *New Jersey*	**Who Can I Turn to**	(37)(38)	Blue Note BST 84204
	Heartaches	(37)(38)	—
	Shiny Stockings	(37)(38)	—
	Very Saxily Yours	(38)	Blue Note CDP 7466812*

June 10
Broadcast,
Jazzhus Montmartre,
Copenhagen

DEXTER GORDON QUARTET
Dexter Gordon (ts); Atli Bjorn (p); Benny Nielsen (b); Finn Frederiksen (d)

Take the 'A' Train	SteepleChase (D) unissued
My Melancholy Baby	—
What's New?	—
Wee Dot	—
Second Balcony Jump – n.c.	—

June 24
Broadcast,
Jazzhus Montmartre,
Copenhagen

Dexter Gordon (ts); Kenny Drew (p); Niels-Henning Orsted Pedersen (b); Alex Riel (d)

There Will Never be Another **You**	SteepleChase (D) unissued
Come Rain or Come Shine	—
I Should Care	—
Blues Walk	—

July 8
Broadcast,
Jazzhus Montmartre,
Copenhagen

Take the 'A' Train	—
Shiny Stockings	—
Misty	—
Cheese Cake	—

August 5
Broadcast,
Jazzhus Montmartre,
Copenhagen

Heartaches	—
Devilette	—
You've Changed	—
So What – n.c.	—

August 19
Broadcast,
Jazzhus Montmartre,
Copenhagen

DEXTER GORDON QUINTET
Add Donald Byrd (tp)

Lady Bird	—
So What	—
Who Can I Turn to	—
Blues by Five – n.c.	—

October 27
Munich

BOOKER ERVIN
Booker Ervin, Dexter Gordon (ts); Jaki Byard (p); Reggie Workman (b); Alan Dawson (d)

Setting the Pace	Prestige PR 7455
Dexter's Deck	—

December 2
Paris

KITTY WHITE
Sonny Grey (tp); Melih Gurel (frh); Dexter Gordon (ts); Jean-Louis Chautemps (bs); Kitty White (p, vcl); Pierre Cullaz (g); Michel Gaudry *or* Jimmy Woode (b); Kenny Clarke (d)
Say It isn't So   Clover (F) CLS 1229
My Kind of Guy   —

1966:
January 6
Broadcast,
Jazzhus Montmartre,
Copenhagen

DEXTER GORDON QUINTET
Pony Poindexter (as); Dexter Gordon (ts); Kenny Drew (p); Niels-Henning Orsted Pedersen (b); Makaya Ntshoko (d)
Stella by Starlight   SteepleChase (D) unissued
Satin Doll   —
Round Midnight   —
Sonnymoon for Two – n.c. —

1967:
June 29
Broadcast,
Jazzhus Montmartre,
Copenhagen

DEXTER GORDON QUARTET
Dexter Gordon (ts); Kenny Drew (p); Bo Stief (b); Art Taylor (d)
Satin Doll   SteepleChase (D) unissued
It's You or No One   —
Darn That Dream   —
Billie's Bounce – n.c.   —

July 20
Jazzhus Montmartre,
Copenhagen

DEXTER GORDON
Niels-Henning Orsted Pedersen (b); Albert Heath (d) replace Stief and Taylor
Devilette   (39) Polydor (E) 2460 108
For All We Know   (39)(39a)   —
Doxy   (39)(39a)   —
Sonnymoon for Two   (39)   —
Misty   Trio (J) PA 6120
Like Someone in Love   (40) Black Lion (E) BLP 30157
Come Rain or Come Shine(39a) Trio (J) PA 6120
There Will Never be
Another You   (39a)(40) Black Lion (E) BLP 30157
Body and Soul   (40)   —
Blues Walk   (40)   —

July 21
Jazzhus Montmartre,
Copenhagen

But Not for Me   (39a)Trio (J) PA 6120
Take the 'A' Train   —
For All We Know   unissued
Blues Walk   —
The Theme   —
I Guess I'll Hang My Tears out
to Dry   —
Love for Sale   —
Devilette   —
Come Rain or Come Shine   —
I Should Care   —
Sonnymoon for Two   —

July 22	**Darn That Dream**	—
Jazzhus Montmartre,	**Now's the Time**	—
Copenhagen	**Satin Doll**	—
	What's New	—
	Nica's Dream	—
	Stanley the Steamer	—
	Amania	—
	Lover Man	—
	Cheese Cake	—
	Society Red	—
	Stella by Starlight	—

1968:

January 25
Concert,
Rome

JOHNNY GRIFFIN–DEXTER GORDON
Dexter Gordon, Johnny Griffin (ts); Hampton Hawes (p);
Jimmy Woode (b); Kenny Clarke (d)

Blues Up and Down	(40a) Joker (J) ULS 2058	
It's You or No One (JG out)	unissued	

Note: Gordon out on other titles from this concert.

c.mid 1968
TV recording,
Copenhagen

BEN WEBSTER
Ben Webster (ts) with The Danish Radio Big Band: Palle
Bolvig, Allan Botschinsky, Perry Knudsen, Palle Mikkelborg
(tp); Per Espersen, Ole Kurt Jensen, Torolf Molgard, Axel
Windfeld (tb); Dexter Gordon, Uffe Karshov, Bent Nielsen,
Sahib Shihab, Jesper Thilo (reeds); Kenny Drew (p); Niels-
Henning Orsted Pedersen (b); Albert Heath (d); Niels Jorgen
Steen (cond, arr–1); Ray Pitts (arr–2)

Stompy Jones – 1	(41) Storyville (D) SLP 4105	
Cotton Tail – 1	(41)	—

Same session

Add Svend Aage Blankholm, Aage Bertelsen, Holger Bjerre, H.
Bjerregard Jensen, Stanley Carlson, Erling Christensen,
Mogens Holm Larsen, Svend Aage Jensen, Kurt Jensen, Anton
Kontra, Per Ludolph, Borge Madsen, Hans Chr. Schwenger,
Helge Willer-Nielsen, Ove Winther, Finn Ziegler (strings)

Going Home – 1	(41) Storyville (D) SLP 4105	
Come Sunday – 2	(41)	—
Danny Boy	unissued	
You'd be so Nice to Come Home to	—	
Greensleeves	—	

1969:

February 5
The Paradiso,
Amsterdam

DEXTER GORDON
Dexter Gordon (ts); Cees Slinger (p); Jacques Schols (b); Han
Bennink (d)

Fried Bananas	(42) Catfish (Du) 5C188.24336/37	
What's New	(42)	—
Good Bait	(42)	—
Rhythm-a-ning	(42)	—
Willow Weep for Me	(42)	—

Junior	(42)	—
Scrapple from the Apple	(42)	—

March 10
Copenhagen

DEXTER GORDON & SLIDE HAMPTON

Dizzy Reece (tp); Slide Hampton (tb, arr); Dexter Gordon (ts); Kenny Drew (p); Niels-Henning Orsted Pedersen (b); Art Taylor (d)

My Blues	(43)	MPS (G) 15.230
You Don't Know What Love is	(43)	—
A New Thing	(43)	—
What's New	(43)	—
The Shadow of Your Smile (DR,SH out)	(43)	—
A Day in Vienna	(43)	—

April 2
New York City

DEXTER GORDON

Dexter Gordon, James Moody (ts); Barry Harris (p); Buster Williams (b); Albert Heath (d)

Montmartre	(43a)	Prestige PR 7623
Lady Bird		Prestige PR 7680
Sticky Wicket		—

April 4
New York City

Moody out		
Those were the Days	(43a)	Prestige PR 7623
Stanley the Steamer	(43a)	—
The Rainbow People	(43a)	—
Boston Bernie		Prestige PR 7680
Meditation		—
Fried Bananas		—
Dinner for One, Please James	unissued	

c.1969
Broadcast,
Gamlingen,
Stockholm

DEXTER GORDON QUINTET

Rolf Ericson (tp); Dexter Gordon (ts); Lars Sjosten (p); Sture Nordin (b); Per Hulten (d)

All the Things You are	(44)(44a)	SteepleChase (D) SCS 1224
Darn That Dream	(44)(44a)	—
Straight No Chaser	(44)(44a)	—
The Theme	(44)(44a)	—
I Remember You	(44a)	Steeplechase (D) SCCD 31224*
Three O'Clock in the Morning	(45)(45a)	SteepleChase (D) SCS 1226
Pfrancing	(45)(45a)	—
Body and Soul	(45a)	SteepleChase (D) SCCD 31226*

Note: Pfrancing mistitled No Blues on SCS 1226.

c.1969
Jazzhus Montmartre,
Copenhagen

DEXTER GORDON

Dexter Gordon (ts); Kenny Drew (p); Niels-Henning Orsted Pedersen (b); Makaya Ntshoko (d)

Fried Bananas   Soundtrack
Those were the Days   —
Note: The film 'Dexter Gordon' was made by Flip Film
Productions in Denmark.

1970:
May 10   KARIN KROG & DEXTER GORDON
Oslo   Dexter Gordon (ts, vcl–1); Kenny Drew (p, org–2); Niels-
                  Henring Orsted Pedersen (b); Espen Rud (d); Karin Krog (vcl)
  take 1   Shiny Stockings   (46) Sonet (D) SLPS 1407
  take 2   I Wish I Knew   (46)   —
  take 1   Everybody's Somebody's
                     Fool   (46)   —
  take 2   Jelly Jelly – 1   (46)   —
  take 2   Blue Monk   (46)   —
  take 1   How Insensitive   (46)   —
  take 3   Blues Eyes – 2   (46)   —
  take 1   Ode to Billy Joe   unissued
  take 4   Some Other Spring   (46) Sonet (D) SLPS 1407

June 18   DEXTER GORDON WITH JUNIOR MANCE TRIO
Concert,   Dexter Gordon (ts); Junior Mance (p); Martin Rivera (b);
Montreux   Oliver Jackson (d)
                  Fried Bananas   (46a) Prestige P–7861
                  Sophisticated Lady   (46a)   —
                  Rhythm-a-ning   (46a)   —
                  Body and Soul   (46a)   —
                  Blue Monk   (46a)   —
                  The Panther   (46a) Prestige PCD 7861–2*

July 7   DEXTER GORDON
New York City   Dexter Gordon (ts); Tommy Flanagan (p); Larry Ridley (b);
                  Alan Dawson (d)
                  The Panther   Prestige PR 7829
                  Body and Soul   —
                  Valse Robin   —
                  Mrs Miniver   —
                  The Christmas Song   —
                  The Blues Walk   —

July 26   GENE AMMONS & DEXTER GORDON
North Park Hotel, Dexter Gordon (ts); John Young (p); Cleveland Eaton (b);
Chicago (afternoon Steve McCall (d)
set)   Polka Dots and Moonbeams Prestige PR 10010
                  I Can't Get Started   unissued
                  Misty   —
                  Wee Dot   Prestige PR 24046
                  Note: A long bass solo has been edited out of Wee Dot. Gordon
                  out on other titles from this set. Prestige PR 24046 issued as 25
                  YEARS OF PRESTIGE.

Evening set	Gene Ammons, Dexter Gordon (ts); Jodie Christian (p); Rufus Reid (b); Wilbur Campbell (d); Vi Redd (vcl–1)

Lonesome Lover Blues – 1   Prestige PR 10010
The Chase   —

July
TV recording,
Chicago

DEXTER GORDON
Ammons out; John Young (p) replaces Christian
Long Tall Dexter (Theme) (unissued)
Love for Sale   J For Jazz JFJ 802
Sticky Wicket   —
The Shadow of Your Smile   —
Rhythm-a-ning   —
Unknown title – n.c.   unissued
Note: JFJ 802 issued as by CHARLIE MINGUS–DEXTER GORDON–CHARLIE PARKER.

c.August
Both/And Club,
San Francisco

Dexter Gordon (ts); George Duke (p); Donald Rafael Garrett (b); Oliver Johnson (d)
Fried Bananas   Chiaroscuro CR 2029
Blue Monk   —
The Shadow of Your Smile (47)   —
Montmartre   (47)   —
Wee Dot   (47) Everest FS 360
The Rainbow People   (47)   —
Note: Fried Bananas mistitled Jive Fernando; Wee Dot
· ·led Oui Dot (Why Not). There is a possibility that this
   ˙· n was actually recorded in 1969.

August 23
North Park Hotel,
Chicago
      18775
      18776

CHARLIE PARKER MEMORIAL CONCERT
Red Rodney (tp); Von Freeman, Dexter Gordon (ts); Jodie Christian (p); Rufus Reid (b); Roy Haynes (d)
Groovin' High   (47a) Cadet 2CA 60002
Billie's Bounce   (47a)   —
Note: Gordon out on other titles from this session.

August 27
New York City

DEXTER GORDON
Dexter Gordon (ts); Wynton Kelly (p); Sam Jones (b); Roy Brooks (d)
Evergreenish   (48) Prestige PR 10020
For Sentimental Reasons (48)   —
Star Eyes   (48)   —
Rhythm-a-ning   (48)   —
If You Coul·ᵗ ˢ·· Me Now (48)   —
The Jump·   ʲ·   (48)   —
Note: Rhyt·.   ·ing mistitled Straight No Chaser.

September 18
Concert,
Zurich

GEORGE GRUNTZ DREAM GROUP
Franco Ambrosetti (tp); Michel Portal (bcl); Dexter Gordon (ts); George Gruntz (p, arr); Beb Guerin, Eberhard Weber (b); Pierre Favre, Tony Oxley (d)
Bunauara   MPS (G) CRF 843

1971:
April 21
Broadcast, Stampen,
Stockholm

DEXTER GORDON QUARTET
Dexter Gordon (ts); Lars Sjosten (p); Sture Nordin (b); Fredrik
Noren (d)

Secret Love	(49) SteepleChase (D) SCS 1206	
Polka Dots and		
Moonbeams	(49)	—
The Shadow of Your		
Smile	(49)	—
Summertime	(49)	—

September 2
Jazzhus Montmartre,
Copenhagen

HAMPTON HAWES
Dexter Gordon (ts); Hampton Hawes (p); Henry Franklin (b);
Michael Carvin (d)

Long Tall Dexter	Arista Freedom AF 1043
Yesterdays	unissued

Note: Long Tall Dexter mistitled Dexter's Deck. Gordon out
on other titles from this session.

September 16
Concert,
Zurich

INTERNATIONAL FESTIVAL ALL STARS
Franco Ambrosetti, Benny Bailey, Art Farmer, Dusko Goyko-
vich (tp); Slide Hampton, Albert Mangelsdorff, Ake Persson,
Jiggs Whigham (tb); Heinz Bigler, Leo Wright (as); Herb Geller
(as, oboe); Don Byas, Dexter Gordon (ts); Sahib Shihab (bs);
George Gruntz (p, arr); Isla Eckinger (b); Tony Inzalaco (d)

The Age of Prominence	MPS (G) 3321277-7
Lonely Woman	MPS (G) 2121437-0

1972:
April 5, 6
Lugano

THE BAND
Franco Ambrosetti, Dusko Goykovich, Virgil Jones, Woody
Shaw (tp); Benny Bailey (tp, flh); Erich Kleinschuster, Ake
Persson, Jiggs Whigham (tb); Runo Ericson (btb); Herb Geller,
Phil Woods (as); Flavio Ambrosetti (as, ss); Eddie Daniels,
Dexter Gordon (ts); Sahib Shihab (bs); George Gruntz (p, elp,
dir); Niels-Henning Orsted Pedersen (b); Daniel Humair (d)

Our Suite Dig	MPS (G) 3321460-5
Pistrophallobus	—
Witch Stitch	—
English Waltz	—
The Tango	—
Gravenstein	—
Saint Charity	—
The Age of Prominence	—

Note: Some titles are spliced together from two different takes.

June 22
New Jersey

DEXTER GORDON
Freddie Hubbard (tp, flh); Dexter Gordon (ts); Cedar Walton
(p); Buster Williams (b); Billy Higgins (d)

Milestones	((50) Prestige P-10069	
Scared to be Alone	(50)	—
We See	(50)	—

The Group	(50)	—
Days of Wine and Roses		
(FH out)	(51) Prestige P–10091	

June 28
New Jersey

Thad Jones (tp, flh); Dexter Gordon (ts); Hank Jones (p); Stanley Clarke (b); Louis Hayes (d)

Ca'Purange	Prestige P–10051	
The First Time Ever		
I Saw Your Face	—	
Airegin	—	
Oh! Karen O	—	
Tangerine	(51) Prestige P–10091	
August Blues	(51)	—
What It was	(51)	—

July 3
Radio City
Music Hall,
New York City

JAM SESSION
Harry Edison (tp); Kai Winding (tb); Dexter Gordon, James Moody, Flip Phillips, Zoot Sims (ts); Roland Kirk (ts, manz, str); Herbie Hancock (p); Chuck Wayne (g); Larry Ridley (b); Tony Williams (d)

Impressions	Cobblestone
	CST 9026–2

Note: Mistitled So What.

July 6
Radio City
Music Hall,
New York City

Howard McGhee, Clark Terry (tp); Dexter Gordon, Sonny Stitt (ts); Gary Burton (vb); Jimmy Smith (org); George Duke (p); Al McKibbon (b); Art Blakey (d)

Blue 'n' Boogie	Cobblestone
	CST 9026–2

August 28
Broadcast,
Jazzhus Montmartre,
Copenhagen

CHARLES MINGUS QUINTET FEATURING DEXTER GORDON
Charles McPherson (as); Dexter Gordon (ts); John Foster (p); Charles Mingus (b); Roy Brooks (d, saw–1)

Jelly Roll Muddy Blues	White label (It)
	unnumbered
Blues for Roy's Saw – 1	unissued

Note: The white label issue is a 2-LP box set.

November 2
Haagsche Jazz Club,
Haag

DEXTER GORDON WITH ROB AGERBEEK TRIO
Dexter Gordon (ts, vcl–1); Rob Agerbeek (p); Henk Haverhoek (b); Eric Ineke (d)

Some Other Blues	Dexterity (Du) ST 1–001
Stablemates	—
The Shadow of Your Smile	—
Jelly Jelly – 1	—
You Stepped Out of a Dream	—

1973:

February 16
Ecole Normale
Superieure,
Paris

DEXTER GORDON–SONNY GREY
Sonny Grey (tp); Dexter Gordon (ts); Georges Arvanitas (p);
Jacki Samson (b); Charles Saudrais (d)

Caloon Blues	(52)	Futura (G) FUT 2054
Fried Bananas	(52)	—
No Matter How	(52)	—
Dexter Leaps Out	(52)	—

June 6, 7
Munich

MIRIAM KLEIN
Roy Eldridge (tp); Slide Hampton (tb); Dexter Gordon (ts);
Vince Benedetti (p, arr–1); Oscar Klein (g); Isla Eckinger (b,
arr–2); Billy Brooks (d); Miriam Klein (vcl)

Comes Love – 2	MPS (G) 2121885–6
What a Little Moonlight Can	
Do – 2	—
You've Changed – 2	—
The Man I Love – 1	—
Big Stuff – 2	—
Fine and Mellow – 2	—
I Cried for You – 2	—
Yesterdays – 2	—
Body and Soul – 1	—

July 7
Concert,
Montreux

DEXTER GORDON
Dexter Gordon (ts); Hampton Hawes (elp); Bob Cranshaw
(elb); Kenny Clarke (d)

Gingerbread Boy	Prestige P–10079
Blues a la Suisse	—
Some Other Spring	—
Secret Love	—

Same concert

GENE AMMONS AND FRIENDS
Add Nat Adderley (cnt); Cannonball Adderley (as); Gene
Ammons (ts); Kenneth Nash (cga)

'treux Bleu	Prestige P–10078

Note: Gordon out on other titles from this session.

July 20
Jazzhus Montmartre,
Copenhagen

JACKIE McLEAN FEATURING DEXTER GORDON
Jackie McLean (as); Dexter Gordon (ts); Kenny Drew (p);
Niels-Henning Orsted Pedersen (b); Alex Riel (d)

All Clean	(53)(54)	SteepleChase (D) SCS 1006
I Can't Get Started	(55)	SteepleChase (D) SCS 1020
Dexter Digs in		unissued
Half Nelson	(55)	SteepleChase (D) SCS 1020
On the Trail		unissued
The Theme		—
Star Eyes		—
Blue Monk		—
The Theme		—

July 21 *Jazzhus Montmartre,* *Copenhagen*	There Will Never be Another You	unissued
	Sunset	—
	Rue de la Harpe	(53)(54) SteepleChase (D) SCS 1006
	Dexter Digs in	(55) SteepleChase (D) SCS 1020
	The Theme	unissued
	Callin'	(54) SteepleChase (D) SCCD 31006*
	Sunset	(53)(54) SteepleChase (D) SCS 1006
	Rue de la Harpe	unissued
	Another Hair-Do	(55) SteepleChase (D) SCS 1020
	On the Trail	(53)(54) SteepleChase (D) SCS 1006

1974:

January 16, 17, 18
Domicile Club,
Munich

SLIDE HAMPTON–JOE HAIDER ORCHESTRA
Benny Bailey, Idrees Sulieman, Ack Van Rooyen (tp); Bob Burgess, Slide Hampton (tb); Eric Van Lier (btb, tuba); Ferdinand Povel (as, fl); Andy Scherrer (ts, ss); Dexter Gordon (ts); Joe Haider (p); Isla Eckinger (b); Billy Brooks (d)

Tribute	(56) MPS–BASF (G) 2922311–6
Grandfather's Garden	(56) —
Think	(56) —
Like a Blues	(56) —
Tante Nelly	(56) —
What is Happening?	(56) —
Quiet Nights	(56) —
Petaluma	(56) —
Waltz for My Lady	(56) —
Time for Love	(56) —

May 24
Copenhagen

DEXTER GORDON QUARTET
Dexter Gordon (ts); Kenny Drew (p); Niels-Henning Orsted Pedersen (b); Albert Heath (d)

Some Other Blues	unissued
Strollin'	—
Old Folks (KD, AH out)	(57) SteepleChase (D) SCS 1025
Mr P.C.	unissued
Days of Wine and Roses	—
There Will Never be Another You	—

September 8
Copenhagen

The Apartment	(57) SteepleChase (D) SCS 1025
Wee Dot	(57) —
Strollin'	(57) —
Candlelight Lady	(57) —
Antabus	(57) —
Stablemates	unissued

1975:

February 21, 22, 23
Copenhagen

DEXTER GORDON AND ORCHESTRA
Dexter Gordon (ts, ss–1, vcl–2) with Orchestra: Allan Botschinsky, Benny Rosenfeld, Idrees Sulieman (tp, flh); Richard

Boone, Vincent Nilsson (tb); Axel Windfeld (btb); Preben
Garnov (frh); Bent Larsen (C, alto & bass fl); Erwin Jacobsen
(eh, oboe); Luba Boschenko (harp); Mogens Holm Larsen, Per
Walther (vln); Age Knudsen (vln–1); Bjarne Boie Rasmussen
(viola); Erling Christenson (cello); Thomas Clausen (p, elp);
Ole Molin (g); Niels-Henning Orsted Pedersen (b); Ed Thigpen
(d); Klaus Nordsoe (cga, perc); Palle Mikkelborg (arr, cond)

Naima – 1	(58)(60)	SteepleChase (D) SCS 1030
Good Morning Sun	(58)(60)	—
Ernie's Tune	(58)(60)	—
Tivoli	(58)(60)	—
More Than You		
Know	(58)(60)	—
This Happy Madness		
– 2	(59)(60)	SteepleChase (D) SCS 1145

Note: Contributions to Good Morning Sun by Kenneth
Knudsen (synth); Mikkelborg, Sanne Salomonsen (vcl) were
recorded at March 27, 1975 session.

<table>
<tr><td>

March 10
Copenhagen

</td><td>

DEXTER GORDON QUARTET
Dexter Gordon (ts, ss–1); Horace Parlan (p); Niels-Henning
Orsted Pedersen (b); Tony Inzalaco (d)

Just Friends	(61)	SteepleChase (D) SCS 1040
Misty	(61)	—
Red Cross	(61)	—
So What	(61)	—
In a Sentimental Mood – 1	(61)	—
Stablemates	(61)	—

</td></tr>
<tr><td>

March 27
Copenhagen

</td><td>

DEXTER GORDON AND ORCHESTRA
Palle Mikkelborg (tp, arr, cond); Idrees Sulieman (flh); Vincent
Nilsson (tb); Dexter Gordon (ts); Thomas Clausen (p, elp);
Kenneth Knudsen (synth); Ole Molin (g); Niels-Henning
Orsted Pedersen (b); Alex Riel (d); Klaus Nordsoe (cga, perc)

The Girl with the		
Purple Eyes	(58)(60)	SteepleChase (D) SCS 1030

Note: Performances by Knudsen (synth); Mikkelborg, Sanne
Salomonsen (vcl) included in Good Morning Sun (February
21–23, 1975) were recorded at this session.

</td></tr>
<tr><td>

August 23
Nova Park,
Zurich

</td><td>

DEXTER GORDON QUARTET
Dexter Gordon (ts, vcl–1); Kenny Drew (p); Niels-Henning
Orsted Pedersen (b); Alex Riel (d)

Tenor Madness	(62)	SteepleChase (D) SCS 1050
Wave	(62)	—
You've Changed	(62)	—
Days of Wine and Roses	(62)	—
Montmartre	(63)	SteepleChase (D) SCS 1090
Sticky Wicket	(63)	—
Didn't We?	(64)(65)	SteepleChase (D) SCS 1110
The Panther		unissued
Rhythm-a-ning		—

</td></tr>
</table>

August 24 *Nova Park,* *Zurich*	Add Joe Newman (tp–2) **There is No Greater** **Love**		(63) SteepleChase (D) SCS 1090
	Darn That Dream	(63)	—
	Jelly Jelly – 1		(64)(65) SteepleChase (D) SCS 1110
	Sophisticated Lady	(64)(65)	—
	Rhythm-a-ning	(64)(65)	—
	Tenor Madness		(65) SteepleChase (D) SCCD 31110*
	Wave		unissued
	Montmartre		—
	Days of Wine and **Roses – 2**		(65) SteepleChase (D) SCCD 31110*

September 13 *Copenhagen*	Philip Catherine (g); Billy Higgins (d) replace Drew, Riel		
take ?	**Freddie Freeloader**		(66)(67) SteepleChase (D) SCS 1136
take 3	**Freddie Freeloader**		(67) SteepleChase (D) SCCD 31136*
	When Sunny Gets Blue	(66)(67)	SteepleChase (D) SCS 1136
	Invitation	(66)(67)	—
	Winther's Calling	(66)(67)	—
	Polka Dots and **Moonbeams**	(66)(67)	—
take ?	**Yesterday's Mood**	(66)(67)	—
take 4	**Yesterday's Mood**		(67) SteepleChase (D) SCCD 31136*
	Note: An extra guitar line by Catherine has been overdubbed on Invitation.		

September 14 *Copenhagen*	Tete Montoliu (p) replaces Catherine		
	Billie's Bounce		(68) SteepleChase (D) SCS 1060
	Easy Living	(68)	—
	Benji's Bounce	(68)	—
	Catalonian Nights	(68)	—
	Four	(68)	—

November 29 *Copenhagen*	DEXTER GORDON Dexter Gordon (ts)	
	The Christmas Song	SteepleChase (D) SCS 1975/6
	Donna Lee	—
	Body and Soul	unissued
	Round About Midnight	—
	Note: The above issue was used by SteepleChase Records as a seasonal greeting, and was not issued commercially.	

1976: *May 17, 18, 19* *Helsinki*	ESKO LINNAVALLI NEW MUSIC ORCHESTRA Kaj Backlund, Allan Botschinsky, Markku Johansson, Simo Salminen (tp, flh); Juhani Aalto, Petri Juutilainen, Mircea Stan (tb); Tom Bildo (btb); Pekka Poyry (as, ss, fl); Juhani Aaltonen

(ss, ts, fl); Dexter Gordon, Eero Koivistoinen (ss, ts); Pentti Lahti (bs, ss, fl); Esko Linnavalli (p, elp, arr); Georg Wadenius (g); Niels-Henning Orsted Pedersen (b, elb); Esko Rosnell (d)

Talking with Mr Jones		Finnlevy (Fin) SFLP 9590
Sari	(59)	—
Eclipse	(59)	—
A Good Time was Had by All	(59)	—

Note: Last title edited on reissue.

June 15
Copenhagen

DEXTER GORDON TRIO
Dexter Gordon (ts); Niels-Henning Orsted Pedersen (b); Alex Riel (d)

Nursery Blues	(69)	SteepleChase (D) SCS 1156
Lullaby for a Monster	(69)	—
On Green Dolphin Street	(69)	—
Born to be Blue	(69)	—
Tanya	(69)	—
Good Bait		unissued

October 22
New York City

COHN/GORDON/HARRIS/HAYES/JONES/MITCHELL/NOTO
Blue Mitchell, Sam Noto (tp); Al Cohn, Dexter Gordon (ts); Barry Harris (p); Sam Jones (b); Louis Hayes (d)

Lady Bird	(70)	Xanadu 136
How Deep is the Ocean	(70)	—
True Blue	(70)	—
On the Trail (AC, DG only)	(71)	Xanadu 137
Allen's Alley	(71)	—
Silver Blue	(71)	—

November 9
New York City

DEXTER GORDON QUARTET
Dexter Gordon (ts); Barry Harris (p); Sam Jones (b); Al Foster (d)

Apple Jump	(72)(73)	SteepleChase (D) SCS 1080
I'll Remember April	(72)(73)	—
Skylark	(72)(73)	—
A la Modal	(72)(73)	—
Blue Bossa	(73)	SteepleChase (D) SCCD 31080*
Georgia on My Mind	(73)	—

December 11, 12
Village Vanguard,
New York City

DEXTER GORDON
Woody Shaw (tp, flh); Dexter Gordon (ts); Ronnie Mathews (p); Stafford James (b); Louis Hayes (d)

Gingerbread Boy	(74)	Columbia PG 34650
Little Red's Fantasy	(74)	—
Fenja	(74)	—
In Case You Haven't Heard	(74)	—
It's You or No One	(74)	—
Let's Get Down	(74)	—

Round About Midnight	(74)	—
Backstairs	(74)	—
Fried Bananas	unissued	
Body and Soul (WS out)	—	

December
New York City

DEXTER GORDON WITH LEON PENDARVIS ORCHES-TRA

Dexter Gordon (ts); Mike Mainieri (vb); Leon Pendarvis (p, arr); Cornell Dupree, Steve Khan (g); Bob Babbitt (b); Chris Parker (d); Erroll Bennett (perc); unknown strings

Isn't She Lovely?	Columbia 3–10565

1977:
June 21, 22
New York City

DEXTER GORDON

Benny Bailey, Woody Shaw (tp, flh); Slide Hampton (tb, arr); Wayne Andre (tb); Frank Wess (as, fl, picc); Dexter Gordon (ts, ss); Howard Johnson (bs, tu); Bobby Hutcherson (vb); George Cables (p); Rufus Reid (b); Victor Lewis (d)

Laura	(75)	Columbia JC 34989
The Moontrane	(75)	—
Red Top	(75)	—
Fried Bananas	(75)	—
You're Blase	(75)	—
How Insensitive	(75)	—

July 24
Concert,
Montreux

VARIOUS ARTISTS

Greg Bowen, Alan Downey, Maynard Ferguson, Stan Mark, Joe Morsello, Woody Shaw (tp); Clifford Hardie, David Horler, Geoffrey Perkins (tb); Bobbi Humphrey, Hubert Laws, Thijs Van Leer (fl); Stan Getz, Benny Golson, Dexter Gordon (ts); Bobby Millitello (bs); Eric Gale, Steve Khan (g); George Duke, Bob James (keyb); Alphonso Johnson (b); Billy Cobham (d); Ralph McDonald (perc)

Blues March	Columbia JG 35005

Add Janne Schaffer (g)

Montreux Summit	—
Andromeda	—

Same concert

Woody Shaw (tp); Slide Hampton (tb, cond–1); Dexter Gordon (ts); George Duke (p); Gordon Johnson (b); Billy Brooks (d)

Fried Bananas	Columbia JG 35005

Add Clifford Hardie, David Horler, Geoffrey Perkins (tb)

The Moontrane	Columbia JG 35090
Laura	rejected

Add Maynard Ferguson (tp); Hubert Laws (fl); Stan Getz (ts)

Red Top – 1	Columbia JG 35090

Note: Columbia JG 35005 & 35090 issued as MONTREUX SUMMIT VOLS. 1 & 2.

November 11 *New York City*	LIONEL HAMPTON WITH DEXTER GORDON Dexter Gordon (ts, ss); Lionel Hampton (vb); Hank Jones (p); Bucky Pizzarelli (g); George Duvivier (b); Oliver Jackson (d); Candido (cga)		

	Cute	(76)	Who's Who In Jazz WWLP 21011
	They Say that Falling in Love is Wonderful	(76)	—
	Lullaby of Birdland	(76)	—
	I Should Care	(76)	—
	Seven Come Eleven	(76)	—
	Blues for Gates	(76)	—
	Lullaby of the Leaves		Who's Who In Jazz WWLP 21014
	Note: WWLP 21014 issued as GIANTS OF JAZZ VOL. 2.		

November 29, 30, *December 1* *Berkeley,* *California*	PHILLY JOE JONES Dexter Gordon (ts); George Cables (p); Ron Carter (b); Philly Joe Jones (d)	
	Neptunis	Galaxy GXY 5112
	Polka Dots and Moonbeams	—

1978:

May 1 *New York City*	DEXTER GORDON QUARTET Dexter Gordon (ts); George Cables (p); Rufus Reid (b); Eddie Gladden (d)	
CO122635	Ruby, My Dear	Columbia JC 35978

May 2 *New York City*		
CO122736	Moment's Notice	Columbia JC 35608
CO122849	Tanya	—

May 3 *New York City*		
CO122850	Body and Soul	—
CO123348	LTD	—
CO123349	I Told You So	—

May 4 *New York City*		
CO126832	Secret Love	unissued
CO126833	As Time Goes by	Columbia JC 35608

May 13 *Keystone Korner,* *San Francisco*	Antabus	(77) Blue Note BABB 85112
	unknown titles	unissued

May 16 *Keystone Corner,* *San Francisco*	It's You or No One	(77) Blue Note BABB 85112
	Tangerine	(77) —
	Come Rain or Come Shine	(77) —
	unknown titles	unissued

September 23	Add Johnny Griffin (ts–1)	
Carnegie Hall,	**Secret Love**	unissued
New York City	**Come Rain or Come Shine**	rejected
	End of a Love Affair	unissued
	More than You Know	—
	Blues Up and Down – 1	Columbia JC 35978
	Cake – 1	—

Note: Cake is the same tune as Cheese Cake.

c.1978:		
Jazz Showcase,	**Gingerbread Boy – n.c.**	Soundtrack
Chicago		

Note: Included in the Film *Jazz in Exile*, directed by Chuck France.

1979:		
January 26	Add Woody Shaw (tp); Curtis Fuller (tb); Eddie Jefferson	
New York City	(vcl–2)	
	Diggin' in – 2	Columbia JC 35978
	It's Only a Paper Moon – 2	—
	These Foolish Things – 2	rejected

February 1	**Alone Together**	—
New York City	**I Fall in Love Too Easily**	—

March 3, 4, 5	CBS JAZZ ALL STARS	
Karl Marx Theatre,	Stan Getz, Dexter Gordon (ts); Bobby Hutcherson (vb–1,	
Havana	mar–2); Cedar Walton (p); Percy Heath (b); Tony Williams (d)	
	Polka Dots and Moonbeams	Columbia PC2–36180
	Tin Tin Deo – 1	—
	Add Woody Shaw (tp); Hubert Laws (fl); Arthur Blythe (as);	
	Jimmy Heath (ts); Willie Bobo (perc)	
	Sounds for Sore Ears – 2	Columbia PC2–36180
	Project S. – 2	Columbia PC2–36053

March 23	DEXTER GORDON	
Keystone Korner,	Dexter Gordon (ts); George Cables (p); Rufus Reid (b); Eddie	
San Francisco	Gladden (d)	
	Sophisticated Lady	(77) Blue Note BABB 85112
	unknown titles	unissued

March 24	**Easy Living**	(77) Blue Note BABB 85112
Keystone Korner,	**unknown titles**	unissued
San Francisco		

March 27	**More than You Know**	(77) Blue Note BABB 85112
Keystone Korner,	**unknown titles**	unissued
San Francisco		

May 30, 31,   Woody Shaw, Richard Williams (tp); Janice Robinson (tb);
June 1   James Spaulding (as, fl); Dexter Gordon (ts, ss); Frank Foster
New York City   (ts, arr); Mario Rivera (bs); Kirk Lightsey (p); Rufus Reid (b);
    Eddie Gladden (d); Ray Mantilla (cga, perc, timb–1)
    Soy Califa – 1   Columbia rejected
    Blue and Sentimental   —
    Twisted   —
    Clap Hands, Here Comes
    Charlie   —

1980:
August 11   Dexter Gordon (ts); Cedar Walton (p); George Benson (g);
New York City   Percy Heath (b); Art Blakey (d)
    CO126886   **Hi-Fly**   (77a) Columbia JC 36853
    CO126887   **Gotham City**   (77a)   —

August 12
New York City   Woody Shaw (tp) replaces Benson
    CO126888   **The Group**   rejected
    CO126889   **The Blues Walk**   (77a) Columbia JC 36853
    CO126890   **A Nightingale Sang in**
                    Berkeley Square
                    (WS out)   (77a)   —

November 4   DEXTER GORDON QUINTET
New York City   Dexter Gordon (ts); Kirk Lightsey (p); David Eubanks (b);
    Eddie Gladden (d)
    take ?   **Have Yourself a Merry Little**
                Christmas   Columbia FC 37551
    take ?   **Have Yourself a Merry Little**
                Christmas   Columbia AE7 1221
    Note: FC 37551 issued as GOD REST YE MERRY JAZZ-
    MEN. AE7 1221 was a promotional record not issued
    commercially, the reverse containing an interview with Gor-
    don.

1981:
November 17   DEXTER GORDON–JOHNNY GRIFFIN
Blackstone Hotel,   Add Johnny Griffin (ts)
Chicago   **Red Top**   Soundtrack
    Note: Included in the film *Jazz in Exile*, directed by Chuck
    France.

1982:
March 8   DEXTER GORDON
Philadelphia   Dexter Gordon (ts); Grover Washington Jr. (ss); Shirley Scott
    (org); Eddie Gladden (d)
    The Jumpin' Blues   Elektra-Musician
                                        E 1–60126
    Besame Mucho (GWJ out)   —
    For Soul Sister   —

March 15 *New York City*	Woody Shaw (tp–1); Steve Turre (tb–2); Dexter Gordon (ts); Kirk Lightsey (p); David Eubanks (b); Eddie Gladden (d); Ray Mantilla (cga–3)	
	The Touch of Your Lips – 1,2	Elektra-Musician rejected
	Soy Califa – 2,3	—
March 16 *New York City*	Sticky Wicket	Elektra-Musician E1–60126
	Skylark	—
	Interview with Gordon	—
June 19, 20 *Hollywood Bowl,* *Los Angeles*	Fried Bananas – 1	Elektra-Musician 60298–1–1
	You've Changed – 1	—
	Note: Elektra-Musician 60298–1–1 issued as THE PLAYBOY FESTIVAL.	

September 1 *Budokan,* *Tokyo*	AUREX JAZZ FESTIVAL '82	
	Clark Terry (tp, flh, vcl–1); J.J. Johnson, Kai Winding (tb); Dexter Gordon (ts); Tommy Flanagan (p); Kenny Burrell (g); Richard Davis (b); Roy Haynes (d)	
	The Snapper – 1	Aurex (J) EWJ 80238
	Minor Mishap (JJJ, KW out)	—
	Milestones	—
	unknown titles	unissued
September 2 *Festival Hall,* *Osaka*	Soba Up	Aurex (J) EWJ 80255
	God Bless the Child	—
	Walkin'	—
	Minor Mishap	unissued
	The Snapper – 1	—
	Milestones	—
	Now's the Time	—
September 5 *Concert,* *Yokohama*	Walkin'	—
	Minor Mishap	—
	Milestones	—

1985: *July 1–12* *Paris*	DEXTER GORDON	
	Dexter Gordon (ts); Herbie Hancock (p); Pierre Michelot (b); Billy Higgins (d)	
	Still Time	(78) Columbia SC 40464
	Add John McLaughlin (g)	
	As Time Goes By	(79) Blue Note BT 85135
	Body and Soul	(78) Columbia SC 40464
	Autumn in New York – n.c.	Soundtrack
	Society Red – n.c.	—
	Lonnette McKee (vcl) replaces McLaughlin	
	How Long Has This Been Going On?	(78) Columbia SC 40464
	Bobby Hutcherson (vb) replaces McKee	

	'Round Midnight – n.c.	Soundtrack
	Now's the Time – n.c.	—
	Add Wayne Shorter (ts)	
	Una Noche Con Francis	(78) Columbia SC 40464

August 20, 21
Paris

Freddie Hubbard (tp, flh–1); Dexter Gordon (ts, ss–2); Cedar Walton (p); Ron Carter (b); Tony Williams (d)

Society Red – 1	(79) Blue Note BT 85135
Rhythm-a-ning	(78) Columbia SC 40464
Chan's Song – n.c., 2	
(FH out)	Soundtrack

August 22
Paris

Palle Mikkelborg (tp); Dexter Gordon (ts, ss–1); Wayne Shorter (ss); Herbie Hancock (p); Ron Carter, Mads Vinding (b); Billy Higgins (d)

'Round Midnight	(79) Blue Note BT 85135

August 23
Paris

Cedar Walton (p) replaces Hancock; Shorter, Carter out

Tivoli – n.c., 1	(79) Blue Note BT 85135

Note: All the above titles were recorded for use in the film *'Round Midnight* directed by Bertrand Tavernier. Gordon is not present on other titles from these sessions.

1987:
New Jersey

TONY BENNETT
Tony Bennett (vcl); Dexter Gordon (ts); Ralph Sharon (p, arr); Paul Langosch (b); Joe LaBarbera (d)

All of My Life	(80)(81) Columbia 38–07658
White Christmas	(80)(81) —

Acknowledgements: As well as previous Gordon discographers Ann Cooke, Johs Bergh and Thorbjorn Sjogren, I should like to express my thanks for their assistance to Arne Astrup, Michael Cuscuna (Manhattan), Steve Didymus, Graham Griffiths (New Note), Keith Knox, Mario Luzzi, Bob Porter, Don Schlitten (Xanadu), Chris Sheridan and Nils Winther (SteepleChase).

Index to Discography

(25)   Blue Note BST 84112/CDP 7 46094 2* (*Go!*)
(25a) Blue Note CDP 7841332* (*A Swingin' Affair*)
(26)   SteepleChase (D) SCC 6004 (*Cry Me a River*)
(27)   Blue Note BST 84146 (*Our Man in Paris*)
(28)   Blue Note BST 84430 (Bud Powell *Alternate Takes*)
(29)   Blue Note CDP 7 46394 2* (*Our Man in Paris*)
(30)   Blue Note BST 84176 (*One Flight Up*)
(31)   SteepleChase (D) SCC 6008 (*Cheese Cake*)
(32)   SteepleChase (D) SCC 6012 (*King Neptune*)
(33)   SteepleChase (D) SCC 6015 (*I Want More*)
(34)   SteepleChase (D) SCC 6018 (*Love for Sale*)
(35)   SteepleChase (D) SCC 6022 (*It's You or No One*)
(36)   SteepleChase (D) SCC 6028 (*Billie's Bounce*)
(37)   Blue Note BST 84204 (*Gettin' Around*)
(38)   Blue Note CDP 7 46681 2* (*Gettin' Around*)
(39)   Black Lion (Du) BLP 30102 (*Montmartre Collection Vol. 1*)
(39a) Jazz Life (G) LP 2273232/CD 2473232* (*For All We Know*)
(40)   Black Lion (Du) BLP 30157 (*Montmartre Collection Vol. 2: Blues Walk!*)
(40a) Lotus (It) LOP 14. 082 (*Johnny Griffin Meets Dexter Gordon*)
(41)   Storyville (D) SLP 4105/STCD 4105* (Ben Webster *Masters of Jazz Vol. 5*)
(42)   Affinity (E) AFFD 27 (*Live at the Amsterdam Paradiso*)
(43)   Jazz Stop–MPS (Sp) JS–002/MPS (G) 821 288 2* (*A Day in Copenhagen*)
(43a) Fantasy Original Jazz Classics OJC-299 (*Tower of Power*)
(44)   SteepleChase (D) SCS 1224 (*After Hours*)
(44a) SteepleChase (D) SCCD 31224* (*After Hours*)
(45)   SteepleChase (D) SCS 1226 (*After Midnight*)
(45a) SteepleChase (D) SCCD 31226* (*After Midnight*)
(46)   Storyville (D) SLP 4045 (Karin Krog & Dexter Gordon *Some Other Spring*)
(46a) Prestige PCD 7861–2* (*With Junior Mance at Montreux*)
(47)   Dargil (Sp) FS 360 (*Gordon's Gotham*)
(47a) Chess CH2–9217 (Various Artists *Charlie Parker Memorial Concert*)
(48)   Fantasy-Prestige (F) CD 98.560* (*The Jumping Blues*)
(49)   SteepleChase (D) SCS 1206 (*The Shadow of Your Smile*)
(50)   Prestige (It) HBS 6067 (*Generation*)
(51)   Prestige (It) HBS 6127 (*Tangerine*)
(52)   Spotlite (E) SPLP 10 (*Dexter Gordon–Sonny Grey with Georges Arvanitas Trio*)
(53)   SteepleChase (D) SCS 1006 (Jackie McLean–Dexter Gordon *The Meeting*)
(54)   SteepleChase (D) SCCD 31006* (Jackie McLean–Dexter Gordon *The Meeting*)

Index

13359918R00140

Printed in Great Britain
by Amazon.co.uk, Ltd.,
Marston Gate.